THE FLESH

SEASON 4: LIBERATION

CARTEL

RACHEL HAIMOWITZ
HEIDI BELLEAU

ANGLERFISH PRESS

Anglerfish Press
PO Box 1537
Burnsville, NC 28714
www.AnglerFishPress.com
Anglerfish Press is an imprint of Riptide Publishing.
www.RiptidePublishing.com

The Flesh Cartel, Season 4: Liberation
Copyright © 2014 by Heidi Belleau and Rachel Haimowitz

Cover art: Imaliea, imaliea.deviantart.com
Editor: Sarah Lyons
Layout: L.C. Chase, lcchase.com/design.htm

ISBN: 978-1-62649-088-8

First edition
March, 2014

Also available in ebook across four episodes:
ISBN: 978-1-62649-072-7 (Episode 11)
ISBN: 978-1-62649-073-4 (Episode 12)
ISBN: 978-1-62649-074-1 (Episode 13)
ISBN: 978-1-62649-075-8 (Episode 14)

THE
FLESH
SEASON 4: LIBERATION
CARTEL

RACHEL HAIMOWITZ
HEIDI BELLEAU

ANGLERFISH
PRESS

TABLE OF CONTENTS

THE FLESH CARTEL

SEASON 4: LIBERATION

EPISODE 11: PERMANENT RECORD

NATE

Nate was contemplating the merits of a third cup of coffee when the manila folder hit his desk.

"Happy birthday," Louise said.

"Oh, you shouldn't have," Nate drawled back, picking up the folder and then realizing there was another underneath. A pair of them. On a Friday afternoon. Wow, thanks. "You really, really shouldn't have."

Louise snorted. "Relax. It's not that bad. We'll still be out of here by five, cross my heart. Practically just data entry. Pair of adult brothers: LVMPD actually closed the case about a month back, says they fled to Mexico, but the former foster father living in Florida plays golf on Sundays with a judge or some bullshit, so the higher-ups want the case in our system at least. Look like we're doing something even if we're not."

Depressing, how often Nate heard that, even if it was always followed up with—

"Not that you heard it from me."

That.

"Gotcha," Nate said.

"Besides," Louise added, quirking a tiny, sly smile, "I think you actually might really want this one, cold case or no."

Oh, really? He couldn't even begin to think of why, but then again, it was Friday afternoon, and he wasn't exactly firing on all cylinders anymore. But Louise was still standing there smiling that little smile, so he gave up trying to guess and just flipped the first folder open.

Douglas Carmichael. Twenty-three. A pretty kid, looking bewildered in the picture clipped to his file: his school ID, actually. Huh, a doctoral candidate. Nate had assumed drug or gambling debts to go along with the fled-to-Mexico thing, but this kid's record was squeaky clean, and not only that, *going places* clean. Hardly the kind of person you expected to jump the border. But then, maybe the brother had more to do with that side of things. In which case, Nate pitied poor Douglas. It wouldn't be the first time one sibling had dragged another into the mud. It never stopped being sad, though.

He glanced up at Louise, who'd folded her arms and leaned one hip against his desk, getting comfortable. Nothing in the file so far to pique his interest more than any other file—he let the question show on his face.

"Keep reading," she said.

That name, Carmichael. That actually was familiar, although Nate wasn't sure from where. He certainly didn't recognize this gawky white kid with his big eyes and crumpled sports coat. Last seen by his academic advisor about four months back. The advisor had been the one to report him missing, too. Nate hadn't expected any parental concern, considering the kid had been in the system since puberty, but didn't he at least have *friends*? Well, maybe not. Not like Nate had many of those, either.

He set Douglas Carmichael aside and opened the second folder.

No. Fuck no.

Nate hadn't recognized poor Douglas Carmichael, but he sure as hell recognized his brother, Mathias.

Or, as Nate knew him, Mat "Stonewall" Carmichael. Six feet of pure muscle, grim-faced in the octagon and fucking gorgeous outside of it. How many times had Nate sought out Stonewall Carmichael's fights, just to watch all that power unleashed? He wasn't the best fighter on the circuit, not by far, but he always left Nate breathless at the way he took pain and punishment and just fucking *overcame*.

How many times had Nate leveraged his connections to worm his way into after-parties, too shy to get close, even though the hunger got so bad sometimes it physically gnawed at him? But oh, he loved to watch that lean face lose some of its guarded fury, become something flirtatious and cocky and the man was like a god on Earth and now he was *gone*? And Nate was supposed to just put him on file, scan his photo, leave him up on some cold case missing persons' website to rot, without even a reward to tempt the bounty-hunting types?

He scrubbed his face, looking at the fierce blue eyes in the photo, half-softened by a crooked smile. The evidence said Mathias had fled to Mexico with his brother, but Nate's gut said something else.

Stonewall Carmichael was a fighter. He would never run, especially not if it meant bringing his brother down with him. It wasn't logical. It wasn't possible.

Should Nate pass on this case to someone else? Admit his objectivity was compromised? Already he was ignoring the facts in favor of his own (lust-fueled, starry-eyed) assumptions.

No. Louise had brought him—well, *them*—this case in particular. She obviously thought he could handle it. And he trusted her more than anyone who wasn't blood—and even more than a few who were.

The Carmichael house was in pre-foreclosure, but it hadn't been cleaned out yet, and the LVMPD still had some evidence in storage. Nate would start there.

Yes, a third cup of coffee was definitely in order.

CHAPTER ONE

Though Douglas's coming-out party wound down around eleven, Allen stayed well past midnight, mostly toying with Mat while Douglas knelt nearby and drifted, barely conscious of his own body.

When it was all over, when Douglas was alone with Nikolai and Roger again, he began to cry. Weep inconsolably, to be specific. And to vibrate so hard with adrenaline that his teeth chattered.

He knew he should be punished for handling it so badly, but punishment never came. Nikolai murmured to him and shushed him and petted him, and then Roger gathered him up against his hard chest and carried him upstairs.

Again, he drifted, wafting in and out of consciousness, crying all the while. They washed him under the warm, gentle stream of the handheld showerhead. Cleaned him inside, too, until all the filthy cum ran down the drain and he was new again. Drew him a bath. Rubbed his body with soapy, caressing hands. Washed his hair. Kissed him, once or twice, in between his sobs. Toweled him off and carried him to bed.

It felt good to be pressed between them, Roger at his back and Nikolai in front of him, cradling his face in warm, steady hands and kissing at his tears, murmuring "That's all right," and "You did so well," and "Let it out, now."

When the crying slowed, they fucked him together, two cocks moving in tandem inside him, Roger's palms tracing tickling patterns over his chest while Nikolai stroked his hair and cupped his neck, and then Douglas turned his face up and the both of them kissed him at once, and kissed each other, too—three sweet, affectionate, lustful tongues tracing each other, and Douglas knew this was where he belonged, and no matter what happened, no matter where he went, he would always have this to keep in his heart and think back on and look forward to, because one day, if he was a Good Boy—maybe not for years, maybe not even for decades—but *one day*, Nikolai would call him home.

Mat woke to a splitting headache and a whole constellation of soreness and hurts. For one brief, beautiful moment, it was just another post-fight morning, all aches and pains and satisfaction and—if it'd been a particularly good night—a hangover and a temporary bedmate and several thousand extra dollars in his bank account.

But then reality kicked him in the teeth, and the languor vanished in a bright hot burst of pain. *Nikolai. Slave. Allen. Dougie. Dougie rap—*

He rolled over the side of the bed and retched.

Nothing in his stomach to eject, but that didn't stop it from trying until he'd managed to wrestle down those nightmare images of him and Dougie—

Wow, Jesus, he really needed to stop thinking.

Tenuous peace with his stomach achieved at last, he rolled onto his back with a groan. Groaned again and curled onto his side when the cane welts Allen had left from calves to shoulders bitched at the pressure. He burrowed under the blankets, shivering as sweat dried on his skin. God, he really was hungover. How was he hungover? He hadn't had a drop to drink. Yet he couldn't remember coming back to his room. Couldn't remember getting clean, though obviously he had; he smelled of soap, not semen. He vaguely recalled Allen forcing half a wine bottle up his ass. Must not've been empty. His fists clenched at the sense memory—burning, pain, the vicious sting of alcohol on raw flesh—and his knuckles twinged. Scraped, bruised. Had he hit someone? Some*thing*, at least. But he wasn't tied down now, which meant he probably hadn't hurt anybody. Or that Nikolai felt they'd deserved it for getting him blind fucking drunk with an alcohol enema.

Or maybe you hurt Dougie and they thought it was funny.

God, he didn't know how to feel about Dougie anymore. His stomach roiled, but maybe it was just the hangover. Because there was no denying it anymore—part of him was searingly, irrefutably *angry* with Dougie. Worse than angry. So far beyond merely *angry* he wasn't even sure how to process it. Enraged. Disgusted. Shattered.

Betrayed.

He tested those feelings for a long moment, let them nestle alongside the throbbing in his head and the ache in his ass and the slicing sting of a hundred cane welts. They felt . . . valid, for starters. Necessary. Important. He wasn't a bad person for being angry. Wasn't selfish for not playing the martyr every single fucking second of the day. He *wasn't*.

But then, Dougie wasn't a bad person either. Wasn't really a *person* at all anymore, was he? More like a robot, Nikolai's little programmable fuck toy. He could hardly be faulted for the things he'd done. Mat had seen what happened when Dougie disobeyed—had been forced to watch those horrors for a week straight. He wouldn't have lasted either if he'd been in Dougie's shoes.

And he knew that—he *knew* that. But the anger didn't fade. The disgust. The betrayal. Feelings weren't logical. He couldn't force them to be no matter how hard he tried.

"You love him," he said to the empty room, the words scraping up and out of his abused throat. He blinked at the wall, shifted his gaze to the family photo on the nightstand, Dougie's bright smile radiating joy. "You love him." The words felt more real this time. Stronger. He tried again. "*I* love him." He blinked at the photo again, and realized that this time he was blinking back tears. "I *love* him. No matter what. Always. Forever. He's my brother and I *love* him."

It was true. It was true. Just . . . could he maybe not have to look at him for a while? Not like Dougie wanted to see him anyway. And he needed . . . "Time, that's all," he mumbled to the family photo, then put his back to it, curling up on his other side. "I just need some fucking *time*."

And like fifty years of therapy. And Nikolai's head on a fucking pike. Allen's too, while he was at it.

On impulse he rolled back over and snatched the framed photo off the nightstand. Couldn't bear to look at it—to look at Dougie, at the happy child he'd once been, at the monster he'd now become, at all the ways Mat had failed him, let him down, let his parents down, let *everyone* down—so he hugged it to his chest instead, lay there curled around it like somehow protecting *it* would protect *them*. It was stupid and sentimental and *bullshit* and he was *furious* again, hatred digging claws into his chest and fucking *nesting* there, right behind his heart, doing its damnedest to squeeze everything else out. His breath hitched, pain and pressure and he was *crying* again, when had he started crying and why couldn't he fucking *stop*? "I'm sorry, Mom," he choked out, because he *was* sorry, he was *so* fucking sorry, but he couldn't apologize to Dougie, *wouldn't* apologize to Dougie, not right now, not with the memory of last night oozing through his brain like some toxic fucking earwig. "I'm sorry. I'm sorry."

"You have nothing to be sorry for, Mathias."

Mat was too wrung out and hungover to startle, too sad and shameful to bother trying to hide his tears. He just pressed the photo harder to his chest—as hard as he dared without risking the glass—and said, "Bullshit."

Nikolai strode across the room, invited himself right onto Mat's bed. Settled by his hip and placed a hand on one hunched shoulder. Mat let him. He deserved this—this twisted paternal patronizing bullshit, this violation of his space. Deserved this and more for his failure. His anger. His weakness in the face of it.

Nikolai gave his shoulder a gentle squeeze. "You're not to blame for anything that's happened here, Mathias. Nor for how you feel about it. About him."

Mat could've hugged Nikolai for not speaking Dougie's name aloud, though how he knew what Mat had been thinking . . . Had Nikolai been eavesdropping via hidden camera? Inferred the truth somehow? Or was Mat simply that fucking transparent to Nikolai now? He could hardly be bothered to care; what did it matter anymore, after all? He was leaving soon. Passing from one monster to the next, a monster himself. With another monster of his own making in tow.

"I hate you," he meant to say, but the words he tasted on his tongue—the words he somehow spat with such venom—were "I hate him."

"A not-unreasonable response." Nikolai said that so matter-of-factly that Mat had to meet his eyes to see if he was mocking him.

The man looked dead serious. Downright sympathetic, in fact. The hand on Mat's shoulder was warm, firm, the thumb stroking a slow, soothing path up and down, up and down.

Mat shrugged out from underneath it, inched back until Nikolai's hip was no longer touching his thigh. Side-eyed the guy. "Why are you being so nice to me?"

One eyebrow and a corner of Nikolai's mouth quirked ever so slightly. "Am I?"

"Yes," Mat huffed, trying not to sound as petulant as he suddenly felt. Whatever—it beat crying like some lost little kid. Or raging at one.

"It's true we've had our differences, but I don't hate you, you know."

Differences, huh? Is that what the kids were calling torture these days?

"Have I *ever* been needlessly cruel to you?" Nikolai tried. "Why would I start now?"

Mat's fingers tensed around the photograph, half-numb already from how tightly he'd been holding it. "I guess that depends on how you define need."

Nikolai reached for Mat, and he flinched back, realizing only belatedly that Nikolai was going for the photograph rather than his face. A moment's halfhearted tug-of-war; Nikolai wasn't pulling very hard, and Mat, for reasons he'd never be able to explain, just sort of . . . let go.

"What you need now," Nikolai said, carefully placing the photograph back on the nightstand, turning it to face Mat, "is to accept the fact that your fate, Douglas's fate, were beyond your control. To accept the fact that you've every right to be angry—at the men who procured you, at Madame, at me, and yes, even at Douglas—and that when the burden of your selflessness becomes too heavy to bear, no one will blame you for laying it down for a time. You've sacrificed so much here for the one you love above all else. It's more than anyone could have asked. And now you look at how he's changed and you think it's all been for naught, but you're wrong, Mathias. You saw with your own eyes how happy he is. You gave that to him. *You.*"

The photograph blurred through a scrim of fresh tears. Mat blinked them away. More replaced them. "I *destroyed* him," he whispered.

"And I rebuilt him better than new." Nikolai's hand curled around Mat's shoulder again. Mat half hoped for pain, but the touch was endlessly gentle. "You hate what he's become because you cannot *see* what he's become. The beauty in it. The glory. The purpose. The *peace*. You cannot have what he has, and though you may not know it, you're jealous of what he has."

Bullshit, Mat wanted to say, yet somehow, for some reason, the word got stuck in his throat.

"But you love him for who he was, who he is, no matter what he's done or what he'll do. Because he's your brother. Because he still loves you too—and surely he must, for the fury he feels toward you can come from no other source. All of these things are okay, Mathias. They're all allowed. None of it makes you a lesser man, or a bad man. You hurt because you care. You *hate* because you love. You must never forget that."

Mat wasn't sure how to respond to that, was still busy contemplating the potential truth of it, when Nikolai stood from the bed and walked away. For a moment Mat thought the guy was simply done with him—had come and spewed his weird Yoda-esque pep talk for some unfathomable reason and then rushed off to squeeze out his last few moments with Dougie—but Nikolai stopped at the table by the door. Where he'd left a covered tray that had completely escaped Mat's notice. Mat smelled eggs when Nikolai lifted the lid, and his stomach rebelled for a moment, but Nikolai only brought him a tall cup of water and two little white pills.

"Hydrate," Nikolai said. He didn't volunteer what the pills were. Mat didn't ask. Just took them. Drank half the water. Then the other half under Nikolai's watchful eye. Nikolai refilled the cup in the bathroom and brought it over with the breakfast tray, set it all next to Mat on the bed.

Jeremy had gone all-out. That was some fancy-looking shit there, plated like in a five-star restaurant. Too bad the mere sight of it made him want to hurl again.

Nikolai sat carefully beside the tray and laid a hand on Mat's thigh like an afterthought, so casually possessive. "This may be the last time anyone ever takes care of you again."

No cruelty in those words, no mocking. Wistfulness, maybe. Maybe even a hint of remorse. Nikolai said nothing else, but Mat heard the unspoken *You should enjoy it while you can.*

He picked up the plastic fork and cut a tiny little corner off the omelet. Managed to chew it sans disaster. It hurt to swallow, but the food stayed where he put it without argument. Nikolai looked pleased, and not in his usual smug unbearable way.

"When do we leave?" Mat asked.

"Soon. A week or two, perhaps. I wasn't certain until late last night if you were ready. But I can see now that you are."

Strange how vehemently a part of him wanted to reject that idea, to shout *No, I'm* not *ready, don't make me go.* After all, a new master meant a new chance at freedom—Nikolai's home was purpose-built to cage unbroken slaves, but his clients might be less careful. They were expecting obedient pets who wouldn't so much as *think* to run away.

On the other hand, this particular new master was a bad, bad man. Evil, even. Certainly in ways Nikolai was not—Nikolai, who hurt Mat only when he "had" to, never because he wanted to or enjoyed Mat's suffering. Nikolai, who showed Dougie such love, fucked-up and twisted as it was. Who took such care with them both when their training allowed.

Allen held no such considerations or affections. The things he'd done last night to Mat . . . The things he'd promised to do, to make *Dougie* do . . .

He sucked in a ragged breath and realized he was halfway to crying again. "How do I *protect* him there?"

A muscle jumped in Nikolai's jaw, the movement barely detectable, and Mat studied him hard because this was important somehow, this meant something, and maybe if he could just figure out what—

"Be what you were bought for. Fight, but not too much. Always obey in the end. Take your licks whether you deserve them or not. Pretend it's all worse than it is, and lie when it suits you. And most importantly, strategize. You already know he'll use Douglas against you. Accept that. Don't make things any harder for Douglas than they may already be. And don't punish him for not finding them hard, if that ends up being the case."

Yeah, 'cause he clearly hadn't found fuck-all hard about tying Mat up and raping him last night.

That muscle twitched in Nikolai's jaw again. "In fact," he said, "it may be best to pretend not to care altogether. I'd say that ship has sailed, but after last night, Allen might well believe your anger. Gods know it's genuine enough. If he thinks you despise Douglas, he'll have no cause at all to harm the boy."

Mat cast his eyes down to the tray, stuck his thumb and forefinger into the center of a slice of sprouted grain toast and tore a bite out. Chewed it thoughtfully. Murmured, "I don't think I can fake that." Even if he wanted to. Even if he *should*. Because Nikolai was right: he *could* love and hate at the same time. And neither one of those extremes lent itself very well to pretending not to care.

"And what about me?" he asked, though he hadn't planned to, hadn't even seen the question coming, selfish as it was. "How do I protect *me*?"

No mistaking the regret on Nikolai's face now for anything but what it was. He shook his head, pursed his lips, gaze frank and unflinching on Mat's face. "The best you can do is remember what I've taught you."

"Remember what you've taught me," Mat echoed, and that thought didn't comfort him at all. Trying to placate Allen, trying to tempt him into being gentle, or at least not provoke him into heedless anger... it was a great idea in theory, but now that he'd met the fucking sadist, he wasn't so sure. "He's going to fucking kill me."

Another absent thigh-pat, mindlessly affectionate. "Not until he bores of you. Don't let that happen and you'll be—" Nikolai swallowed the automatic—and obviously untrue—*fine* like it tasted bad. "Well," he said instead, and patted Mat's thigh again. "Eat your breakfast."

Asshole. That was all he had for Mat? The end of his sage fucking advice?

Nikolai stood from the bed and folded his arms across his chest. "That wasn't a request," he said, raising a meaningful eyebrow at the tray, then at Mat. Mat pulled another piece from the middle of his mutilated toast and chewed as obnoxiously as he knew how. Nikolai just shook his head, chuckled ruefully. "Definitely not boring."

Angry and *interesting*. Great. Just what he'd always fucking wanted.

CHAPTER TWO

N ikolai would have thought, after all these years, that Roger had long grown past that awkward tendency slaves sometimes had to . . . well, lurk. Skulk around in the corner of a room, waiting for nothing, unable to find something to keep them busy and too obviously uncomfortable to be as unobtrusive as a slave ought to be.

And yet, despite all his years of service and training, Roger was lurking now.

There, standing at the edge of the bedroom with his hands behind his back, jaw tense, silently watching—but never approaching—as Douglas sprawled wantonly on the bed between Nikolai's legs, sucking his cock with his now-familiar sweet enthusiasm. Tinged, as it had been since his coming-out, with perhaps the slightest hint of desperation—as if he tongued well enough, sucked deep enough, maybe Nikolai would keep him.

He reached between his legs with a pointed sigh aimed at Roger, and petted Douglas's bobbing head.

Roger's gaze fell to his feet, shoulders tense, back ramrod straight. Douglas briefly pressed his head into Nikolai's cupped hand without ever breaking stride, humming with pleasure as he did.

Nikolai suddenly found it hard to enjoy himself.

Hand holding Douglas's head in place—*don't stop, my pretty, don't stop*—he said to Roger, "Would you care to join us, then?" Maybe he was feeling left out. It was true, they'd certainly made a habit of sharing Douglas of late. Not that Nikolai was under any kind of obligation to share one slave with another, of course.

Roger didn't step forward, though, not even when Douglas lifted his ass plaintively. He twitched as if Nikolai had struck him, as stiff and restrained as the well-trained slave he was, but obviously hurting. Had Nikolai said something wrong? Perhaps his tone *had* been a bit on the acerbic side.

"Only if it pleases you, Master," Roger finally said. To his feet. Not so much as a suggestion of looking at Nikolai as he replied. His shoulders tightened, straightened in a way that said he was clenching his hands behind his back. This was more than jealousy. Was he . . . was he *nervous*?

That set off alarm bells so rusty with disuse that Nikolai almost didn't recognize them for what they were at first. His erection began to wilt in Douglas's talented mouth; his boy made a little distressed noise, mostly confusion and determination, but it quickly slid into fear as Nikolai went completely soft.

"It's all right, Douglas," he hastened to assure the boy.

Douglas lifted his head, rubbing his swollen lips with the back of his hand. "Should I bring you your cane, Master?" he asked. Not a trace of fear in his words; he was long past his fear of physical pain, but there was no mistaking the crushing disappointment on his face. The *failure*. As if this were *his* fault, instead of blasted Roger's. His precious boy . . . had Nikolai truly taught him to think that? No, of course not. The boy was just offering his pain because it was one of the only things he *could* offer to a master with no sexual need.

"No," Nikolai said, voice as gentle as he could make it. He stroked a hand down Douglas's head, cheek, jaw, ran the pad of his thumb over those lush lips. "You were exemplary. I'm tired, that's all. Come here." He opened his arms to the boy, who crawled up Nikolai's body and slotted against his chest, basking in the warmth Nikolai offered. Nikolai kissed the crown of his head. "I've another task for you tonight."

Douglas glanced up at him, eagerness in every line of his body.

"Go help Jeremy prep for tomorrow's breakfast, and then spend tonight showing him all I've taught you. A massage first, I think—he's not as young as he used to be, and it can't be easy leaning over sinks and counters all day. And then perhaps a leisurely rimming—he always did love those. Whatever he asks of you, be a good boy and give it to him." Douglas looked ever-so-slightly stricken (and very much like he was trying to hide it), so Nikolai kissed his head again and added with a smile, "He won't hurt you. Make me proud. Represent me as only my special boys can. You can tell me all about it in the morning."

Ah, there was the light coming on. He was a clever, clever boy; he might have been too preoccupied to sense the tension between Roger and Nikolai, but he could certainly see this task as a test run for what was to come with his new master—and, likewise, the promise to hear about it after as a promise not to leave him with Allen forever. Sent away, but only temporarily, and never as a punishment.

"Of course, Master," he said, fresh determination in his voice. And even a hint of mischief on his face as he added, "I'll make him come so hard he forgets his name, Master."

"There's my good boy," Nikolai said, putting on a smile for Douglas and kissing him one last time. "Off you go, now."

As anxious as he'd been, he practically skipped out of the room now, so eager to serve that it nearly broke Nikolai's heart. But there was no time now for sentimentality. He had other issues to attend to.

"Roger," he said, voice cold and clipped, in direct contrast to the sunny, comforting tone he'd taken with Douglas.

The man slunk forward, his usually perfect posture ruined by a distinctive flinch. "I didn't mean to interrupt, Master."

"And yet you have." He sat up, swung his legs over the side of the bed. His cock and balls, still damp with Douglas's spit, were cooling uncomfortably in the evening air.

Without looking at him, Roger handed him clean underwear from gods knew where. He snatched it up and stood to pull it on, and the fact that he was having this argument three-quarters naked infuriated him even more. "So, out with it. What was so important it couldn't wait until I'd taken my pleasure?"

Roger flinched again. "I . . . I didn't—"

"Mean to interrupt, yes, yes." He snatched his waiting pajama pants from Roger's hand and pulled those on too, then the top. "And somehow you thought that turning down my gift of affection and the use of my favorite boy"—another flinch; *Roger* had always been his favorite—"wouldn't be disruptive in the slightest."

"I really am sorry, Master, I meant to wait until you'd finished with Douglas. I know he's leaving soon, and I didn't want . . . I didn't want to take advantage of your generosity, Master, knowing that you won't be able to enjoy him for very much longer."

The frost around Nikolai's heart began to melt at that, just a little. Roger's gesture may have been disruptive and inept, but at least it'd been well-meaning. But then, why had he come into the bedroom in the first place?

"And actually, Master, that's why I was here. I . . ." His eyes darted up to Nikolai's and down to the floor again, tongue sweeping hesitantly across his lower lip. Whatever had him so nervous, he cleared his throat and soldiered on. "I came to tell you I've laid the coal fire and all your tools, Master. Everything's ready for you."

"You did *what*?" he roared. "Without my order?" And suddenly Roger was kneeling on the floor, cheek clutched in one hand and blood dribbling down his lip before Nikolai had registered he'd backhanded the man. He hadn't meant to strike. Hadn't hit Roger out of anger in *decades*. He cradled his smarting knuckles and lifted his chin, defiant to his own guilt. "And who here, exactly, is the master? Who decides when my slaves are ready for the ritual? Are you the master now, Roger? Has all my pampering and generosity gone to your fucking head?"

Roger squeezed his eyes shut, likely more hurt by Nikolai's tone than by his hand. Any other slave would've been trembling. Begging for forgiveness. Any *sensible* slave would've thrown himself at Nikolai's feet by now. Not just . . . *sat* there looking so calm, so determined, so . . . sad. "No, Master. Of course not, Master. I only—" He sighed heavily. "I only wanted to help you and serve you, you know that. But it's just . . . it's been over a week since Allen signed the contract, and I thought maybe you were having a hard time working past your emotional attachment to Douglas to get him packaged, so I thought that if I . . ."

His *emotional attachment*? Did Roger think him a child? An animal, bound to his base instincts and emotions? His fingers curled with the urge to strike the man again, and Roger must've seen it despite his bowed head because he raised his chin, turned his cheek to Nikolai, offering himself: *Punish me if you must, you're worth the pain.*

When seconds passed and Nikolai didn't strike, Roger darted a nervous tongue over his split lip and said, "I'd never presume, Master, just . . . a gentle reminder. Because I love you, and I couldn't bear the thought of Allen badmouthing you to his—" His face twisted up briefly, half disgust, half confusion. "Does he *have* friends?"

Nikolai couldn't help it. He laughed.

The tension bled from Roger's shoulders, jaw, eyes. He sat back on his heels, seemed to arrange himself automatically into proper position—except, of course, for how he was looking Nikolai directly in the eye. "I know you love Douglas, Master, and I love him too. I don't want him to go, and that's why I worry that maybe, unconsciously, you don't want him to go either, and that's why you're putting off . . ." He circled a hand through the air, as if to represent all of it: the ritual, the sale, packaging and sending away Douglas and Mathias once and for all. To Allen. For gods-knew-how-long. Nikolai's heart squeezed. It was true, the thought of sending such a beautiful boy as Douglas to an underappreciative brute like Allen rankled, and terribly. Even the thought of sending Mathias there, after all they'd been through together and all he'd learned about the man, upset him.

But that wasn't the reason for the delay, was it? Nikolai sat back on the bed, and after a moment, patted the space on the mattress beside him. Roger was quick to rise from his knees and sit, placing a tentative hand on Nikolai's thigh.

Nikolai dabbed at the blood on his lip with the pad of his thumb, then kissed the split softly: *I'm sorry I hurt you when you were only trying to help.* But a master never apologized for such things, not even when a lover might. Roger kissed him back anyway: *All is forgiven. Always.*

Just as Douglas would forgive him for sending him to Allen. Would wait for him, patient and obedient, and do Nikolai proud until the day he came to fetch him back. But Mathias . . . That was a different story. And also, he realized, the reason for his delays. Of course.

"You know I don't sign my work until it's finished," Nikolai said, and squeezed Roger's hand on his thigh in frustration. "I can't in good conscience go through with signing Mathias. He's—"

"Absolutely perfect, Master," Roger interrupted, returned to his usual bold self. "Trained exactly to the client's specifications. Not as you'd have him, no, but perfect in his own way. I think you know that, Master."

Hmm. Perhaps Roger *was* speaking sense. Except . . . if that was true, if Mathias really was perfect, then why was Nikolai still keeping them here? Why was he delaying?

Because Roger knows you better than you know yourself, you fool, and you'd best not compound the problem with cowardice as well.

He loved Douglas. He *loved* Douglas. And he wanted to keep him.

Same damn mistake he'd made with Roger all those years ago, except this time he had no excuse. He wasn't some green teenage trainer working his first project, high on his accomplishment and sentimental about the art he'd created. He wasn't young or weak or silly anymore. He was a businessman first and an artist second. He'd been doing this for nearly *twenty-five years* now. He'd seen many slaves, all of them as perfectly trained and conditioned as Douglas or Roger, come and go. He'd sent them away to masters he'd approved of, and masters whose wallets he'd approved of. He'd gotten them back whole, or twisted, or in ashes, or never at all—mostly never at all—but above all else, he'd always moved forward. One project to the next. No procrastination. No stalling. No remorse.

No excuse. No excuse at all.

He'd do this. First thing tomorrow.

And only not tonight because he didn't want to go back on the orders he'd already handed down to Douglas.

For now, though, he owed Roger an apology a master *could* give. And a thank-you.

He swept a hand down the man's nape, toying with the short hair there, as his other hand wandered into Roger's lap, over to cup his heavy cock through his trousers. "It's a shame Douglas isn't here to service us tonight."

"Yes, Master," Roger murmured, head tipped back and eyes closed, canting his hips ever so slightly into the pressure of Nikolai's hand. He only indulged himself for a moment, though, before starting to slide off the bed and to his knees.

Nikolai tightened the fingers of one hand in Roger's hair and the other around Roger's cock. "No," he whispered. Licked his lips meaningfully, eyes on Roger's crotch as he did so.

Roger's pupils flared and his chest hitched. "Oh," he breathed.

"'Oh' indeed," Nikolai said as he guided Roger back, unbuttoned the man's pants, and set to work.

As gruff as he was, Jeremy was a surprisingly gentle lover—wooed, perhaps, by a rimming so long and thorough that Douglas could barely feel his tongue when he was through. After they'd finished a leisurely, affectionate fuck, Jeremy had rolled over onto his back and gone immediately to sleep, leaving Douglas alone with his thoughts for the night.

He knew there was something going on between Nikolai and Roger, something that made Roger quite anxious, but he didn't know what, and he *did* know it wasn't his place to care. Still, he couldn't help lying awake and thinking about it while Jeremy snored away beside him. It was almost time for him to leave. He knew that. Roger did, too. Mentioned it sometimes, always gently, with the intention of comforting Douglas and offering him a sympathetic ear. The master himself had refused to mention or acknowledge it, though. His prerogative, of course, but Douglas wished sometimes that the master would take more care in this regard—talk to him, warn him, *prepare* him. Not that he hadn't been doing that since Day One, but Allen— *my new master*—was a frightening man, one Douglas wasn't sure he'd know how to please. There'd be no more safety net, no more Nikolai, no more Roger, even no more Jeremy. No one to help him when he was lost or confused or afraid, no one to hold him when he was weak or praise him when he'd done well. Allen didn't seem the type. And Mat . . . well, he couldn't be counted on for *anything*, could he.

Douglas tossed carefully, too restless to stay still, but fearful of waking Jeremy. The clock by the bedside shone 4 a.m.; Jeremy's alarm would be going off soon. Douglas should sleep at least a little. Sure, he'd pulled all-nighters before, but he'd never had a demanding master to please the next day, never felt so keenly the drive not to let someone down, not to fail them—or worst of all, disappoint them. How could he anticipate Nikolai's needs if he couldn't keep his eyes open? He needed to stop worrying about Nikolai and Roger, Mat and Allen. It wasn't his place. It was irresponsible. He was being careless. Foolish. *Bad.*

Hadn't Nikolai warned him about this very thing? He should request the cane when Nikolai summoned him today. He hated it, oh how he *hated* that sharp, biting pain. But it was so much better than failure. Scrubbed his sins from his flesh in hot sparks of agony and brought absolution in its wake. Life hadn't always been so simple, mistakes so easy to fix, love so easy to reclaim. He'd take the pain and be grateful for it.

Grateful. Simple. Those words and the understanding of them washed over him, and before he knew it, he'd drifted off into easy, contented sleep.

Which was shattered all too soon by Jeremy's alarm. Both of them jolted at the noise, though only Jeremy climbed right out of bed. He'd stayed up far too late last night, too, but that didn't stop him from heading straight for the shower. Douglas, clutched in the grips of exhaustion and with no specific orders for the morning, slid back into sleep until the snooze alarm went off. Then again, and again, and again. When he finally worked up the energy to turn the damn thing off, Jeremy was gone. No one had come for him, or called for him. It was barely six. He went back to sleep.

And woke three hours later to Roger's hand on his shoulder, shaking gently.

"Oh God, I'm sorry," he muttered as he sat up, ready to leap out of bed, but Roger shook his head as he sat beside him.

"It's all right. Master said to let you sleep in. You have a big day ahead of you." He crossed one ankle over his knee and gave his foot an absentminded pat.

Big day? Oh, God, was he ... was *today* ...

He wasn't ready to leave yet. It couldn't be time already. *Couldn't* be.

He could ask Roger, though. It wouldn't be insubordinate from one slave to another.

He had to ask.

"Is he—" He flinched, heart pounding so hard he couldn't speak. "Is today the day? That we go?"

Roger smiled fondly, a little sadly, but he was shaking his head, so Douglas could breathe again. "No. Not quite yet. Today's the day the master reminds you that no matter where you go, or for how long, you'll still always be his."

Douglas knew that already, right down to the bottom of his heart, to the very last hair on his head. He needed no reminder of the truth that would sustain him through his time with Allen.

But nor was he about to argue with any choice his master made for him. And Roger looked so ... was that pride? Yes, for him. Douglas was sure of it. He didn't know what he'd done to deserve it, but it warmed him through. Shook the sleep from his mind. He tossed the covers back, stretched until his back popped.

"Should I shower first?" he asked.

Roger nodded. "But be quick. Five minutes. You can use Jeremy's."

Oh, he bet Jeremy would just *love* that. The thought kind of tickled him, even after the lovely night they'd shared. The man was still a grump, after all. Douglas headed into the bathroom and turned the hot tap, snickering at the thought of leaving his hair in the drain.

Except, watch the surly jerk keep it and bake it into your next meal.

There was no time to agonize over the issue, though, so he quickly scrubbed clean under the hot water, made use of Jeremy's enema attachment, and was out and dried in the allotted five minutes.

Roger was waiting for him outside, still vaguely anxious, and he greeted Douglas with a kiss on the nose. "Master's in his study," he said. "He'll tell you what's happening when you get there. I'll warn you, though, there's a bit of formality to it, so try not to crack any jokes, all right? But don't let that stress you out or panic you. I'll be there the whole time, and so will Master."

Douglas still didn't understand what he had to be stressed or panicked about, exactly, but he appreciated the sentiment just the same, slipping his hand into Roger's larger one and giving it a gentle squeeze. "You're always there for me," he said. "The both of you. Thank you."

"Now stop, you're getting me all sentimental." Roger cleared his throat. Was he . . . was he crying a little? Would he really miss Douglas that much?

Douglas squeezed Roger's hand, and Roger squeezed back, and together they walked down the hall to the master's study. The paneled double doors were open, warmth from the lit fireplace wafting invitingly. Inside, Douglas spotted Nikolai first, as he should have—a slave's attention should always be drawn to his master. But then, beyond Nikolai, in that plush antique recliner he'd never once seen used, was Mat. Wearing the big black bit gag that made him drool all over his own chin, and looking ten kinds of nervous and pissed. Jaw clenched. Resolutely avoiding Douglas's eyes, or face, or . . . anything, really. Staring up at the ceiling in silent rage. And, Douglas realized, tied down very, very thoroughly.

Douglas turned his attention back to his master, downright delighted to realize that Mat's presence hadn't upset him. Hadn't thrown him off-balance. In fact, he felt nothing at all toward the slave. No anger, no resentment, nothing. Just a vague sense of obligation—one placed there by Nikolai rather than any familial bond: *keep your brother under control for me at your new master's.*

"Master," he said, ignoring Mat entirely, and knelt. And strangely enough, Roger knelt beside him. Roger only rarely knelt; Douglas was used to and happy with the difference in authority between them. But apparently today those lines were blurred, though not enough for Roger to go naked, the way Douglas always did.

Nikolai was standing by the study's huge fireplace, where Douglas had so long ago burned up his clothes. Something smoked there now, red hot, and Nikolai prodded it as he turned to acknowledge Douglas's presence. "Ah, good morning, my sweet. I trust you're well-rested?"

"Yes, Master. Thank you, Master." No asking what was going on here, why Mat was here, why Roger seemed so . . . off-balance today. No questions at all, just patient obedience. Simple. Happy.

The master seemed happy too. He gestured for Douglas to stand, to approach him. Cupped Douglas's cheek when he drew close enough. Kissed him, nearly chaste and painfully sweet, long and lingering like he wanted to imprint this moment in his mind forever. If that was the case, Douglas was happy to stay in the moment with him, perfectly preserved in his contentment.

"There comes a time in every new boy's training when he's learned all I have to teach him, Douglas."

Douglas's empty belly clenched, as did his fingers by his sides. *He's saying good-bye. Please don't let this be good-bye.*

And then, *If this is good-bye, then please let me be strong and brave and a good boy. Please let me not cry.*

Nikolai's hand returned to his cheek, so, so gentle, thumb sweeping away the tears Douglas wasn't letting fall. "When with every thought, every breath, every action, he shows me all he's learned, makes me so very proud, full to bursting with it. When he's transformed into his best possible self. He becomes . . . art."

The master paused—a strange, expectant silence Douglas itched to fill, but didn't know how to. He thought back on Roger's warning—*a formal moment, no jokes*—bit his tongue and waited.

"Like any artist proud of his creation, Douglas, I sign my work when it's finished. A mark to show the world who made you. A mark to remind *you* who loves you more than anyone. A keepsake and a promise, if you will."

A tattoo? Was he getting a tattoo? He imagined *Nikolai* in calligraphic script, flowing across his heart, or maybe the inside of his thigh. How it'd warm him at night in Allen's house, to brush his fingers across the script and *remember*. But . . . he hadn't seen any tattoos on Roger, or Jeremy, or anyone here, come to think of it. As much as Douglas loved the idea of a tattoo in a special place, would his new master appreciate seeing Nikolai's name every time he spread Douglas's legs?

No marks at all, in fact. Nothing marring their perfect bodies. And the master always said Douglas was special, sure, but he couldn't possibly be *that* special. Nikolai said he did this with all his boys. So what was he missing?

"Will you show him, Roger?" Nikolai cast Roger a fond look. "My very first, and I was so proud to sign him, the same way my mentor had signed all his creations before me. The same way all trainers sign their completed works."

Roger nodded once and began to strip, slowly and methodically removing every item of his fine tailored clothing to reveal the handsome body underneath. Shoes and socks, too. He set it all aside, and when he was done, he walked to Nikolai's side and knelt. No, didn't kneel—prostrated himself, back to Douglas, forehead to the floor, and Douglas wasn't sure, exactly, what he was supposed to be seeing at first, until he *did* see it, a faint shining mark on the sole of Roger's left foot, where the skin wasn't as perfectly smooth as his right.

A scar. Douglas inched closer, and when the master issued no reprimand, inched closer still. Knelt right behind Roger and pressed his palm to the mark, feeling it out.

Not a scar. A *brand*.

"NP," the letters no bigger than a silver dollar. Just as ornate as Douglas had imagined the tattoo would be, but subtler, and somehow *more* permanent. Strangely old-fashioned, too, reminding Douglas of stories of ancient Rome. Of gladiators sworn to fealty to their dominus, fighting and bleeding and dying for their master's glory.

Such devotion. Such clarity of purpose. He felt akin to those men. As fierce in his determination to serve. As strong.

And he'd wear Nikolai's mark just as proudly.

No, more so.

"I'd be honored, Master," he said. "I'd be so, so honored. I love you."

"I love you too, Douglas, and I'm proud to call you mine. But . . ." He turned to face the fire, stirred it with a poker—no, the brand, it was the brand, glowing red hot and making the air around it shimmer like a mirage, and Douglas thought he should be terrified, but he wasn't, not even a little bit. ". . . I'm saving the best for last. Mathias first—" And Nikolai had barely gotten those words out when Mathias howled behind his gag, thrashing against his bindings, but getting nowhere, not really. The chair was heavy, the straps tight. And, Douglas realized, his left foot wasn't just tied across the footrest—no, it was strapped into a frame, purpose-built to expose the sole, immobilized as thoroughly as if it'd been casted.

Nikolai strode forward, brand in hand, and Douglas followed close behind, wanting to see, to know how it would be when his own time came. Not like this, though—not whimpering and shaking and reeking of fear sweat, pupils dilated and teeth bared in a feral snarl around a bit gag. Not struggling to get away (and failing, of course, as Mat failed at everything in his life), not filled with disgust and fury.

Cowardice, all of it. Cowardice and disloyalty and base, animal fear. It was fucking disgusting. Mat *disgusted* him.

"Be quiet, you ungrateful beast."

Mat's panicked gaze snapped, shocked, to Douglas's face, and Douglas realized he'd spoken aloud, issued an order he had no right to issue, and he hated Mat even more for that, for making him slip up in front of the master. He apologized, but Nikolai was paying him no mind, squatted level as he was with Mat's bound foot, studying the sole like an artist seeking out the hidden shape of his canvas.

He brought the glowing end of the brand to bear, and Mat lurched again as the first wave of heat hit his sole. His gagged screams turned to whimpers, high and broken, an animal in the throes of its own violent destruction. Douglas was half-surprised Mat wasn't pissing himself.

The brand drew nearer. Nearer. Nikolai reached out with his free hand to stroke Mat's calf, then drew it back to steady the brand. Mat's whimpers grew higher, more urgent. The coward was crying. No, *sobbing*, and the brand hadn't even touched him yet.

"Be brave, Mathias," Nikolai said. Not scolding, not a command. Just . . . gentle. Kind. Understanding. So much more so than Douglas could've been to Mat now.

Mat didn't deserve Nikolai's kindness. He deserved to piss and cry like the animal he was. He deserved pain and shame, and he deserved for Nikolai to feel as disgusted by him as Douglas was.

But Nikolai was so much better than Douglas, so much more kind and good and generous, and he shushed Mathias like a parent would an exhausted, tantruming child, firm but loving. And then he pressed the brand to the sole of Mat's foot, right in the center of the arch, and Mat screamed and *screamed* and sucked in a ragged breath and screamed again through his tears, kept screaming long after Nikolai pulled the brand away, replaced it with a thick pad of sterile gauze dripping with cool water. Screamed and sobbed and struggled, though he had to know it was pointless now, too late to break free and stop this, screamed until his voice cracked behind the gag and his bulging muscles went limp and all the color drained from his skin.

Roger returned the brand to the fire as Nikolai stood watching Mat cry. Surely the pain couldn't be *that* bad—surely they'd all been through worse since they'd been procured. But Mat looked so pale, covered in sweat, chest heaving, pulse pounding way too fast at his temples and throat, and if it wasn't the pain making those fat tears roll down his cheeks, then what was? Douglas swallowed hard, caught a faint whiff of burnt skin, and had to swallow again. He didn't want to be afraid. He wanted to be strong for Nikolai. But *could* he be?

Nikolai stood by patiently, waiting for Mat to exhaust himself. *Yes*, Douglas decided. *I can be. Mat's a coward. Weak. An animal. He can't control himself. He doesn't know what he's fighting for. I do. I can.*

At last Mat's sobs eased down to the occasional whimper or hitching sniffle, and his body went limp in his bonds. Nikolai nodded to Roger, who swapped the wet gauze pad for a dry one shimmering with ointment, pressed it carefully to Mat's foot and wrapped it in place with a bandage. Nikolai unbuckled the gag and offered Mat water from a bottle.

Douglas half expected Mat's pride to interfere, but Mat didn't hesitate; he opened his mouth and drank.

"If I untie you," Nikolai said, "will you make a scene?"

A moment's pause, and then, eyes downcast, voice scratchy and broken, "No."

"If you put so much as a single ounce of weight on that foot, I will strap you to your bed with a catheter for the next week, do you understand me?"

Another pause, another scratchy, despairing, "Yes." No *sir*, no *master*. Such disrespect. It made Douglas furious, but Nikolai didn't seem to mind at all, so maybe Douglas shouldn't either.

"I'd let you rest here awhile," Nikolai added, "but Douglas needs the chair."

Yes, I do, and I won't shame our family name when I'm in it, you coward. You untrained beast.

Mat nodded, looking weary beyond comprehension. Douglas realized Mat was still crying, though at least he was being quiet about it now. His fingers itched to hit Mat, give him something *real* to cry about. But Nikolai was unstrapping him with such care, such gentle kindness, that Douglas felt guilty for the thought.

When all the buckles were undone, Roger helped Nikolai get Mat to his feet—well, foot. Nikolai gestured at the now-empty recliner with his chin. "Make yourself comfortable," he said to Douglas. "We'll just be a moment seeing him to his room."

Douglas nodded, fixing Mat with a glare as they passed one another. He went obediently to the chair and sat, feeling the slick of Mat's sweat all over the leather. The stench.

He'd ask for another shower when all this was over.

At least the pathetic animal hadn't pissed himself.

Douglas settled back in the recliner, surprisingly comfortable despite its intended use. Or maybe that was the point. A cradle purpose-built to support the first emergence of a fresh new slave. The straps that'd been holding Mat down were curled on the floor, not a part of the chair as Douglas had originally thought. Then again, why would they be? Who among Nikolai's boys, *except* his animal of a—*brother, go on, it's okay to say it; it's not your fault you're related*—except his animal of a brother would feel anything but elation at the prospect of receiving their master's mark?

The brace for immobilizing the foot was very much a part of the chair, though. Which made sense too; even the strongest new boy might not be able to resist jerking away from that kind of pain and ruining the fine brand. He leaned forward to examine it. Molded steel padded with thin foam. A tangle of leather straps. This one went behind the toes, that one across the heel, two crisscrossing around the ankle, one higher up the shin. He buckled himself in. Pulled the straps tight until he couldn't move his foot even a centimeter. Sat back and waited.

"Ah, there he is."

His master's voice. Full of pride.

Douglas sat up in his seat with a bright smile. "Ready for you, Master."

"I see that."

"Not afraid at all, Master." That was the most important part. Not afraid. Excited. Ready to face the pain and receive his master's most precious gift.

Nikolai practically beamed at him. He felt the warmth of it even over the crackling fire, right down to his toes. Then Nikolai's fingers were *on* his toes, checking the straps, making sure everything was right. Of course it was; Douglas wouldn't screw up something like this, and wasn't Nikolai always telling him what a clever boy he was? The master ran a tickling finger down the sole of his foot, and while the rest of his body lurched a little, his foot remained immobile. Nikolai, still grinning so broad, so proud, turned away from him and went to retrieve the brand from the fire.

"You don't have to watch if you don't want to." Roger's voice, soft as a caress, right near his ear. He'd actually forgotten about Roger for a second, as focused as he was on his master.

He kept his eyes on Nikolai as he replied, equally soft, "I want to."

He sensed Roger nod, and then Roger's hand was slipping into his own, fingers squeezing gently. Douglas knew there'd been a time, not so long ago, when his fists would've been clenched with fear here. But he wasn't an animal anymore. Wasn't a baby. Didn't need anyone to hold his hand. He appreciated the sentiment, the support, but he didn't squeeze back. Nikolai was approaching now, brand glowing hot. It looked like such a simple thing, such a little thing, but it held so much meaning, so much *power*.

Roger let him go with a chuckle and said, "I'll be right here the whole time." He settled his hand on Douglas's forearm.

The master squatted down before Douglas's foot like he had before Mat's, the artist contemplating his canvas. Douglas clenched his jaw—just a precaution, didn't want to embarrass himself—but didn't close his eyes, didn't turn his head away.

When Nikolai pressed the brand to Douglas's arch, Douglas didn't even scream.

The pain was *enormous*, though, so big it took a shockingly long moment to even travel from his foot to his brain. He lurched as it hit, but kept his scream behind teeth clenched so hard his jaw ached, hands clawing into the armrests of the chair. So, *so* grateful for the brace. And for Roger at his side. And for his master, too, eyes shining with love and pride, trading the brand for a dripping wad of gauze that he held to Douglas's foot, damping those terrible, consuming flames.

Douglas met his master's eyes, blinked back tears, and smiled the goofiest, drunkest smile he'd ever felt on his own face. His master smiled right back. "See?" Douglas said, partly to Roger but mostly to the only man in the room who truly mattered to either of them. "I did it."

"You did it," Nikolai agreed, and leaned forward to kiss him.

Douglas would have kissed him back, he really would have, except just then he passed out.

CHAPTER THREE

The pain in Mat's foot pulsed with every beat of his heart. Had kept him up half the fucking night, weepy and exhausted and feeling filthy in his own skin, like ants crawling all over him, like invisible fingers touching uninvited, everywhere, all over, outside and in, and he couldn't stop it anymore. Would never be able to stop it again.

Well. At least the horror was so huge he was just . . . numb with it. Everywhere but his fucking foot. He'd have hacked it off in a heartbeat if he'd had the right tools. Or even the wrong ones. Had come *thisclose* to digging his own fingers into the fresh wound and ripping it away. Only the knowledge that Nikolai would strap him down and do it to the other foot, then *keep* him strapped down until the wound had healed, had stayed his hand.

When he got out of here—not if, *when*—he'd cut the skin right off if he had to. For now, he'd just have to try to live in this skin without tearing himself out of it. Find a way not to let the despair beat him. He still had a brother to save, after all.

No matter how much contempt had been in Dougie's eyes when Mat had fought to stop this.

Congratulations, Nikolai. Dougie hates me now as much as I hate him sometimes.

He wasn't gonna let the bastard win in the end, though. He *wasn't.*

He tried to hold on to that conviction for a while, let it calm him enough to sleep. There was no hiding how big of a setback this was, though. Permanent physical scarring to go with his permanent mental scarring.

At least it hadn't crippled him.

That's a low bar, Mat, Jesus.

But then, better to lower the bar and step over it than to keep it high and have no hope of crossing it at all. These were extreme circumstances. It wasn't wrong to adjust his worldview, was it?

After all, before this he'd have never so much as contemplated a circumstance that would make him use the words "hate" and "Dougie" in the same sentence, unless it was something like "I hate seeing Dougie unhappy." In the outside world, they were brothers, and you loved your brother and stood by him and forgave him no matter what. But this wasn't the outside world anymore, it was Nikolai's world. And soon it'd be even worse: it'd be *Allen's* world, that's-right-pretty-pup-ride-your-brother's-cock world.

Nausea surged at the thought, spurred on by the throbbing in his foot, the relentless, painful beat of *you're marked now, you're marked now, you're marked now* as steady as his pulse in his ears. He bit it back. Crutches were waiting for him by the bed, but he wasn't ready to use them. That'd mean admitting he *needed* them. It'd mean admitting *why*. He couldn't face that yet.

So he curled up tight beneath the covers and squeezed his eyes closed instead. Tried to shut off his brain. Tried to pay no attention to the pain in his foot, the fist around his heart, the jumbled fuckery in his head. Just sleep. Sleep. Sleep, damn it.

He must've for a little while, because the sound of a knock at the door startled him awake again.

"It's me," Roger called softly through the door.

Mat didn't say *Come in*, because Roger would do that anyway. Oh well, better Roger than Nikolai. Roger was still his not-ally, after all, someone he couldn't quite hate, but who was still Nikolai's man in the end—a fact that Mat couldn't let himself forget, as much as he sometimes wanted to.

But at least Roger hadn't *marked* him.

"I brought you some breakfast," Roger said. "And a change of bandages." He put a tray down by the table, picked up a little white bottle and shook it. "Painkillers too. No reason for you to lie there and suffer, after all."

Mat actually scoffed at that. Yeah, like anything that came in a fucking bottle could solve his problems right now.

"I'm not hungry," he said instead.

Roger's expression fell a little, but he brought the pills and a cup of juice—pineapple, Mat's favorite—over to him anyway. Mat took them because he couldn't stand to see that fucking *pout* on Roger's face, and Roger sat down by his hip, close but not touching. "It can't be *that* bad, surely? I mean, it's you. You've definitely had worse."

Worse pain? Yes, probably. That electric shock butt-plug nightmare came to mind. The serum came to mind. The sight of Dougie wrapping his mouth around Mat's junk came to mind.

But this was…it was permanent. It was public. It was recognizable. It was fucking *personalized*.

And it was something he had no way to fight.

But Roger wouldn't understand any of that. Was *proud* of his brand, like Dougie had looked so proud to know his was coming. *Wanted* it to be permanent. Personalized. Public.

The three P's. Mat wanted to be sick. He wanted to rip Nikolai's head off with his bare fucking hands. He wanted to punch that judgmental, contemptuous look right off his brother's worshipful fucking face.

He wanted to be *strong* again. Not feel so fucking helpless and scared and angry all the time.

"What's for breakfast?" he made himself ask.

Roger perked right up, as if all the world's problems had been solved by that one simple question, no more worries, no more concerns. As if Mat were healed. "Chocolate chip pancakes with fresh whipped cream and a side of bacon."

"Not my usual diet," Mat said, eyebrows lifting—and, surprisingly, mouth watering.

"No, but shhh, don't tell Master." Roger's green eyes twinkled. "It's tradition to have a bit of pampering after the branding, and I don't see why you should miss out. So I thought maybe you and I could have a little fun."

"Fun," Mat echoed mechanically. Had he just stepped into the fucking twilight zone? How in the hell could Roger even think about having fun in a place like this? At a time like this? And why did the idea sound so impossibly tempting to Mat?

Roger eyed him mock-sternly. "Yes, fun. I have a laptop loaded up with the entire *Fast & Furious* franchise, and Jeremy promised to make his famous caramel popcorn. For the next few days, at least, you're off your feet *and* off your diet, and I'm at your beck and call. And if you get bored with Vin Diesel eye-fucking Paul Walker"—he smiled and winked—"we can always just make out in the back of the theater."

Was he seriously propositioning Mat?

God, that sounded tempting too.

Except he's Nikolai's man first and foremost. He can't be your ally for real, no matter how kindly he acts and no matter how good it sounds to just let yourself go.

"You know," Roger said, that fucking *pout* creeping back onto the corners of his eyes and mouth, "most people don't scowl quite so hard at the prospect of free movies, junk food, and blowjobs."

"My foot hurts," he said, because it was easier than any other explanation he could offer.

But then of course Roger nodded at the fucking pills and pineapple juice Mat had been holding this whole time. He swallowed them. Drank the juice. Roger smiled. Shit, but the juice was good. It didn't seem right, somehow, that he should enjoy anything that much when he'd been *marked*, when he was stewing with rage toward his own brother. People who hated their families weren't supposed to have good things. People who failed to protect their little brothers weren't supposed to be sitting around sipping fucking pineapple juice and watching action films. And yeah, maybe he'd gotten over blaming himself for letting Dougie be taken, but it was nobody's fault but his own that he'd let himself grow to *hate* the kid.

Pity, too. Don't forget pity. And grief. So fucking much of it. More even than he'd felt at his parents' graveside, watching the dirt piling on their coffins and knowing he'd lost so much more than just his mom and dad—that life would never, *could* never be the same again.

But at least Mom and Dad were at rest, either in heaven or in nothingness. Dougie was trapped in a nightmarish living hell—

"Here." He must've zoned out, because he snapped back to Roger settling a tray over Mat's lap, piled high with contraband. His mouth watered despite the turmoil in his head; he'd almost never been one of those people put off their food when upset. He plucked up a crisp strip of bacon between thumb and forefinger, ate half of it in one bite. Embarrassed himself with the little moany noise that escaped his throat. Jesus, that was good. He couldn't remember the last time he'd had bacon. Years.

But then he dropped the other half back to the plate, wiped his fingers on the linen napkin beside it. "You can't placate me with food, you know."

Roger crawled into bed beside him, back propped against the headboard, and finished the piece of bacon Mat had abandoned. He settled a laptop on his lap, let it boot. "I'm not trying to *placate* anyone. This isn't a competition, Mathias. Breakfast isn't a consolation prize. If something's upsetting you, let's talk about it, but I really wish you'd stop punishing yourself all the time."

The whipped cream on the pancakes was melting. Mat swiped a finger through it and sucked it clean, eyes closing on a single moment of bliss that was knocked clear away by the sense memory of sucking so many *other* things clean, unwanted things forced on him, as white and drippy as the whipped cream.

PTSD, he realized. Jesus fucking Christ, he had fucking PTSD. Well, TSD, he supposed—couldn't be *P* until he'd gotten the fuck out of here. And really, was it any wonder?

"Nothing's upsetting me." He picked up his shitty plastic fork and cut a wedge from his stack of pancakes—*See? I'm fine. I'm eating.* It was a patently ridiculous lie, and they both knew it. *Everything* was upsetting here.

Well, except the pancakes. The pancakes were really fucking amazing.

Roger's hand came to rest atop his forearm, the touch gentle, unobtrusive. Surprisingly welcome. Mat found himself holding still for it, pressing into it just a little. "I won't tell Master, if that's what you're worried about. He said I could keep your confidence. I want to *help*, Mathias."

"Call me Mat," he said. "Please."

Not Mathias, that formal name Nikolai insisted on using. The name his mother had used when he'd gotten into *real* trouble—*Mathias Robert Carmichael, get your butt down here right now!*—the name irrevocably and forevermore associated with Bad Things.

Roger nodded. "Let me help you, Mat."

"I—" Mat stared down at his pancakes, stomach flip-flopping. "I don't know that you *can*. I understand what you're trying to do and I think you're a nice guy—a really nice guy—for wanting to do it, especially after I— After I got you beaten . . ." God, how was Roger still *talking* to him, let alone being so *kind* to him? Shaking his head and smiling that soft little smile like Mat was an idiot for blaming himself? Well, if Roger could forgive it, maybe Mat could eventually forgive himself for it, too. "But . . . I don't . . . I don't deserve it, damn it! It's a joke! It's a joke for me to be sitting here eating these pancakes and flirting and watching movies—"

He thumped his fist on the breakfast tray, rattling the plastic pancake plate. Rather than risk knocking it to the floor—because he wouldn't do that to Roger again, make him clean up his fucking messes and get his ass fucking beaten to hell and back, not anymore— he lifted it from his lap and set it on the nightstand. Roger watched him the whole time, saying nothing, radiating silent support. And, okay, maybe vague disapproval that Mat was letting his treats go cold. And a little confusion, too. He clearly *wanted* to understand, but he couldn't. Of course he couldn't.

Matt scrubbed a hand across his face and then flopped his arm out, encompassing the room, the house, the whole ugly fucking situation. "It's not . . . it's not just because of where we are and what's happening to me and what's about to happen, but because I don't *deserve* good things. I don't deserve fucking chocolate chip pancakes and movies in bed and . . . and *you*."

Roger's brows creased, and he captured Mat's wildly gesturing hand in both his own, but he still said nothing. Maybe he sensed that Mat wouldn't listen right now. Or maybe he had no idea what to say to make things better. Because there *wasn't* anything that would. No magic fucking words here.

Just the ugly, ugly truth: "Don't you get it?" he asked, pulling his hand away from Roger's, and Roger's face creased even further, head shaking once, back and forth. "I don't deserve to even pretend to be happy as long as my brother . . . I'm supposed to love him, and I'm supposed to take care of him and forgive him and I do, I *do*, I swear I do, but I can't help but *hate* him too. I don't want to hate him, and then I want to hate him so bad because maybe it would hurt less and maybe it would be the right thing for *both* of us, and I just don't know. I don't know what to do, there's no fucking rulebook for this, there's nobody to look up to, no coach or cornerman except *Nikolai*, and

I can't even look up to him the way you and Dougie do because he won't even fucking brainwash me! So there's nothing."

He slumped back against the headboard, panting and drained, feeling bizarrely like a snake who'd just shed his skin: tender, vulnerable, raw, and too exposed—everything too vivid, too bright, too fresh and on the surface. So lost, knowing everything safe and familiar was behind him, knowing he might not even recognize himself if he looked in a mirror.

Roger reached out with a tentative hand—slowly, cautiously, like approaching a strange and maybe violent dog—and, when Mat didn't rebuff him, touched his fingertips to Mat's cheek.

Only when Roger wiped away the tears did Mat realize he'd been crying.

And then things got weirder, because Roger raised himself up onto his knees beside Mat, took Mat's face in both hands, and laid a gentle kiss on his mouth. Not a chaste condescending peck, not a pornographic tongue kiss, but something soft and sweet and kind, so full of understanding and love that for a moment—a long, long, *long* moment—Mat was shocked into inaction. Sat there. Leaned into it, even. Let Roger kiss him. Closed his eyes and just . . . *basked* in it.

Kissed back. Wrapped his arms around Roger and pulled him close and moaned softly into that tender, loving mouth.

But then he remembered he was a terrible, hate-filled human being and a bad brother and a failure and *marked forever*, and people like him didn't deserve nice things, didn't deserve such compassion and generosity, and he drew his hands back to Roger's shoulders and gently pushed him away.

"I can't," Mat whispered. The words Roger hadn't said—hadn't needed to say, Mat had known all along—the last time they'd kissed.

Roger crooked a smile at him, like he was the world's most adorable idiot, and said, "Of course you can. You just don't *think* you can." He settled back on his heels, touched Mat's face again, and Jesus, Mat wished he'd cut that out because he wasn't strong enough to stop him again, not this time. "Tell me," he said, hand still cupping Mat's jaw, not letting Mat look away from him, "when you and Douglas go to Allen's, will you watch out for him?"

"Of course," Mat said, automatic as breathing.

"And protect him? Even if it means taking a proverbial bullet for him?"

A little less automatic this time, but that was just the fear talking; it was easier to profess you'd take a bullet for someone before you knew just how terrible that bullet could be. Still, the answer was as screamingly obvious as ever. Mat nodded against Roger's palm. "Yeah."

Roger looked relieved. "Good. I've gotten pretty close to him this past while, you know. I worry. He's sensitive. I really don't want to see him hurt." Roger's thumb stroked a single line up and down Mat's stubbled cheek, and he tilted his head, smiling ruefully. "Of course, I don't want to see you hurt either, but . . ." *But that's what you've been built for. Were bought for.* They both knew that. "But one more question. If you were really such a bad person, if you were really so vengeful and hateful, do you think you'd still sacrifice so much to protect him?"

"I—" Mat blinked. Ducked his head away from Roger's hand. "Penance," he said. "It's . . . I'm just trying to make things *right* again." Well, as right as they ever could be in this place.

Roger seemed momentarily surprised, said nothing. Like he'd been so sure of getting a different answer and didn't know what to do with the one Mat had given him instead. Finally, he said, "Evil men don't bother with penance."

Mat shrugged; he was pretty sure that wasn't true. You didn't have to be evil all the way through to still be a bad person. You could care about some things but not others. Lots of things, even.

"Do you still love him?" Roger asked.

"Yes!"

They both blinked at Mat's instant reply, so forceful it'd nearly been shouted. Then Roger raised an eyebrow at him—his *you adorable idiot* face—and said, "Well, there you go."

It . . . couldn't really be that simple, could it?

"You're hurt," Roger said, reaching out again, but this time he went for Mat's hand where it was fisted on his thigh, laid his own over it. "People aren't rational when they're hurting. They lash out. They hurt back. They think nasty, uncharitable things. Even about the ones they love. That doesn't mean they love those people any less. And it certainly doesn't make them undeserving of being loved back."

Being loved back. God, Mat wished he could be loved back, wished someone, *anyone* still loved him. But Mom and Dad were long gone, and he hadn't gotten a shiny new foster family like Dougie had, and yeah, sure, Coach Darryl *liked* him well enough, but he was ultimately just a meal ticket (and a shit poor one, at that) for the guy. And Dougie . . . poor Dougie was too far gone to love him. Maybe Roger was right and Mat's own hate was just out of hurt and didn't—couldn't—change the way he loved Dougie. But Dougie's hate wasn't out of hurt; it was manufactured, manipulated, specifically designed to leave no room for love.

And that wasn't Dougie's fault. Mat *knew* that. Knew it down to the marrow of his bones. And if it wasn't Dougie's fault that he hated Mat, then . . . well, then possibly, maybe, it wasn't Mat's fault that sometimes he hated Dougie too. Maybe Roger was right. Maybe he *was* lashing out. Like an injured dog, scared and hurting and biting the hands of the folks who'd loved it its whole life. Because he did still love Dougie, somewhere under all the anger and betrayal and pain. Not even deep under. He could feel it brimming right there beneath the surface, right on the tip of his tongue, the first thing that came out of his mouth when he spoke. *Yes, I love him. Yes, I will protect him, no matter what.*

So maybe there was redemption for them yet.

For both of them.

Maybe he wasn't a monster. And maybe Dougie—poor sweet Dougie—wasn't really one either. Maybe Mat could still *fix* this.

Maybe Roger wasn't a fool to keep giving him chances, to keep coming to his side over and over again no matter how much he lashed out, no matter how much his actions hurt Roger.

Maybe Mat could learn a thing or two from Roger. From his kindness and patience and trust. Maybe he could learn to manage these two sides of himself until he could repair the tear, rather than let the one overpower the other.

Roger smiled at him, and damn it all, he realized he was fucking *crying* again—when had he become such a fucking *girl* about everything down here (*only don't let Coach Darryl's daughter hear you say that; she'll kick your ass into next fucking* year)—and his fist unclenched and he flipped his hand up, laced his fingers with Roger's and gave him a little tug.

Roger came to him so eagerly—not lustful, not hungry, just proving his point. Kissed Mat again, free hand sliding up Mat's shoulder, neck, into his hair. Petting him, almost. Mat closed his watering eyes and sighed into Roger's parted lips, let himself feel loved, let himself *have this*.

"That's better," Roger murmured against his lips. And then, pulling back, "Your breakfast's getting cold. And Paul Walker."

No verb in that sentence; did Roger have a little actor crush? Mat chuckled, sniffled, swiped at his eyes with one hand and reached for his tray with the other.

He could have this. This brief escape, this single moment of pleasure and companionship and happiness. It'd only make him stronger, after all, for what was to come. And he'd need every ounce of that strength if he was ever going to get them home again.

Douglas barely got out of bed for a week. He and Nikolai ate all their meals there, and spent their waking hours reading and watching movies and talking and just generally fucking like rabbits, none of which Douglas minded in the slightest. It made him sad, sometimes, to think that he'd be losing all this soon, but he also knew what he was sacrificing it *for*, and that he wouldn't be away forever, and remembering that always made things okay.

He was even okay with all the girly stuff Nikolai had spent this past week teaching him. How to tuck his cock and balls so they wouldn't bulge out the front of the little lace panties Nikolai was making him wear. How to put on mascara and eyeliner and lipstick and blush without looking like a clown. How to alter his voice to sound more feminine. How to use a garter belt and pull up his stockings without poking his fingers right through them. The only thing he hadn't practiced was walking in high heels, because of his foot.

All for Allen, Nikolai explained. Allen, who insisted he didn't like men, only liked to punish male slaves for tempting him with their unabashed whoreishness.

Douglas didn't like the idea of dressing as a girl for some sadistic closet case, but it was what he had to do to return to Nikolai, so he embraced it.

Even enjoyed it, a little, when Nikolai tucked him and called him beautiful and made love to him face-to-face, kissing the lipstick right off his mouth. He'd try to remember that transgressive sense of happiness and security when it was Allen stroking between his legs.

Now Nikolai was checking the sole of his foot, dropping little kisses on his heel, each toe, skirting around the healing brand and making Douglas shiver. It didn't even hurt anymore, not really, though he still limped a little when he walked. Nikolai assured him that was normal, that he'd be limp-free in another week or maybe just a few more days, that it might take several months for the mark to rise to its finished form.

He could hardly wait. But then, he'd gotten good at patience lately, hadn't he. And he'd need to get better still in the days to come.

"I've something to tell you," Nikolai murmured against the ball of Douglas's foot.

Douglas's heart skipped—*good news or bad?*—but he forced calm. "Yes, Master?"

Nikolai rose to his hands and knees, kissed his way up Douglas's calf, knee, thigh. Douglas shivered, let his legs fall open, tried not to hope too hard that his master might pleasure him. (Allen would probably never pleasure him, not if he couldn't face his bisexuality.)

"It's my going-away present to you; that's why I didn't tell you sooner."

Douglas's shoulders untensed. Good news, then. "That's okay, Master. You know you don't have to explain yourself to me."

Nikolai nipped the inside of his thigh, playful but rough. Douglas's cock sprang up, but he forced himself not to draw attention to it. "I want to. Hush. Now, I've made some alternate arrangements with Allen regarding your sale."

"A-alternate arrangements, Master?"

Nikolai nodded, and his hand swept up Douglas's legs to frame the base of his cock between thumb and forefinger. Douglas moaned softly, but didn't move. "That's right. Something I've never done before with a client. But this is a special circumstance, and you are a very special boy."

A very special boy.

"After all, Allen is only buying you to use against your brother, and I don't expect him to last long." He paused and met Douglas's eyes, as if to see if that prediction affected Douglas in any way. It didn't. It *didn't*. "And since I'd prefer for you to come back in one piece, I've arranged not to sell you outright under the usual terms, but instead to lease you to Allen. He pays a comparatively small monthly fee, and when he disposes of your brother or bores of you, he'll return you to me."

Now *that*, on the other hand, affected Douglas very much. He gasped, swallowed it down with an apology for his lack of control.

Nikolai waved it off. "However, there's a catch, and this is the part I need you to listen to very closely, Douglas. Allen wants assurances that you won't perform badly in order to encourage him to tire of you quicker and thus return you at an earlier date. He wants assurances that you will perform to the best of your abilities. So I've agreed that if he no longer wishes to keep you because of poor performance on your part, he won't return you to me. He'll sell you on to another master or auction house and keep the profits for himself. It will cost me a small fortune, and more than that, you'll likely be lost to me forever then."

Another gasp he couldn't control. Except this time, he couldn't seem to start breathing normally again. His hands flailed out, clenched in the sheets. His eyes squeezed shut. Lost to Nikolai forever? *Forever*? Oh God, what if nothing he did was good enough, what if he couldn't make Allen like him, what if—

"*Breathe*, Douglas." Nikolai's hands stroked up his chest, cupped his face. "I have no doubt you'll do fine. You are a work of art, remember? My creation. My favorite pupil. You will perform perfectly for Allen, your brother will wear out his welcome as he's meant to, and then you will come home to me."

Home. To his master. "And I won't leave you again?"

Nikolai shook his head. "You'll be all mine."

"Oh, Master!" Douglas threw himself forward, arms around Nikolai's shoulders. "Thank you, Master, thank you."

Nikolai kissed him, as hungry and eager as Douglas felt, and next Douglas knew he was being pushed back to the bed, purple lace panties shoved to the side, Nikolai's cock pressing swift and deep inside him. A flash of pain at the lack of prep, but he was still slick from this morning's fuck, and he'd gotten good at relaxing—Nikolai had trained him so, so well—and then it was nothing but sweat and friction and pure sweet bliss, Nikolai's taut belly rubbing across Douglas's cock with every thrust until they both came.

"I love you," Douglas said when it was over.

"And I'll miss you," Nikolai offered in return. But Douglas heard the real truth beneath those fondly spoken words: *I love you too, Douglas.*

"Now go clean up, get dressed, and do your makeup. You're leaving after lunch, I'm afraid."

Douglas faltered halfway out of bed, the world banking sharply sideways. But he was ready. He was. His master loved him, and had bought him a reprieve, a reprieve that even Roger hadn't been given.

"I said go," Nikolai chided, and swatted him on the ass. "And if you ruin your makeup with tears, you'll be going to Allen's with more than just a sore foot, am I clear?"

Douglas stood tall, straightened his shoulders, ducked his head. "Yes, Master." Nikolai was just protecting him, that was all. Protecting them both. Making sure he didn't screw this up right out of the gate—something he couldn't even bear considering, not when the cost of screwing up was so high.

So he went into the bathroom and made himself as pretty as he could for his temporary new master.

And when he came out again, Nikolai was gone and Roger was waiting to take him away.

"He doesn't do good-byes," Roger said at what must have been Douglas's puzzled look. "You look . . . well, you look like Allen will like you." He smiled a little sadly. "I prefer the natural look on you."

"Oh, Roger . . ." Douglas's heart jumped in his chest and a thickness settled into his throat. He ruthlessly swallowed it back. *Don't cry, don't cry, you'll ruin your makeup and Nikolai will beat you and Allen will hate you and—*

"Shhh." Roger pulled him close, tight against his chest. "I know it's scary. But you'll do fine, and you'll be home before you know it. I'll miss you every day of it though, you know that? My little guy." He ground his knuckles against the top of Douglas's head, not hard enough to mess up his hair.

Douglas huffed out a watery little laugh. "I'll miss you too." He tightened his arms around Roger's waist, tilted his head back to press a kiss to Roger's cheek. "Thank you, Roger. For everything."

"Don't mention it. You make Master happy. Happier than I've seen him in a long time, truth be told." Roger kissed his forehead, likely mindful of the lipstick Douglas was wearing. "And you make me happy too. It was my pleasure. Every moment of it." This time it was Roger's turn to force back tears. He sniffled, rubbed one eye. "Now come on, before I get all sentimental. Allen's people are waiting."

They walked together to the front foyer, where they found Mat already waiting, both arms strapped behind his back in an unforgiving leather sleeve and his ankles hobbled by a short length of chain. Wearing the black bit gag, too. Somehow, Douglas bet he'd still find a way to make trouble. But he was docile as Roger settled one hand atop the leather sleeve and said, "Ready?" Actually nodded his head. Shuffled forward without protest when Roger led them outside.

Mat froze on the porch, though, blinking hard in the afternoon sunlight. Douglas got to go outside all the time now, but he suspected Mat hadn't left the house in, well . . . ever, probably, beyond that one pathetic escape attempt. The sun was high and bright, the air crisp and cold, the deciduous trees all bare. Still winter, Douglas figured, though that could've meant November or March, maybe even April this high in the mountains—who knew. He supposed it didn't matter, anyway. Not for slaves.

"This way."

Roger led them down the stairs—an almost comically difficult process for Mat with his too-short hobble and his arms bound; Roger practically had to lift him with both hands—and around the back of the house toward the detached garage. Douglas's foot throbbed dully in his dress flats, and his bared skin pebbled in the cold. He'd have killed to feel Nikolai's blue cashmere sweater wrapped around him right now, but those days were over, at least for a while. He'd do best not to think about them at all.

From now on, it was scratchy lace lingerie and corsets and, once his foot healed, probably high heels, too. All of it meant to humiliate and unman him, but it wouldn't work, because Douglas had the memory of Nikolai to hold onto, the memory of Nikolai saying he was beautiful and making love to him with such passion that he believed it.

Four figures emerged from the garage, tall and broad-shouldered and—*female*, Douglas realized as they drew closer. Beautiful, intimidating women, the kind he'd have run from once upon a time, blushing and stammering and feeling unworthy. Now he simply trusted them to get him where he needed to go.

"Hey, Cutie, how's it hanging?" the one in the lead said, stopping well within Roger's personal space and kissing him on both cheeks.

"Oh, you know, to the left, usually." They shared a laugh. An old joke, then. Douglas wondered how many times they'd done this before. How many men had Allen bought from Nikolai? How many had ever returned?

"What's up with Hannibal over there?" she asked, jerking a thumb at Mat. "Allen said we didn't need to worry."

Roger took a long look at Mat, who met his eyes without venom, and then turned back to the woman. "You don't. Just a precaution. If you brought less cruel restraints, don't be afraid to swap them out; it's a long drive."

Now it was the woman's turn to study Mat, and then Roger. The three women behind her stood in a perfect line, perfect posture, taking everything in, saying nothing. Professionals, all of them. Too forward to be slaves, too put together to be the kind of minimum-wage tyrants Madame had on hire.

At last she nodded. "Yeah, okay." She must've seen something in Roger's face, because there sure as heck wasn't anything in Mat's to inspire trust like that. Frankly, Douglas thought it was a stupid idea. But it wasn't his place to comment, so he didn't. Heck, let Mat be an idiot and get himself killed on the ride over. That'd get Douglas back to Nikolai all the faster.

She nodded to one of the women behind her, who pulled a pair of handcuffs from her belt and went to work replacing the binder on Mat's arms. Mat stood stock-still for it, eyes averted, head down, a submissive beast baring its neck to its pack master. Douglas knew better than to be fooled by that. Mat was probably just biding his time.

Or maybe the coward was too afraid of being beaten by a bunch of women to present a threat.

The leader watched this for a moment, then turned her eyes on Douglas. Her gaze was assessing, nonjudgmental, neither hard nor soft. She seemed to approve of what she was seeing; at length she nodded, a little smile twitching at the corners of her mouth. "You're prettier than I am," she said, mock-bitter.

Douglas felt his cheeks color beneath the blush. "I'm sorry, miss. Although I really don't think I am."

She turned to Roger with a pout. "Aww, he's nervous! Poor little sex kitten." She winked and smiled. "He's cute, we'll take good care of him. Until he gets to Allen, at least."

Roger nodded, expression sober. "That's really all we can hope for."

She squeezed Roger's shoulder. "Don't worry, Allen's going to like him, I can tell."

Douglas was pretty sure that was exactly the problem, though.

"Anyway, long drive, we'd better be on our way." Roger nodded. "Kiss for the road, Cutie?"

Roger grinned, leaned in, and planted one right on her, rough and wet and dirty, both hands threading up into her hair and pulling. Douglas couldn't help it—he stared. Okay, *gaped*. Where had *that* come from? But then, it made sense. Roger had been trained to please people, just as Douglas had. If that was what this woman liked, then he would give it to her with a smile. The perfect slave. Douglas envied him.

"Phew!" she said with a laugh when Roger pulled away again, and shook out her hair. "Wish I could afford someone like you. Maybe I'll win the lottery."

Roger winked. "I'm sure Mat would pull your hair if you let him."

She barked out a laugh. "Yeah, right out of my scalp. No thanks. Besides, Allen would kill me. Literally." She eyed Mat up and down, clearly impressed with the sight; Douglas didn't get the appeal, but supposed he could concede the beautiful body. "Assuming Mat didn't first. Anyway, see you in six months or so? Give Nikolai my regards."

Six months.

Was that how long Mat was expected to last?

Six months. A death sentence. People with terminal cancer had more optimistic outcomes.

Well, Douglas wasn't going to think of it that way.

Six months until I'm home with my master again.

With one last look at Roger, he followed the strange new woman to her RV and into his new future.

NATE

"Heya, partner."

Nate started at the voice so close behind him; he'd been so engrossed in the fight video that he hadn't heard her coming. He hit pause, turned from his laptop to see Louise holding out a mochachino from the coffee cart outside their building. "Oh God, *thank you*." He took a long swallow.

Louise raised a perfectly sculpted eyebrow. She had no business looking that put together at the end of a day this long. "It's past seven," she said pointedly.

Was it really? He tilted his head, stretched a crick out of his neck. "Oh."

"You've been here for over twelve hours," she said even more pointedly.

He tilted his head the other way, winced at the burn. Straightened out and threw his free hand up. "I know, I just . . ." He pointed at his laptop, at the underground cage fight paused on the screen, a battered Stonewall Carmichael balanced perfectly on one foot, the other mid-strike toward his equally battered opponent.

Louise's judgmental eyebrow finally unfroze, relaxed. She put her own coffee down on Nate's desk and perched beside it. "Look, whatever you're hoping to find that the entire LVMPD missed, it's not going to happen if you're exhausted."

She was right, he knew that. He wasn't twenty-five anymore; eighty-hour weeks were getting harder and harder to pull. But he *was* missing something, he knew that, felt it in that place in his gut he'd learned a long damn time ago never to ignore.

Louise put a hand on his shoulder, squeezed at sore muscles. "Come on, let me take you out for a bite to eat. If you must, you can talk it out with me over a meal that doesn't come from a vending machine."

He took one last glance at the paused fight, then gave in to the inevitable. "Fine." He snapped the lid shut, pointed a finger at his partner. "But you're buying."

Louise insisted they walk to the restaurant, which was just fine with Nate, who was craving the fresh air and exercise. The little Americana joint they favored was nearly two miles from the office, but sitting all day digging through dusty evidence boxes wasn't exactly conducive to staying field fit. He only wished he'd been smart enough to change his shoes first, like Louise had. Clever, how she had a pair of sneakers under her desk for when her high heels (and the sorely needed three inches of height they gave her) weren't of any use.

The waitstaff knew them, seated them at their favorite table. Nate ordered a rare steak and the house microbrew. Louise got the same; she was enviably fit, but no delicate flower, and despite how short she was, she could pack it away with the best of them.

"So tell me again," she asked between little sips of her beer—she'd nurse that one the whole meal, barring extenuating circumstances, "why you've decided to kill yourself over this? I mean, I knew you'd be interested—I've seen you drool over this guy more times than I can count. But there's interested and then there's *interested*, like in the John Hinckley, Jr. way, if you catch my drift. And the LVMPD *did* already close this case."

Nate flushed, and not for the first time in his life thanked the powers that be that his skin was too dark to show it. "It just doesn't feel right," he said.

The Dubious Eyebrow of Doom returned. "Uh huh."

Nate snatched a roll from the basket between them and buttered it with entirely too much focus. "Seriously," he said to the roll. "So the cops' entire theory hinges on two sketchy informants' claims that this bookie Gerald Alvardo caught Stonewall throwing a fight for this other bookie Will Curran."

Louise laid a hand over Nate's, which apparently was still buttering his roll. "But it *is* true that Curran was trying to elbow in on Alvardo's territory, right? And they also have proof that Alvardo took a multimillion-dollar hit on that fight, and every penny of it flowed into Curran's pocket. It *did* upset the balance of power there. If I were Alvardo, I'd want to take it out of Carmichael's ass too."

"Or," Nate said, "he lost the fight legitimately and Alvardo *still* wanted to take it out of his ass. After all, either way, it cost Alvardo the same. And if that's the case, then those informants were lying."

Because Stonewall Carmichael would never throw a fight. He *wouldn't*. And okay, maybe Nate wasn't the most unbiased—or even informed, really—person to ask about Carmichael's character, but still. He wouldn't. The guy wasn't like that. Nate refused to believe it.

Even if he hadn't known about the underground cage matches before this case.

He took a bite of his roll—man, he really was hungry; he'd worked right through lunch without realizing—followed it up with a swig of his $7-a-bottle beer. "But that's just the thing, right? Look, guy's aboveboard career is on the rocks. Money's tight. His house is worth half what he paid for it, and on top of that he's trying to put his kid brother through grad school. I went through those financials with a friggin' microscope; the guy was *selfless*, I'm telling you. Not one movie ticket, not one restaurant receipt, nothing. Photos of the house show no flat-screen TV, no gaming systems. They're not underwater—not desperate, still making their payments every month okay—but it's clear the guy's thinking of nothing but his kid bro. So why would he take a huge risk he doesn't *need* to take, with bad, bad men, that he's gotta know puts kid bro in the line of fire?"

He took another swig of beer, watched Louise process. Predictably, she said nothing, just waited for him to continue arguing his case.

"I mean, I get why he's doing the underground fights; his manager and coach both said the UFC paychecks had fallen off and the bonus payouts were few and far between, and his bouncer salary wasn't much to write home about either. But he was earning mid-four figures every time he stepped into that underground cage—and didn't have to carve a slice out for the manager *or* the coach because they didn't even know it was happening. Enough to cover *his* bills, considering he lived like a monk. I could see it if he gambled, or if he did drugs, or if he and his brother had fifty K of credit card debt from living above their means. But they didn't. Mat Carmichael didn't *need* to run dirty on the side."

"Well," Louise said, "maybe he was tired of living like a monk."

"Sure. But tired enough to put his brother in danger? He sacrificed everything for that kid. No way he'd up and decide to throw all that away because he wanted a new car and some flashier clothes."

"Hmm." Louise took another long, slow sip of her beer, picked at a roll. The waitress came and dropped off their appetizer—something Louise had ordered, gloriously battered and fried. Nate snatched one up without even knowing—or caring—what it was.

"Maybe," Louise said around a mouthful of what turned out to be mozzarella sticks, "it wasn't about a new car. Did you check the medical records? I mean, guy's getting old, right?"

Hey now. Nate scowled. "He's *my* age."

Louise chuckled. "Yeah, and you say all the time you're getting too old for all-nighters. Now imagine you're this poor guy, getting his ass kicked for a living. Coming up on the big three-oh. Fighters are like actresses, okay? They age in dog years. Selling the house won't pay off the mortgage—which, by the way, is over two grand a month. His bouncer money's not gonna cover that, let alone things like keeping food on the table or the lights on. Maybe he's looking ahead. Seeing he won't be able to do this forever. What would you do in his shoes?"

Nate shrugged and stuffed a whole mozzarella stick in his mouth because he didn't want to have to admit she might be right. Or that he hadn't checked the medical records. How had he not *thought* of that?

"I know it's not what you want to hear, partner. But it makes sense. You know it does."

"Maybe," he conceded. Except . . . "But all fighters age out eventually. The vast majority of their end-games don't involve illegal activity. Especially ones like Stonewall. They coach. They open gyms. They become talent scouts or agents or announcers or analysts. Or they do what Carmichael was already doing part-time: they go into security, work as bouncers or bodyguards."

"True," Louise conceded back. "But maybe Carmichael knows he won't be able to keep working in security." Right. Mental note: check the damn medical records. "Plus, the smart fighters all have put money away for retirement, and the popular ones can coast off endorsement deals for years. Carmichael never managed to save much that didn't go into his house or his brother's education; he had less than ten grand in his bank account when he cleared it before they fled. And his manager said the endorsement deals were drying up. The one with K-Swiss was only paying two grand a fight, and he hadn't done an ad shoot in nearly a year. On the books, and *counting* the part-time bouncing job, he made just under $70K last year. Take out the cuts for the manager, the coach, and Uncle Sam . . ."

"Yeah, yeah." Nate chewed dejectedly at a cooling mozzarella stick and waved over the waitress for another ridiculously overpriced beer. It felt wrong, somehow, to be dropping $7 on a microbrew while dissecting the sad financials of a missing person. Not that $70K a year was exactly *sad*—Nate made about the same and lived plenty comfortably, but then, Nate didn't have an underwater house and a bunch of folks dipping fingers into his pie and a brother to put through school. And *his* job came with a pension plan.

The waitress came back with his beer and their steaks, and the conversation lulled for a while as they dug in. But Nate's mind kept spinning as he ate. He barely even tasted the food. "Hey," he said, waving a fork full of mashed potatoes at Louise, "so what's the endgame for Alvardo, then? How does *that* make sense?"

Louise looked up from her steak for the first time since the waitress had brought it over. "What do you mean?"

"Well, if Stonewall's dive really did cost Alvardo millions—assuming he even *did* dive—and Alvardo expects him to pay it back like the informants claimed, then what's he get out of just sending some thugs over to rough the brother up? That's not going to make Stonewall magically any more able to cough up the cash—and might've made it worse if the kid needed medical treatment. It would've made a lot more sense just to kill the kid. Then Stonewall doesn't have to feed or house or school him, *and* he gets the payout from the university health insurance Douglas had. What is that, two hundred and fifty grand? That's a big chunk of cash. But instead they deliver a warning that gives Stonewall time to flee?"

"Hmm."

If Nate knew Louise's *hmms*—and he definitely did—that was a thoughtful one. He'd *finally* piqued her professional curiosity. "And," he added, pressing his luck while he had it, "why would they flee to Mexico, of all places? They've got no family there, no connections.

They don't even speak the language. And why ditch the car? And why use what limited funds they had to pay a coyote rather than cross legally when it wasn't the Feds they were running from?"

Louise shrugged. "Alvardo runs a big racket. Maybe he's got his fingers in border patrol and Carmichael didn't want to risk it."

Yeah, maybe . . .

"And why not Mexico? It's faster and cheaper than Canada—or anywhere else, really—and I wouldn't blame him for not feeling safe in the States anymore."

"Oh, come on. Alvardo's a bookie, not Marlon Brando in the *Godfather*. Like he's gonna chase Carmichael more than a couple states. If he changes names and keeps his head down, he could probably get away with it. But Mexico or no Mexico, the story still doesn't make sense."

Another shrug. "Well, maybe he wasn't thinking clearly. Would you be, if you came home to find someone had beaten the shit out of the brother you'd sacrificed everything for, and you knew it was your fault?"

Nate sighed, put down his fork with enough force to clank. "Just . . . work with me here, would you?"

Louise looked momentarily taken aback, then chagrined, then dead serious. "Always, partner, you know that."

Yeah, he did. He also knew she was just doing her job, playing devil's advocate, forcing him to think up all the angles. *Like the medical records, you asshole.*

"But you've got to promise me you won't kill yourself over this. *I* brought us this case; don't make me un-bring it."

He picked his fork back up, took a deliberate bite of his steak—*look, Ma, I'm eating.* "I promise. I'll go straight to bed after dinner."

She was polite enough not to call him on his bullshit.

After their meal, he promised Louise he'd go straight home, and he meant to, he really did. But somehow he ended up swinging by the office for his laptop first. He'd just check the medical records real quick, and then he'd go to bed. He would. Louise had poked enough holes in his theories to let him sleep without feeling like his time resting was time stolen from an imperiled Mat and Doug Carmichael.

That was the theory, anyway. But when he got home and accessed the medical records, all it did was light a bigger fire under his ass.

Because other than the expected bumps and cuts and the occasional concussion or cracked rib, Mat Carmichael's record was nearly perfect. He'd never even broken his hands or gone unconscious for more than a few minutes at a time. Yeah, he was almost thirty, but he had *years* left in him at least. Douglas's record was clean, too. No hospitalizations. No surgeries. No major illnesses.

No crushing debt.

No reason for Mat to take that so-called fall.

Mexico, my ass.

THE FLESH

SEASON 4: LIBERATION

CARTEL

EPISODE 12: PARADISE ISLAND

CHAPTER
ONE

The guards hadn't been kidding when they'd said it was a long drive from Nikolai's to Allen's. In fact, they weren't kidding around about anything. They were professionals, and Mat knew better than to let the fact that they were all women—or that they'd exchanged the cruel arm binder for a pair of handcuffs—fool him.

Dougie had settled comfortably on the couch—unbound, and basically outside the guards' attention—with his nose buried in a book one of the women had offered him. He seemed happy, looking occasionally out the tinted windows or offering the guards a smile (genuine ones, Mat was pretty sure). He even mentioned at one point that he was up for giving backrubs if they got tired, or cooking if they got hungry. Or more, even—all of which the guards politely declined. And no wonder; Mat would've bet his freedom that Allen had sent them under strict orders not to leave sticky fingerprints all over his new goods. Orders he obviously didn't think men were capable of obeying.

Dougie never looked at Mat once, not the whole fucking time. Which was just as well, he supposed, because he was having an awfully hard time looking at Dougie without his blood pressure spiking. How could the kid seem so *at home* here? So comfortable and placid about wearing whorish women's lingerie and makeup, being sold off as chattel? And to a fucking monster, no less.

Sadly, the guards watched Mat much more closely than they watched Dougie. They clearly knew he was dangerous. And they were clearly professionals, just like the men who'd originally brought him and Dougie to Nikolai's from Madame's. At least the women were hands off—no touching, no hurting. But they kept him cuffed to the RV the entire time. When he'd grown weary of staring out the window—which shocked him; after so long cooped up indoors, he'd never thought it'd be possible to grow weary of the sight of the outside world again—and asked if he could lie down, one guard moved him while the other two stood back, outside of grabbing range, their Tasers trained on him, until he'd been cuffed down to the new piece of furniture.

And then they left him again. But they never gave him any chances to leave them. No way to escape. No way to crash the RV. They kept him away from pointy things and fire and even heavy loose objects. They gagged him before every stop for gas. They ate and pissed in shifts in the otherwise ever-moving vehicle. They didn't sleep. Sometimes he heard Dougie talking to them, but they never came close enough to Mat to talk to him. But then, Dougie was domesticated, and by the way they'd treated Roger, they were obviously comfortable around domesticated slaves.

They finally drew to a stop sometime well into the night. Not a gas station this time. Mat hadn't allowed himself to sleep, but he realized—with more than a little guilt and anger—that at some point he'd stopped being so focused on getting away. He perked up now, though. Things were happening. This might be his chance.

He peered out the windows and saw . . . was that water? It was dark out, the kind of dark you never got in cities, and the tinted windows weren't helping, but regular rows of lights were definitely reflecting off something. Now that he was paying attention, he realized he could smell the ocean. Those lights must be dock lights.

Oh God. Were they taking them out to sea? They'd never get home. There'd be no escaping, not with water on all sides.

He realized he'd started to hyperventilate a little. His chest heaved. His nostrils flared. Ice cold fear hit him right in the guts, and he didn't know how to get back up from it, not this time . . .

"Easy, big guy." One of the women was standing by the bed, watching him. "Gotta get you ready for your master now. No use fighting it, okay? Don't make us knock you out; you're too damn heavy to carry." She held up the bit gag, showing it to him like a collar to a fucking stray dog. "I'm going to put this on you. Bite me, and I'll tase your balls until your pubes smoke."

She smiled then, and that was all it took.

He broke.

"Let us go," he begged. "Please. Please, look. We're here against our will. I'm Mat. My brother's Dougie. They kidnapped us. If you don't let us go now, we're never going to get out of here. And that Allen guy? He's going to kill me. Please, if you have any compassion—no, screw compassion. How much is he paying you? I fight with the UFC—or I did. I could get you money."

The woman snorted and shoved the gag between his teeth. He didn't fight her; he couldn't afford to be unconscious when they moved him. "He's paying me plenty, tiger. And if you *do* run away? He'll pay me plenty more to track you down and send you back to Nikolai for some"—God, her smirk was nasty; so much for compassion—"reeducation. And trust me when I say you don't want that. Or me on your ass."

Yeah, no, he didn't need her to tell him that. If he never saw Nikolai again, it'd be too soon. She turned him until his back was to her, uncuffed him from the bed (backup guards with Tasers at the ready), and strapped his arms tight into the leather sleeve. Six straps, he felt her buckling them. From the top of his biceps right down to his wrists, and then his hands stuffed into a tight little pocket. Totally immobilized. Flexible as he was, his shoulders and chest strained enough that they hurt almost instantly.

"Sorry," she said, and she kind of sounded like she meant it, for all the tough talk from a moment ago.

"You shouldn't be, miss," Dougie said. He was standing just behind her, unbound, waiting patiently. He met Mat's eyes with a hard stare and added, "He's trouble."

"Is he now," she replied as Mat's heart shattered into a thousand new sharp-edged pieces, slicing at his chest and making his blood boil. His fists clenched inside their little leather pouch, though whether from anger or despair, he couldn't say. Both, probably. It was always both, now. "Well, you'd know best, wouldn't you, kiddo?"

"Sadly, yes." He frowned deeply. "Can I go to the bathroom and do my lipstick, please?" And just like that, Mat stopped existing again.

"Sure." She waved him off. "Damn, Allen's posh little trophy wife is gonna *love* you, prettyboy."

Mat caught Dougie's shy little smile before he skittered off. The guard who'd bound him gave him a once-over, then grabbed a coat off a hook and draped it over his shoulders, buttoning the top button so he couldn't shrug it off. For the security cameras on the dock, probably. Someone might notice if they saw a guy walking bound and naked and flanked by security. Then again, maybe not. Maybe Allen had the marina guys on his payroll. Maybe it was just cold out.

"Hey, Lauren," the woman called, never taking her eyes off Mat. "Come help me get this one in the boat while Pretty back there puts his face on."

Lauren materialized almost instantly, Taser at the ready. "Yes, ma'am," she said. "Tammy's already out there prepping."

Which left one guard in the RV for Dougie, who'd probably find the damn boat on his own if they tried to leave him behind.

Lauren went out first, and a wall of moist heat hit Mat the moment the door opened. Middle of a winter night and it was this hot? God, where had they taken them, and where were they *going*? Texas, maybe, or Louisiana, or Florida. "Ma'am" led him down the stairs with a firm hand on his shoulder and another on his bound wrists. He briefly entertained the idea of striking her and throwing himself down the stairs onto Lauren, but Ma'am was standing just too far away to headbutt, she'd probably break his arms if he kicked her, and he didn't like his chances of hitting Lauren before she could pull that trigger, especially since she, too, was standing just far enough away to be out of easy reach. Definitely professionals. He wouldn't have been surprised to learn they'd once fought on the same circuit he had. Or served in the military, maybe. Mercenaries.

He went without fighting. Half of winning was being patient and picking the right moment to strike. Now wasn't it.

They moved him quickly, but didn't stop him from looking around. The lights here were dim, bulbs out in two of the three nearby dock lights. Probably on purpose. They were at the far end of the marina, the last berth by the look of things. Lots of big boats here, luxury crafts worth more than his house. A couple of boats down a ways had lights on, but he didn't hear any voices carrying. So, occupied, but probably only crew awake this time of night . . . whatever time it was. Late.

The boat they were leading him to, though, was downright modest. Bigger than a speedboat but not by much—maybe twelve, fifteen feet from stem to stern. He didn't think it was big enough to have a cabin belowdecks. Which meant they couldn't be taking them too far, thank God.

Not leaving the country, then. Relief hit him so hard he stumbled, and would've fallen on his face if not for Ma'am's grip on his arm.

Who must've thought he was trying to pull some trick, because she asked, "You gonna make me hurt you?" perfectly conversational, even as her hand tightened so cruelly he had to swallow a yelp.

Just tripped, Mat tried to say around the gag. Gave up and shook his head instead.

"Good boy."

They got him onto the boat, and then down into the hold he went. He was right; it wasn't big enough for a cabin—more like a coffin. He couldn't even sit up. In fact, Ma'am used her boot to push him onto his back—Christ, the pressure on his arms and shoulders was *awful.* And then along came Dougie, with a polite protest of, "But my makeup . . ." and an answering reassurance of, "It'll be fine, better than getting your hair all blown out up on deck, trust me." So in Dougie climbed, right on top of him because this hold had clearly only been built for one, chest to chest and—ugh, God, no—junk to junk. Mat squeezed his eyes shut and tried not to think of the last time he'd been this close to his brother. Funny how once upon a time this position would have brought memories of long hugs, of lying together in bed on stormy nights, his arms around his innocent little brother, hugging him, protecting him.

So much for that. He was never getting that back. Never.

Luckily, he didn't have to keep his eyes shut for long, because once they were both horizontal, someone shut the door on them, cloaking them in blackness. For a while, all Mat could hear was Dougie's breathing and his own, and the distant sound of water lapping against the hull of the boat. Then the motor started up and drowned out everything else.

His new master. His new master. Douglas was determined to be poised, to do Nikolai proud, to continue to earn the treasured mark on the sole of his foot.

But God, it was hard to keep his composure through all this. Being in close quarters with Mat—no, being pressed against him, right against him, hearing him breathe and feeling his heart thumping away panicked—and getting seasick on top of it. He wished they'd let him stay on deck; after all, he wasn't going to try to escape, wasn't going to try to flag down any passing boats. Not like Mat.

Luckily, the boat ride wasn't so long, and probably not half as long as it felt, either. Plus, the hold was air-conditioned, not humid at all except for the stickiness of Mat sweating beneath him.

Eventually the sense of motion eased, and then the motor cut out, and then, shortly after that, the trapdoor over his head opened. Small hands hooked under his arms and pulled him upright.

"Thank you," he gasped, and meant it. The warm air smelled sweet and fresh, and a light breeze tossed his hair. The dawn was just breaking, one half of the sky still dark enough to twinkle with stars, the other half a deep purple turning pink at the horizon. What he assumed was a tropical island was silhouetted against it—he could make out the shapes of rising hills and maybe a forest of palm trees and what he thought might be a very large house—but it was still kind of too dark to tell. Beautiful nonetheless. Not remotely the same as the view from his master's—no, Nikolai's, he wasn't Douglas's master anymore, not for now—but it was beautiful in its own way. Maybe Douglas would come to appreciate it.

Or maybe he'd count down the days until he could leave.

The days until Mat is dead.

No, he wouldn't think of it that way, because how could he possibly serve to his fullest capabilities if he was constantly thinking of Nikolai and leaving? He needed to live in the now. Serve in the now. Revel in the salt air and the sound of surf washing up on the beach and the glorious tropical warmth after a long winter in the mountains. Revel in making Allen—*Master, he's my new master*—as happy as he'd made Nikolai. Revel, even, in keeping Mat on his damn leash like he was supposed to. Of making sure the beast didn't hurt anyone.

Or most of all, didn't hurt Nikolai's reputation.

One of the women was tying the boat up to a dock. On the other side of the same dock was a boat much like the one they were on. Off to the left, two fishing trawlers shared a dock. And to the left of that, one of those boats like you see on water tours of Hollywood or Boca Raton, or in movies, owned by drug kingpins. The kind of thing that could comfortably hold a hundred people and was probably made of solid mahogany. He didn't have much time to stare, though. Three of the guards led Mat off the boat, down the dock, to a boardwalk on a pristine beach dotted with the occasional palm tree and hammock and lounge chair. The last guard guided Douglas after them, a steadying hand on the small of his back lest he trip in his dress shoes on the dock. Not high heels yet—his brand was still too tender for that—but the dock was swaying gently with the surf and he felt a little unsteady on his platforms, so he was grateful for the assist.

The sky was getting brighter by the moment, and slowly unveiling the scenery of the island. Palm trees. Soft sand. A little boathouse. A long driveway of paving stones. And there, a house coming into view. A . . . an English country manor? A huge mansion, but it didn't match the scenery at all, looking more like a building out of a boring BBC TV special than the beach house getaway it should have been. It was absolutely absurd.

A man in a stiff tuxedo met them at the huge carved-wood double doors.

A tuxedo, really?

At that exact moment, Mat snorted around his gag.

Well, that settled it. Douglas wouldn't be judging his new master anymore. That was for Mat. Douglas would unquestioningly accept his master's taste in houses and the pretension of his house's staff.

"Ah, the new blood," Tuxedo Man said in a nasal English accent that was just as stiff as his outfit. "Thank you, Adriana. I trust your journey here was pleasant and uneventful?"

More noises of derision from Mat. One of the guards rabbit-punched him in the kidney with a stern "Watch your tone, boy," which shut him right up.

"Yes, thank you," Adriana replied as though Mat didn't even exist. "Would you like some tea? Breakfast, perhaps, before you go?"

"No thanks. Time for bed and all that."

Tuxedo Man—the butler, probably?—nodded like he understood perfectly. "Very well, then. Master sends his gratitude, and your payment will be wired as usual."

Master? Was the butler a slave, then? A man like Roger, probably, trusted to run the household. Douglas didn't have time to ponder more than that, though, because the guards said their good-byes and headed back to the boat, and the butler fixed his eyes on Mat—Douglas bore no consideration or concern, apparently—and said, "Whatever you're thinking, don't. You are on an island, you realize. A *private* island."

Mat just sort of . . . deflated at that. Even *he* wasn't dumb enough to think he could escape from here with his arms bound and a gag in his mouth. Not exactly conducive to swimming back to civilization.

"Now then. My name is Nedry"—another snort from Mat, nearly a choking cough; Nedry scowled but let it go—"and I am the head of the service staff here at Smythe Hall. I've been tasked with showing you your new home and detailing your duties. I suggest you mind me closely; I do not care to repeat myself."

"Yes, sir," Douglas said, snapping to attention, even as Mat made a huffy little noise and rolled his eyes.

Nedry's eyes narrowed at Mat. "I have full authority to punish the slaves under my province here, you should know." He squared his shoulders in his tailored livery—God, he must've been unbearably hot in all that—and added, "As I see fit." Then he turned his back on them—on Mat; not smart, Douglas felt a moment of panic coming on—and threw open the grand front doors.

Onto an even grander front hall.

Mat didn't try to attack the man.

Douglas let out a long breath and followed him inside, where a wash of dry, cool air settled over him like a fresh sheet. His flats clicked on large marble tiles laid out in circular patterns, the sound echoing off the vaulted mosaic ceiling. Nedry paused in the foyer for a moment, as if pride prevented him from rushing them along when Douglas so clearly wanted to take it all in, to marvel at the sheer, stupefying *grandeur* of it. Like something right out of *Upstairs, Downstairs*—the curved double staircases with their hardwood treads and oriental runners and intricate carved wood railings (and no doubt a third staircase, somewhere in the back, for the slaves to use). The open ceiling four stories high, the massive crystal chandelier, the carved balconies and paneled hallways leading off in all directions, the occasional young woman (or was that a man, like Douglas?) in revealing maid uniforms dusting or hurrying by. The arched entryways, the Victorian furniture (real antiques, he had no doubt), every surface dripping with silver and lace and fresh flowers, every wall covered with rich deep paneling or woven tapestries or giant paintings in gilded frames.

And this was just the foyer.

"Come on, then," Nedry said, and led them to a small side door tucked away behind one staircase. "This is the entrance to the slaves' corridors, which will be how you will get around unless accompanied by the master, the mistress, or their associates."

Through the door was a small, dim, windowless hall, as plain as would be expected, leading to a narrow little staircase going up and down.

"Down to the cellars and kitchen and laundry. Up to our quarters. The slave hallways run parallel to all the halls through the house. Anywhere you wish to go, you can reach through here."

As in, don't let me catch you in the main house uninvited. Point taken.

"Are we meeting our new master soon?" Douglas asked, after Nedry had led them through the maze of halls, pointing out the various doors to parts of the main house—unlabelled, of course, so they'd have to memorize their way.

"Master will meet you when he's good and ready. You may be an *expensive* toy, but that hardly makes you his priority, no more than his art collection is his priority, or his yacht. You are still a slave. Still a possession. So if I were you, I would nip that entitled attitude right in the bud."

"Yes, sir." Douglas burned with humiliation, not only at being told off, but at having it happen in front of Mat. He had to be perfect. He had to show his beast of a brother up.

"Now, Mathias, I'm not yet sure of your place in this house—I expect Master has something special in mind for you. But you, Douglas, will be staying here, in the pleasure slaves' quarters." He opened a door briefly, letting Douglas peek in. A long room of narrow beds, all made with military precision. A row of theater-style dressing tables at the end, cluttered with makeup and wigs, their surfaces crowded but well organized. Several doors on one wall no doubt led to closets stocked with . . . interesting things.

"There are six of you in all. All men; the mistress won't have it any other way. The boy whose bed you are taking was recently demoted to hallboy in the guard staff's quarters. Master tires quite quickly of your lot. Some enter the general staffing of the house and work in housekeeping or the kitchens, some are sold on, some are—how do I put this delicately?—disposed of, and others are put to their original use but in less glamorous settings . . . as our dear hallboy, who I hear spends most nights taking a line of sweaty cocks up his once-prized ass. The guards are terribly rough with such expensive merchandise, secondhand or no. I suggest if you don't wish to meet the same fate, you make sure to keep things novel for Master, and keep your precious little hands out of any honeypots you come across."

"Understood, sir, th-thank you for the advice." Douglas was unable to keep the tremble out of his voice. As if Allen wasn't scary enough, now there was a possibility of being passed on to be used by his staff? Douglas remembered his time at Madame's. His time in the hunters' cabin. Going to sleep on the floor with a belly full of piss and cum and an ass stretched out by a line of cocks. He wouldn't go back to that. He *couldn't*. He'd be good for Allen. He'd be *so* good. Whatever it took.

Nikolai had taught him well. He'd do fine. He would. He was ready for this. He was ready for *anything*.

"I expect you'll meet your fellows later tonight, and they'll brief you on their particular schedule. I tend not to bother myself with the comings and goings of your set, except inasmuch as it affects the business of the *proper* house slaves."

Your set. How he said it, dripping with malice. He might as well have called them whores.

No shame in being a whore, Nikolai's voice soothed, *as long as you're a good one.*

He wished Nikolai were here now. To advise him. To strengthen him.

To be his master.

But he wasn't, and instead Douglas was stuck with the dubious guidance of Nedry over here—who clearly hated him, though God knew why—and the millstone of his beastly brother around his neck. Well, maybe the other pleasure slaves would be his friends. And maybe he'd figure out fast how to make Allen like him, and—dare he hope it?—even love him. And then maybe things would be okay. Better than okay. Great, even. Happy. Good.

"I'll take you to the master's study now. He retires there after breakfast each morning to attend his work. You'll wait quietly until he can be bothered to instruct you. Don't touch anything. Don't get in the way of the real slaves' work. Don't speak unless spoken to. Am I clear?"

Douglas nodded fervently. "Yes, sir, very clear, sir."

He'd be good and silent and still, all right. Obedient to the letter. But if Nedry thought he was going to just disappear into the furniture like one of the master's expensive paintings, he was dead wrong. The master would notice Douglas. He was a Petrovic, after all.

CHAPTER TWO

The trail had gone cold.

Hell, it had been cold to start with. But now, it really was hopeless. The LVMPD had shipped over the evidence from the Carmichael house, but if there had been any foul play—that is, any beyond the picked lock from the garage where Alvardo's thugs had let themselves in, the struggle in the living room where the younger Carmichael had been attacked, the few splotches of blood the boy had left on the carpet—they'd cleaned up after themselves well. Especially for a gang of bookies, or their hired help, who tended not to put "finesse" high on their priority list. And yeah, maybe that struggle hadn't just been a warning like the informant had said; maybe it had been a kidnapping instead, or even a murder. It had been *something*; he *knew* something was wrong here. But he couldn't find it.

He'd pored over hundreds of hours of security footage from the underground fighting cages Stonewall Carmichael had appeared in, looking for that fateful thrown match. He'd combed through statements from the neighbors (painfully sparse, nobody had seen a damn thing) and evidence photos of the house, looking for anything suspicious, any sign that the brothers had left in any way other than rushing off voluntarily to Mexico after some thugs had beaten the tar out of one of them. All he saw were two dressers of drawers hastily ripped through, some suitcases and toiletries missing, a couple blank spots on the walls where family photos had probably been. A door they'd locked behind them. A full fridge, which was a little odd for people going on a road trip, but then, they'd left in a hurry. Maybe they'd just gotten food on the road. Whatever, because a full fridge wasn't evidence of jack shit, and while Nate trusted his gut, his boss was growing much less inclined to, especially when he was chasing some deadbeat who'd run off to Mexico instead of looking for kidnapped kids and missing teens.

He knew his boss was right. Knew that his time and resources were better spent elsewhere. He was letting his personal feelings get in the way of his common sense. Yeah, Mat Carmichael deserved to be found—not dead, Nate was pretty sure of that at least—but so did that pair of siblings kidnapped by their noncustodial father and spirited across state lines. So did that sixteen-year-old girl who'd vanished out of a shopping mall. So did the thirty-four-year-old pregnant woman who'd have had her baby by now. (Probably dead, but her parents and friends deserved closure.) But it was Mathias he couldn't get off his mind. Taken somewhere kicking and screaming, baby bro held for ransom to ensure his cooperation as Alvardo fought him like a dog in some cage so underground even FBI informants didn't know about it, earning his money back one blow at a time.

Which was how Nate wound up at the Carmichaels' house, he supposed. He'd told his supervisor it was because the house had finally been foreclosed on and this was his last chance to sift through it personally before the cleanup crew came to flip it for sale. The last chance for him to look at the scene with his suspicious eyes before the contents of the place wound up in a charity bin or the trash. But really, it was because he couldn't let it go.

He picked his way through the shin-high grass of the front lawn up to the porch, pulled the key for the bank's padlock out of his pocket, and opened the door.

The air was predictably stale inside, the house dim—the windows were grimy, and small anyway to keep the Nevada sun at bay. For a long moment he just stood there in the front hall, overcome by that feeling of *otherness* and *wrongness* that hit him every time he walked into a victim's abandoned home. There'd been life here once. History. Memories. Private things no one else was meant to see. These brothers had been ripped from their space—somehow, he was sure of it—and now here he was, ready to trawl through it for clues, details of their lives they never thought anyone would see. Things they'd never have shared, given the choice. He shouldn't be here. He wished he didn't have to be.

And yet he was, because otherwise the brothers might never get to be here again either. They'd forgive him his trespass if he brought them home safe. Or maybe they wouldn't, but that was a price he'd gladly pay for their safety.

He headed for the living room first, the scene of the one crime they actually had evidence of. The walk there was short—Carmichael had an awfully small house for a prizefighter, but this close to the city he supposed location cost more than size—but he kept an eye out for . . . well, everything on the way. The place was pretty barren, as simple as expected by their spending habits. But it was clean. Really, *really* clean, actually; no dishes in the sink, no clutter on the table. Other than an unopened bag of chips and an energy drink on the kitchen counter, the place was basically spotless. No grime except for dust, which Nate bet dollars to donuts hadn't been here the night they'd been taken.

Come to think of it, hadn't he read a statement from the younger brother's foster father about the kid being almost obsessively neat? Maybe he did the chores to make up for the fact that his brother paid the bills.

Or maybe being in foster care had taught him to make himself useful and problem-free, lest he be cast away. Nate had seen that behavior repeat itself more than once in kids like that.

He spent half an hour in the living room, though he wasn't really sure why. What little evidence there'd ever been was long gone. The path from the living room to the mudroom to the garage had been wiped clean by the thugs. The lock had been picked by experts—once again he found that a little suspicious for a job organized by a bookie, but alas, it was nothing even close to evidence of the kidnapping he suspected. They'd left no traces in the garage; a neighbor had claimed she'd seen a white windowless van pulling into the garage sometime before sunset, but there'd been no way to prove it, and she couldn't even recall what hour it'd happened. And a white windowless van? It sounded like one of those things witnesses came up with when they felt like they should have seen something, they should have, and after racking their brains and agonizing over the guilt of it, some new knowledge would miraculously appear, accurate or no, just to soothe their conscience.

Which was probably *exactly* what he was doing right now. This was stupid. He was wasting his—and the Bureau's—time. He was good, yeah, but it was pure hubris to think he'd spot something, six months later, that an entire CSI team had missed.

But still, since he was here already, it couldn't hurt to take a look in the bedrooms, could it?

He trumped down the hall leading to the two bedrooms and the second bath. Douglas's room was first; Nate knew it was his because of the bookshelf stuffed with textbooks and the neatly made bed. No computer. Dresser torn open, most of the clothes missing. A couple of framed photos left behind on the dresser. Douglas and Mat, Douglas wearing a grad gown and cap—high school, by the looks of the pimples all over poor Douglas's face. Box of tissues next to the bed. Nice one. And underneath? Boxes of papers and binders. Schoolwork. Novels in the bookshelves—eclectic tastes, everything from Stephen King to Khaled Hosseini to *Star Trek* tie-ins. Definitely a nerd. A nerd who went running, by the looks of the expensive trainers Nate found behind the door, cushioned with custom insoles. Hadn't Stonewall's coach said something about the brothers going running together every morning? Well, didn't seem like the kid had any other hobbies except that and reading. There was an old pair of boxing gloves slung over a bedpost, screen-printed with a bulldog mascot, but Nate didn't think Douglas had worn them. Probably Stonewall's, from high school.

The next room was the bathroom. Tiny, and clean as the rest of the place, except for two towels crumpled on the floor. Toilet, pedestal sink, tub/shower. Now that was weird—the curtain was ripped halfway off the rod. Had something happened here? Some kind of struggle? Well, it fit the narrative, and also explained the two towels, which the Douglas forming in Nate's mind would never have failed to hang up. Alvardo's goons could have snuck up on poor Douglas in the shower before they laid into him. Damn, he wondered if they'd let him get dressed before they kicked the shit out of him, or if they'd just beat his ass naked.

Except . . . if they'd found him in the shower, why had they dragged him into the living room to send their little message? The bathroom was too small for much, but either bedroom would've made more sense. Closer, less opportunity for a struggle. And more importantly, less opportunity for escape. Take a runner near an exit and you risk him, well, running right out the front or back door.

He gave the little bathroom a much more careful search. Floor, walls, ceiling, fixtures. No blood that he could see. And surely the CSI team had been up here with a black light and the rest of it.

Just to be thorough, he checked the medicine cabinet. Pain pills, and a lot of them. Mostly NSAIDs, a couple of them prescription strength, all with Mathias Carmichael on the label. Had he been abusing prescription drugs? Had that been why he'd needed the money? Nate made a note to check with the coach again, but surely the medical records would've reflected an addiction. Not to mention the fact that Stonewall had fought literally the night he'd disappeared. The UFC tested very, very carefully for this kind of stuff. And anyway, none of these particular pills—even the prescription ones—were habit-forming. No narcotics whatsoever, except a single, ten-count bottle of Tylenol with codeine dated two years back—probably from that fight at the Mandalay when he'd gone down so hard from a knee to the ribs that the ref had stopped the fight—and eight of the pills were still inside. Not exactly the behavior of a junkie.

Other than that, there was a half-empty bottle of cough medicine, a wide assortment of basic wound care supplies and muscle rubs, some aftershave that Nate shamelessly opened up to take a sniff of—yeah, it was Mat's all right—and a couple disposable razors. Their toothbrushes were missing. He shut the cabinet with a sigh.

With the bathroom and open areas combed over, that left one last room. Mat's. As he exited the bathroom, Nate very nearly walked right down the hall again, afraid and ashamed to invade Mat's personal space. But then he remembered he was here as a professional, and that after sacrificing everything else for his brother, if Mat were here, he'd have given Nate permission to go through his room if it meant bringing Douglas home. So he made himself cross the threshold.

Mat's room was a good deal messier than Douglas's. Unmade bed, dirty laundry on the floor, posters of fighters on the wall, many of them autographed. Trophies and championship belts were scattered across nearly every horizontal surface, but carelessly somehow—dusty, some covered up, some hidden behind lamps or pictures—as if their owner wasn't sure why he bothered to keep them. Six separate photos of Douglas in various stages of childhood and adolescence were scattered throughout the room, plus one of the dead parents and one of the whole family on the nightstand. Three unfaded rectangles on the wall where other pictures must've been. Inside the nightstand, a mess of condoms and wrappers and a big bottle of lube, and a— Oh God, Nate tried very, very hard not to think about Stonewall using that particular eight-inch item on himself. Not in his room, not after Nate had just talked himself into coming in here by reminding himself he was a professional. He slammed the drawer shut and forced himself to turn away. Turn away from the thought of himself in that rumpled queen-sized bed with Mat, on top, on the bottom, fuck, it didn't matter.

The rest of the room. Focus on that.

In the corner by the closet was a rolled-up workout mat, a rack of light free weights, a speed bag, and a chin-up bar mounted with no care for aesthetics. A letter jacket hung from the corner of the door. He must have looked sexy as hell in it, once upon a time—

Christ. Bad Nate.

The dresser was turned out, just like Douglas's. Almost . . . too much like Douglas's. In fact, now that he thought of it, it seemed kind of strange that Douglas would have left his drawers hanging open, clothes falling out onto the floor, instead of taking what he needed and then neatly closing them behind himself purely out of habit. Mat, sure. A turned-out dresser totally fit the general look of his messy, manly room. But Douglas's room was pin neat *except* for the dresser.

Had someone staged these rooms to look like the pair of them had made a hasty exit?

Or else Mat had packed for both of them.

Which, really, made more sense than anything, if the kid had just gotten his ass beat. He'd probably been hurting, scared, not thinking straight. Stonewall would've done what he always did: think fast on his feet, take charge, take care of the kid.

Get them the hell outta Dodge.

If Nate had had a crush on Mat before, and a boner for him two minutes ago, well, he was kinda in love with the guy now. Too bad Mat was gone without a trace.

Or maybe not. Maybe, just maybe, there was something here in all this mess that could fill in the missing pieces. Something like the dressers, but *without* a logical explanation that dismissed foul play. Of course, in order to find that something, he'd have to get to know these boys like he'd raised them him-fucking-self.

Well, he had a pile of empty evidence boxes in the rental car. Best go get them and get started. And if it just so happened that Nate's "evidence" included all these trophies and photos and that letter jacket, all with sentimental value, all due to be chucked in the garbage by the end of the week?

So sue him.

Nerdy—Nedry, whatever; he was lucky Mat wasn't calling him Assclown—led Mat and Dougie into a large study and made them kneel on a rug on the hardwood floor. Dougie, being the overachieving little shit he was, fell into position like there was nothing he wanted more. Mat went down just as fast, but mostly because he was too damn tired to fight.

The room matched the theme of the rest of the mansion: gaudy Victorian Gothic, with its dark wood paneling and heavy carved antique furniture and massive hearth—unlit, thankfully—and a wall of leather-bound books that Mat bet Allen had never even unshelved, let alone read. "Be ready for the master," Nerdy said with a derisive little sniff—as if the very idea of them ever being worthy of the master's attention was beyond absurd—and then left and shut the door behind him.

Mat shifted and wriggled a bit, vainly searching for some relief from the stress on his shoulders and arms and chest. The pain was terrible; he was naked in an air-conditioned room and still sweating like he'd just gone three rounds. The hard floor beneath his knees didn't help any. Neither did the gag—God, what he wouldn't give to just be able to close his aching mouth and wipe the fucking drool from his chin. Even his fucking foot still ached, though it was easier not to think about the healing brand when the arm binder and gag demanded so much of his attention.

And Dougie—or rather the effort it took not to notice him—demanded even more. Because looking at him like that, all peacocked up for his new master and proud of it, eyeliner and mascara and lipstick and blush, little lavender lace bra and matching G-string, frilly white garters and white and lavender striped stockings and seriously *where* did you find heels to match that particular shade of purple and still fit a guy's foot? The perfect posture, the determined-to-impress expression . . . it broke Mat's heart and made him want to smash his fist into the kid's face all at once. Throw him down and rip that stupid shit off him and slap some fucking sense into his brainwashed fucking head.

But he couldn't, so he stayed where he was.

And waited.

And waited.

And waited.

What felt like ten hours later, in his own good fucking time, Allen finally sauntered in. And then he . . . walked right past Mat and Dougie, chatting away. The fucker was wearing a Bluetooth. He'd spent how much money on Mat and Dougie, and he wasn't even fucking *looking* at them.

"Well, have Tsing's people break his fucking knees then. My assistant has his number. I'm sure he'd be willing to help collect. Or I don't know. He have a kid? Take the kid and I'll have my new dog tear the little shit's throat out, how about that?" Allen's eyes finally flicked down to Mat. Didn't even register Dougie. And then he looked away again. "We have to come down hard on these rats. That's part of the business."

Mat hadn't heard a single dog bark since they'd gotten here. But then, it was a whole entire *island*. God knew where Allen might keep a pack of man-eating hounds.

"Well fucking learn to get your hands dirty. You want people to think we're a bunch of pussies?" Angry, now. Mat watched Allen pace across the room, right up to where he was kneeling. And then Allen pushed the sole of his leather loafer down on Mat's dick and ground it.

Mat grunted, bared his teeth around the gag. Made a split-second decision to hold still for now—tempting as it was to put Allen on his ass while the fucker was posturing like some big man to an underling. He needed a better lay of the land before he risked getting buried beneath it. "Bugs. That's all they are to you and me. They stop being profitable, you *squash* them." Punctuated, of course, by an even harder push on Mat's dick and balls.

This time he couldn't help it. He roared through the gag, hunched over and drew his knees together, eyes watering. Allen kept his foot wedged firmly in Mat's groin. Nothing Mat could really do about it with the binder on his arms.

"Oh, nothing. Just my new pet getting fixed. Yes, yes, the big purchase from Petrovic. Shady Commie fuck wrangled me into picking up two of them, though. I'm suffering from some serious buyer's remorse."

Dougie, as perfect a slave as he supposedly was now, let out a tiny little noise of distress beside Mat, quickly swallowed.

Yeah, well, boo hoo, so sorry your new master doesn't want you enough to grind his heel into your *balls. Let's switch places; he can ignore* me *for a while.*

"No you can't have him." The foot moved from Mat's crotch to his chest, pushed him vertical again. "I dunno, some bullshit about the one I wanted being rabid. I guess the other one's the dog whisperer. Pretty enough, I suppose." Allen turned his sneer on Dougie at last. "Yeah, well, take care of the damn problem, and maybe I'll let you have a go with his little dog whisperer cunt."

Dog whisperer. So Mat was the dog. Allen really thought he was vicious enough to rip a kid's throat out? Unless the kid was a rapist, he had another fucking thing coming.

"Don't call me until it's solved, or else I'll give *your* cunt to the dog." He turned on Dougie. "Get your ass in the air, cunt."

Dougie blinked, stunned, then quickly spun and slammed his upper half to the floor, lifting his ass.

"What the fuck is this? Spread, for fuck's sake. I spent seven figures on your ass and you're too fucking stupid to show me your cunt properly?"

Dougie yelped as Allen booted his ass, but was quick to reach back and spread himself, the flimsy scrap of cloth on his panties riding up his crack. Mat looked away.

"Dog. *Dog.*"

Oh, that was Mat. He swung his head around again, carefully avoiding catching Dougie in his peripheral vision but still leveling what he hoped was a withering stare at Allen.

"Look at your brother's cunt, Dog, and tell me. Does that look like a sloppy wet pussy ready for breeding to you?"

Like hell Mat was answering that.

Luckily, Allen seemed satisfied to listen to himself talk. "Because to me it looks like a stuck-up frigid little asshole with no room for my dick, and what's the fucking use of that? Does Petrovic just not give a shit anymore, is that it? He pawned this little girl off on me and his work is done, and now I have to fuck some dry little fist of a hole?" He grabbed Dougie by the hair and yanked his head up, then slammed it down hard, cracking Dougie's cheekbone against the floor. Mat winced, even as he couldn't help but think, *Good, maybe it'll knock some fucking sense into him.*

"Listen very closely, my little whore. Instead of the froufrou lingerie that's way too pretty for your filthy, used-up body, next time you come to me I want to see your cunt stretched nice and wide and dripping wet for me. You understand? *Dripping.* I'm an important man, and I don't have time to fight to get my dick in a cunt. So you'd best be sloppy twenty-four-seven, or else."

"Y-yes, Master, I'm sorry, Master," Dougie stammered, cheek still pressed to the floor, hands still spreading his ass wide. Mat focused on his face, his face, nothing else. He looked downright *wounded*, tears gathering in his eyes, running his mascara.

Allen slapped Dougie's upturned ass, just once, but hard enough to rock him. "Oh my *God*, are you *crying*, you stupid little bitch?"

"N-no, Master," Dougie lied. Well, half lied. He seemed to be getting himself under control, which was good, because Mat did *not* want to have to watch what would happen if he didn't.

Allen slapped him again. "What's your name, cunt?"

"D-Douglas, Master."

"Right. Donna. Get up here and suck my dick. Let's see what kind of blowjob a million dollars buys me, since your cunt is out of service."

That perked Dougie up. He sniffled and straightened, sweeping his hair out of his face and taking a deep breath, and then he shuffled forward until he was level with Allen's crotch.

"May I, Master?" he asked, voice perfectly composed. And fake. So very fake. The voice Mat had used when the social worker had told him Dougie would be going into foster care. *Yes, thank you for letting me know. I understand. I understand. Thank you.*

"May I, Master?" Allen mimicked in a simpering tone. "Did I or did I not just tell you to suck my dick? What do you need *more* permission for? Just get the fuck on with it, you priss."

Again, Dougie startled as if he'd been slapped, but then shook it off and gracefully opened Allen's fly, drawing his half-hard cock out.

"Thank you, Master," he said. "Thank you for letting me taste your big cock."

"Shut up."

Dougie's jaw twitched in annoyance, but he carried on. Gave Allen's cock a couple of pumps and then leaned forward to draw the head into his lipstick-smeared mouth with a theatrical moan.

"Are you watching this bullshit, Dog?" Allen sniffed imperiously as he fucked into Dougie's face with one punishing stroke. "Of course you are. How could a faggot animal like you resist the sight of your brother sucking dick? I bet you wish you were humping his cunt right now and getting your knot in there like you did the last time we saw each other. Don't worry, I'm sure you'll get another chance to pump him full of cum soon enough. He's an eager little whore, isn't he? So desperate for dick—any dick—that he pretends it doesn't make him mad that I keep insulting him."

Dougie's eyes flicked up briefly to Allen's face, but Allen didn't notice; his eyes were on Mat, along with what seemed like ninety percent of his attention, which was bizarre considering whose mouth the guy's cock was in. Maybe he was basically impotent. It had taken him a damn long time to get off at Dougie's coming-out party; that poor slave whose throat he'd been using had sucked him for like an hour.

"Harder, Daisy. I'm not a fucking lollipop. Less tongue, more throat."

Dougie swallowed him right down, no gagging, no watering eyes. Mat turned his head away, but Allen grabbed him by the hair, yanked him back. "Don't get jealous now, Dog. You'll get your turn soon enough."

Which was bullshit; there was nothing "soon" about any of this. Dougie kept sucking, and Allen kept making Mat watch, and Mat's whole body throbbed with the pain of his bondage, the pain of the fucking situation, the pain of holding fucking still the whole time against the urge to launch up and ram his shoulder straight into Allen's pudgy stomach. On and on and on it went, and Dougie was starting to look a little desperate, a lot concerned, like all his studiousness at Nikolai's feet was maybe going to be useless here, like maybe he wasn't so good at sucking cock after all, until at last, at *last*, Allen let out a moan and said, "Fuck, Daphne, *swallow*," and Mat was sure that meant Allen was going to come down Dougie's throat, but instead he pulled out at the last second, took himself in hand, and shot his load all over Dougie's ruined makeup and hair.

He laughed at his handiwork. "All that time spent tarting up, and the whole time all you needed was a faceful of jizz." He pressed a thumb to Dougie's swollen red bottom lip and smeared a line of cum and lipstick down his chin. "Maybe from now on I should just send Dog here up to your room every morning to paint your nose before I see you. But that robs me of the fun of watching him humping your face."

Yeah, like that was *ever* gonna fucking happen.

Allen smeared another line of cum and makeup across Dougie's cheek. "God, look at you, you filthy fucking whore. Get out of my face. And clean the fuck up."

Dougie hesitated for just a moment, looking confused. As dismissals went, Mat thought that one was pretty clear, but he could see how he might be afraid to fuck up if he were in Dougie's patent-leather shoes. "Yes, Master," Dougie said, and instead of rising to his feet, he lowered himself to his hands and knees. He made no attempt to wipe the jizz off his lips or out of his eyes. Just crawled out of the study, back the way they'd come, slowly enough for Allen to stop him if he'd misjudged the man's intent, quickly enough not to piss the guy off if he hadn't.

Turned out he hadn't misjudged. Allen watched him go, tucking his cock back into his pants. Which left just the two of them now. Not a pleasant thought. Mat couldn't even take solace from the fact that Allen wouldn't be able to get it up again for at least twenty minutes. He knew damn well there were worse things—so many, *many* worse things—than being fucked by some guy's unimpressive cock.

"So Nikolai tells me," Allen said, circling around Mat—no doubt intending to be predatory but instead just coming off kind of clunky, "that his secret to keep you from biting is your little whore brother."

Dramatic pause, like he actually expected Mat to answer through the gag. Well, fuck that; Mat wasn't even going to nod for this asshole.

"Who is," Allen continued, still circling, "of absolutely no value to me. Not even the best cocksucker I've had." Another dramatic pause. Was Mat supposed to defend Dougie's cocksucking honor here?

"So let's just get this out of the way up front, Dog. You bite *me*, and I will do things to your brother there aren't even *words* for, do you understand?"

Mat showed Allen his teeth, but he nodded, because he was Not a Bad Person, no matter how uncharitable his thoughts toward Dougie had been today. So much for his resolution not to give Allen the satisfaction of a reply.

For Dougie. Always for Dougie.

Allen smiled a victor's smile and unbuckled Mat's gag. Pointed with his chin at Mat's bound arms. "That looks painful, Dog."

Mat slowly eased his jaw shut, breathing through the pain and the relief, and went back to not talking.

"I guess you don't want out of those straps, then?"

Oh, tempting. To answer, or not to answer? Allen didn't seem like the type to show mercy either way, but . . . could Mat really afford to pass up the chance?

No. Not really. He sighed, conceded, "I do."

Allen slapped him so hard he fell over. "Try again, Dog," he snapped as Mat struggled back onto his knees without the use of his hands. "Didn't Petrovic teach you *anything*?"

Mat sighed again, worked his jaw to ease the sting. This shit was gonna get old fast—Nikolai had taught him that much, at least. Taught him to concede the battles that didn't matter. Like this one. "I'm sorry, master," he said, though the words burned in his mouth. Whatever. Give the fucker that—it didn't cost Mat anything but a scrap of his already-tattered pride.

"For what?" Allen asked.

Of course if Mat gave him a scrap, he'd want more. Of course he would.

Interesting conundrum, though: did Allen actually want a proper answer, or did he want Mat to snarl and growl? Which one would end up hurting less in the end? God, he needed a fucking roadmap, here.

Well, maybe better to start off safe and work his way out toward lippy one small stretch at a time. "For not addressing you properly, *master*," he said. Okay, sneered a little. Straddling the fence just a bit.

Seemed to be the right choice. Allen smiled. "Oh, you," he said with a shake of his head, like a dad on a sitcom. But then he turned around and walked to the door. Was he leaving Mat here? Was this it? But no, he just opened the door and poked his head out. "Barclay, I'm ready for my rigger now."

Barclay? Jesus, where did he find these guys?

Scratch that. Mat already knew the answer.

When Allen came back in, he was wearing the most insufferably smug smile Mat had ever seen. And here he'd thought *Nikolai* was up his own ass? Nikolai was in the Little Leagues.

"Shouldn't be too long now," Allen said, settling behind his desk and shuffling some papers while he waited, and not long after there was a knock at the door. A man walked in, dressed all in black, with a mass of rope tied into some kind of daisy chain and looped over one shoulder. Allen didn't even look at him. "String him up, would you? I don't really care much how, as long as it's entertaining to look at."

"You got it, boss."

The man approached Mat casual as could be, and nudged the inside of Mat's thigh with his booted foot. Mat eyed him warily, but spread his legs a little and let the guy look him over. On the one hand, it probably meant he'd finally be getting out of this fucking arm binder. On the other hand . . . his eyes zoomed in on the rope again, so much of it, coarse-looking and thick and . . . Just *no.*

"Gorgeous piece you've got here, boss," the rigger said after a long, contemplative study of Mat's body.

Allen was engrossed in something on one of the two computer screens on his desk, and just shrugged. "If you like that sort of thing."

Out of Allen's view—but not Mat's—the rigger rolled his eyes, as if to say *Can you believe this closet case?*

"You want me to bind his dick and balls?"

Said dick and balls promptly tried to crawl up into Mat's body, but Allen just flapped a hand. "Don't care. Busy now."

The rigger rolled his eyes again. "You want him hurting or no? Come on, boss, give me *something* to work with here."

Allen finally looked up from his screen, derision dripping from every pore. "No, I bought him to have tea parties with, Jason."

Jason just shrugged; he was probably well used to Allen's abuse by now. "Whatever you say, boss." Jason dropped the loops of rope from his shoulder and hooked his hands under Mat's armpits, hauling him to his feet and then, thank fucking God, undoing the buckles on the arm binder. When the last one came free and the leather pouch slid from his hands, Mat's arms flopped to his sides. And then he was on the floor again somehow, shoulders hunched forward and arms curled against his chest, stiff and burning and Jesus he couldn't even *breathe* it hurt so bad. Jason was beside him, strong fingers digging into flayed muscle and shredded joints, massaging, assessing, and Mat couldn't decide if he was helping or just making things worse.

"How long you been in that?" Jason asked, mouth close to Mat's ear as if he knew somehow that Mat could barely hear him over the rush of blood and his own whimpers.

"Dunno," Mat gritted out. "Dawn."

Jason's face twisted, mild concern but mostly just irritation, like Allen had left a metal tool out in the rain to rust, not twisted a human body until it'd broken.

Or not broken, maybe. The pain was starting to dull to something he could think around. Jason's massaging hands were starting to feel good—great, even—not like instruments of torture.

"Yeah, okay. We'll just keep your arms natural, then. Come on, on your feet."

Jason had to help him up again, but once he was standing, he managed okay on his own. Jason found the loose end of the rope and tugged, pulling one loop free and straight, then another, measuring by eye as he went. He draped it over Mat's shoulders, looped it around his back and chest, started tying off knots as he went. Mat's arms, as promised, went straight by his sides, pinned biceps to chest, elbows to waist, and wrists to thighs by three coils each. He had to kind of like Jason for that, even if his warier half kept reminding him the guy was on Allen's payroll. But the other half of him—the half desperate for comfort, for allies, the half that had come in Roger's mouth and then kissed him and kissed him and kissed him—that half was absolutely head over heels. Jason didn't want him hurting too much. Jason hated Allen too. Mat clung to that.

"Okay," Jason said after what seemed like a forever of standing still, moving where Jason put him, voluntarily letting someone restrain the ever-loving crap out of him. "Here's where things get tricky. Stand here." He maneuvered Mat a couple paces back, close to a spot on the wall opposite Allen's desk, then grabbed one of the guest chairs and plunked it down next to Mat. For a second, Mat actually thought he was being invited to sit, but Jason said, "Stay," and then stepped up onto the chair, loose end of the rope in his hands. Mat tilted his head back, saw a little network of steel rings and bars and pulleys bolted to the ceiling. Jason started threading the rope through them.

"You're being too nice to him," Allen commented midway through the process. "He's not fighting you at all. Are you defective, Dog? Didn't Nikolai leave you half-feral for me? Or are you as docile as your whore brother after all?"

Little late for fighting now, though so far his legs were still free. But he didn't want to kick Jason. Jason hadn't hurt him.

And anyway, was fighting still fighting if you fought on explicit command? Seemed like it would be a bigger *fuck you* to be completely cooperative, but only for another man. If Allen got close enough, Mat would spit in his face and ask, *"How's that for feral, fucker?"* But for now, he was determined to play along, no matter how Allen taunted him.

Allen's eyes narrowed at Mat's silent stillness. "Maybe the dog needs poking with a stick before he'll snarl."

"Too bad your stick's too small to reach through the cage bars," Mat snapped. Even if he did feel ridiculous hurling insults with his arms bound to his sides.

Jason gave him a wide-eyed and very amused *Oh no you didn't.*

Allen didn't looked perturbed at all. Rather, he grinned, all teeth. "Your brother seemed to think my stick was plenty big enough. Should I call him down and have him demonstrate?"

Sorry, buddy. If you wanted to make me sweat by threatening him like that, you're about eight thousand rapes too late. But apparently he still loved the brainwashed little shit enough not to say so aloud and tempt Allen into calling his bluff.

Allen switched tacks. "Ever been whipped, Dog?"

A sudden, powerful sense memory of cowering like a child beneath the endless lash of Nikolai's belt. He blinked, swallowed it back. Met Allen's eyes—*I'm not afraid of you.* "Yes."

"Well, clearly not enough."

So not a bluff then. Would he untie him? Do it now?

"Finish, Jason. I want him sweating."

Great. So something to look forward to later, then. Jason climbed down off the chair, rope end still in hand. "Got it, boss," he said, and maybe something else too, but Mat was too busy playing the scene back in his head, trying to figure out if he could've changed the outcome at all, if anything he could've said or done might've made things better—or worse. Things had been so simple with Nikolai; the rules were clear and he followed them or faced the consequences. Hard to believe he actually *missed* that now, faced as he was with Allen's random cruelty.

Jason pulled him back to the present with a flick to one nipple, weirdly sensitive in its position between two coils of rope. "I said left foot on the chair." Well, at least he didn't sound angry about having to repeat himself. Mat complied. Jason gave the rope in his hand a little tug, and Mat realized it'd been woven down and through all the loops around his arms and torso on the left side. He felt the pull lifting him a little, throwing him off balance but that was okay because Jason was keeping him upright with his grip on the rigging.

Jason started tying his left leg, binding calf to thigh and then pulling the whole thing out to the side somehow, straining Mat's groin muscles nearly as painfully as his arms had been. "Nice to work with someone so flexible," Jason said, still so bizarrely casual, like he and Mat were just having a friendly conversation over a cup of coffee or something, or like Mat was a paid model for some kind of fetish shoot and Jason the guy who'd hired him for a generous day's pay.

"I can kick you in the face over my shoulder," Mat said, deadpan, in lieu of *thank you* or maybe *fuck you*. Still stuck between both extremes. He wondered if he'd ever truly like and trust anyone again. He knew from Allen that he could definitely still hate someone wholeheartedly.

Jason seemed to find him funny. "I'd like to see that one day."

"How about you untie me and I show you n—?"

Allen slammed his hand down on his desk. "Will you *shut that dog up* and get out of here?"

Jason just shrugged and finished tying off Mat's left leg, but Mat was feeling bold. He already had a whipping coming later; what else did he have to lose? "What," he asked, "no more flirting?"

Allen stood abruptly, shoving his chair back, and stomped over to a cabinet in the corner. Mat followed him with his eyes, pulse picking up, but he wasn't so afraid. Actually, weirdly, despite the terrible stretch and burn in his leg and the fact that he was being strung up like a fucking Christmas turkey, he was almost . . . giddy. He'd thrown Allen off-balance more than once already and they'd only been together an hour or so.

The guy was nothing like Nikolai. Mat really could get under his skin, make him lose control. He liked it. He had *power* here. Power he'd one day leverage to escape. He was sure of it.

Allen rummaged through the cabinet. Said, back still turned to Mat, "If you were so hungry for a cock up your ass, Dog, all you had to do was ask." No surprise, then, when he turned around with a dildo in his hands twice the size of his own cock. He tossed it at Jason, where it landed with a rubber plop at the guy's feet. "Since you two are feeling so fucking friendly, why don't you get that stuffed in him, eh? See how much he likes you then. No lube necessary, I don't think."

You'll have to do better than that.

Jason stooped to pick up the dildo, and Mat opened his mouth unprompted. Jason seemed to find *that* amusing too, stuck it in there for Mat to lick and drool on.

"I said no lube," Allen barked, at which point Jason kind of shrugged with his eyebrows—*Sorry, buddy, I tried*—and pulled it back. At least Mat had gotten it a *little* wet. But this was gonna *hurt*. Strange how he kind of didn't even care.

Jason was as gentle as he could be, given the circumstances, but even going slow and easy, it burned and tore and made Mat grunt.

He didn't miss the bit where Allen rubbed the heel of his palm against his groin at the sound.

Sick fuck.

When Jason finally got all eight or nine inches wedged up Mat's ass—an agonizingly time-consuming process, but he supposed that beat the alternative of forcing it fast—he took the long loose end of the rope dangling from Mat's left thigh and wove it over and through Mat's legs and waist to hold the dildo in place. Almost as bad as the dildo was the rough wrap of the rope—hemp, he thought, or something equally scratchy—wedged up between his balls and framing his cock.

"You ever been suspended before?" Jason asked—softly, almost a whisper, not meant to reach Allen's ears. Mat shook his head. "This is going to be a little uncomfortable—" Mat snorted. More uncomfortable than pulling his leg half out of joint? More uncomfortable than rope burn on his junk? "—but just trust the rigging, it'll hold you, and nothing's going to cut off circulation anywhere. I'm a professional, and as much as he hates it, Allen knows I won't be responsible for anybody's injuries. Now pick up your right foot and tuck your heel to your ass for me."

Mat wasn't thrilled about it, but at this point he didn't really see what choice he had—either he'd cooperate or he'd be forced—so he sucked in a deep breath and slowly, slowly lifted his foot off the ground. The ropes bit as they took his weight, but none of the knots seemed to tighten, and no one point of contact created too much pressure. Which wasn't to say it didn't hurt; resting all your weight on narrow coils of rope, even a couple dozen of them, wasn't fun at all. But at least bits of him weren't going to go numb and fall off anytime soon. A low bar, but there it was.

Jason made quick work of binding his right leg to match his left: ass to heel, thigh spread wide enough to burn from groin to knee. He was basically splayed wide open now, like a frog on a dissection tray with a probe up its ass. All he needed were a few pins in his organs.

Jason stepped back, checked his work with a critical eye, nodded at length. Stepped close again, ran his fingertips over and beneath some of the knots and joints. Checked every pulse point on Mat's body, smoothed his hands up Mat's thighs, made sure the ropes weren't digging dangerously into his junk. Mat appreciated the attention to detail, the care for his well-being, even if the guy had put him in the position of needing it in the first place.

Finally, Jason stepped out of the way altogether, replaced the chair by Allen's desk, and asked, "Good, boss?"

Allen glanced up from his computer screens, nodded once, and wordlessly flapped his hand at Jason—*Shoo.*

When he'd gone, Allen finally looked up, unmistakably pleased by what he saw. "I hope it hurts as much as it looks like it does," he said. "Although if not, I'm sure I could find a way. Now, I've got some work to do, so why don't you just hang there for a while?"

Was he kidding? "No, I kinda thought maybe I'd go for a walk, check out that nice private beach of yours."

"You going to shut up, or do I have to shove a cock down your throat, too?"

Okay, yeah, shutting up. Allen might want his dog to snarl, but Mat didn't much feel like choking on his own vomit.

And if this was going to be his life now—*don't think like that, don't, this is only temporary*—then he really did need to follow Nikolai's advice. Pick his battles. Play it smart. Stay novel, stay one step ahead, stay alive.

And wait for his opportunity to get the hell out of this hell.

CHAPTER THREE

P artway down the slaves' hall, Douglas got to his feet and started walking. Seemed safe enough, now that Allen was gone.

Allen. He shuddered at the thought. Of the way Allen had used him, spoken to him, treated him like absolute dirt.

He was a slave, yes, but with Nikolai he'd been valuable and treasured. With Allen, he felt lower than an animal. Maybe even lower than Mat.

Well, he could still prove himself. He just had to regroup. Maybe the other pleasure slaves would give him some advice on how to get into Allen's good graces. How to seduce him, how to please him, maybe even how to make him smile. Douglas was clever, and a quick study. He'd work it out.

When he found the room Nerdy—ahem, Nedry—had pointed out as his quarters, he forced himself not to knock. This was his space now. He belonged here. He opened the door.

Despite it still being midmorning, the room was dark inside, and quiet. There were six beds, just like before, but now five of them were occupied. Five men, all as slight as him, all fast asleep. Maybe they'd just worked a night shift? The one closest to the door had his blanket thrown off, and in the light from the hallway, Douglas could see he was covered in body glitter, and both nipples were pierced with gold rings. Douglas flushed and quickly looked away.

He wished they were awake to welcome him and tell him their names. He wanted to ask them questions, wanted to know what their schedule was—whether they worked nights and slept days as a matter of course, or if this was a one-time thing—what the expectations were. He wanted so badly to know his role. He felt unmoored, untethered, terrified. But they were all fast asleep, and he knew he wouldn't make too many friends if he woke them. So he gently shut the door behind him and crept into the room, headed for the empty bed. He toed out of his shoes—*ahhh,* God, it felt so good to be rid of those things, especially with the brand still tender—and sat down. Unclasped his itching bra and rolled down his thigh-high stockings. He felt almost human again.

Douglas Petrovic, cherished pet. Not a nameless whore with a sloppy cunt.

He wanted a shower and to wash his face, but he didn't know if there was protocol about the bathrooms. He didn't want to do anything wrong. Was terrified of it, actually. And he was tired, too, despite the hour. Could use the rest. If the others were sleeping, maybe he was supposed to, as well. He drew back the covers and climbed into his new bed, narrow and not very comfortable, not compared to his bed at Nikolai's, and definitely not compared to Nikolai's massive four-poster with its thick duvet and piles of pillows he could sink into.

He supposed he should feel happy he had a bed and a pillow at all. He didn't want to think of where Mat was going to wind up sleeping tonight, if he slept at all.

He sighed and laid his head on the pillow, stubbornly shutting his eyes and willing himself to sleep. And then sat up again. There was something cold and sticky on his ear. He lifted his hand. It was in his hair, too. Sticky and slimy and tacky. Cum. It was all over his pillow. A congealed puddle of it. Not just a little bit. A lot.

If he had to guess, he'd say five men's worth.

For a moment he just sat there shaking, torn between anger and despair. *Why* had they done this to him? He hadn't even had a *chance* to upset them yet. If he were in their shoes, he'd be falling all over himself trying to help the new guy fit in, learn the ropes, stay out of trouble so that they could all please their master better, and maybe, when their master didn't need them, keep each other company during their off time. Wasn't that what it was all about? Taking care of each other? Taking care of their master?

A sob tore its way out of him, and then another. He put his face in his hands and cried. Cried and cried, all the tears he hadn't shed during his last lovemaking session with Nikolai, and saying goodbye to Roger, and in the RV with those strange women, and with Allen getting his face fucked. Big, helpless sobs, and tears to match.

"Oh, shut up," someone mumbled blearily. Behind him, one of the other slaves was quietly . . . *laughing at him*? "And go to fucking sleep before I give you something real to cry about."

Oh God, not even a day and already everything was so awful here. Everything. How was he going to survive the rest of his time? With a sniffle, he flipped his pillow over and lay down again, curling up into a ball on his side and yanking the blankets up to his chin. Cold. And lonely. So alone. He'd never felt so alone.

He squeezed his eyes closed and pictured Nikolai, and Roger, and even Jeremy. Drew Nikolai's face in his mind's eye one line at a time—the sweep of his brows, those strong cheekbones, the slightly pointed chin, the kind gray eyes, and oh, best of all, his smile, the smile he only smiled when Douglas was his Good Boy.

Be strong for me, my precious boy. My good boy. Be strong.

As bad days went, Mat supposed this wasn't much more than a six or seven on the Nikolai scale. A ten, of course, being the day Dougie had stabbed him with the serum and then raped him . . . or the day Dougie had gotten him hard and made him rape himself.

No coincidence that both worst days revolved around Dougie.

Jason came in every so often—four times now, by Mat's admittedly not-too-focused count—to untie and retie him in a different position. Always suspended, but punishing different muscles and joints, putting his weight on different pressure points. It was miserable, sure, but he was used to that. Humiliating, but he was used to that, too. Sometimes he thought the worst part of all this was how infrequently Allen bothered to pay attention to him. Why put him through this if the fucker wasn't even enjoying it? He didn't even seem to want to *hear* Mat suffer; Mat's grunts and moans were met with silence, or worse, sighs of irritation.

But maybe that was for the best, because when Allen *did* pay attention to him, shit got ugly. Mat didn't mind the balled-up papers Allen occasionally chucked his way—once, when Jason had suspended him face-up from his arms and legs, Allen had made a brief game of seeing how many wads he could get to collect on Mat's stomach and chest—but then Allen . . . escalated. Stood up irritated from his desk just before lunch, cracked his knuckles and his neck and his back, and then fished a set of darts from a desk drawer. They weren't sharp enough to puncture, but they left nasty welts, and Allen kept aiming for his junk.

The fucker didn't even take Mat down when he disappeared for lunch. Didn't feed Mat either. Which was maybe for the best, considering how badly he had to piss. Thank God he'd gone before Nedry had led him in here. He wondered what Allen would do if he just let it loose on the hardwood floor. Hmm, no, on second thought he didn't. Because if the guy threw darts at his junk unprovoked, what would he do if Mat really made him mad?

He supposed his entire purpose here was to find out. But he wasn't ready to, not yet. Not until he found his footing, felt out Allen's moods and triggers and—he shuddered—*consequences*. How much was bluster and how much was follow-through. How bad the follow-through would actually be.

Jason came in to reposition him again, and he wanted to beg the guy for just a little fucking mercy this time, but then it turned out he didn't have to. Maybe Jason had heard Mat's little swallowed whimpers when he'd untied him and actually felt bad for him, or maybe he was just looking out for Allen's property—after all, bending and flexing and immobilizing a body that uncomfortably for that long could surely have long-term repercussions—but whatever the case, all he did was make patterns with the rope, interlocking diamonds up and down Mat's arms and legs and chest that actually might've been pretty if they hadn't been inflicted on him, and left him standing there, perfectly comfortable, feet shoulder-width apart on the floor and arms anchored out to his sides. Allen didn't bitch, so maybe this was normal. Whatever; Mat wasn't questioning his good fortune.

Or the fact that it left him clearheaded enough to pay attention to Allen, who seemed to be responsible for some kind of online gaming empire—poker, digital casinos, sports betting, that kind of thing. He spent a lot of time clacking away on a keyboard, but nearly as much time on the phone. He talked to pretty much everyone the way he talked to his slaves: barked and bitched and puffed out his chest and threatened and insulted. There were some exceptions—clients, maybe; people he was trying to impress—but the polite phone calls seemed to take a lot out of him. He'd retrieve his darts after every one of them, and take out his irritation at having been made to behave, even only for a few moments, on Mat. One particularly hard throw must've come in at just the right angle, and the tip pierced right through the meat of Mat's thigh, dangling there heavily by the quarter-inch or so that'd dug in beneath the skin. Mat sweated and swore and tried to shake it loose, teeth clenched and hands fisted around the ropes. If this was going to be his life now—living, breathing statuary-slash-dartboard—he wasn't gonna last very long.

If nothing else, he'd die of boredom. At least Nikolai had left him with the treadmill and punching bag to keep him occupied.

God help him, he was wishing he was back at Nikolai's.

There was an alarm clock in the room. Douglas hadn't seen it when he'd come in—too busy dealing with the pillow covered in cum to really notice—but it certainly made its presence known when it went off a few hours later. The overhead lights came on shortly after that, and all around him the other men stirred and sat up, grunting and groaning and stretching and not looking at all like the expensive sexual playthings they were.

They greeted each other, asked one another how they'd slept, joked with the man covered in body glitter about bukkake with fairies. None of them acknowledged Douglas, and for a moment he was terrified, *absolutely terrified* that he'd have to do this without their guidance, but then a redheaded boy covered head to toe in freckles turned to him and said, "All right, new guy, shower time."

Directions. Directions were good. He followed the line of them through a door and into a huge bathroom, complete with toilet stalls and a wall of showers just like the ones he'd been bullied in after gym class in high school.

Well, if the cum-pillow and the way the five of them were giving him the cold shoulder right now was any indication, then it seemed maybe the more things changed, the more they stayed the same. He stepped up to the sixth shower and turned on the spray, let the hot water run over him.

Relief. Pure relief, there was no other word for it. Showering after a long trip always felt even more cleansing than usual. To be washing off the perfume and makeup he'd put on for Allen—fat lot of good it had done him—was the cherry on top.

"Here, scrub." The redhead shoved a loofah and a bottle of shower gel at him. "We only have an hour between the alarm and presentation upstairs; don't waste it."

Dougie did as told. Beneath the showerhead to his left, two boys, no older than he was, were taking turns scrubbing each other's backs. Laughing, smiling, whispering into each other's ears. They looked so *happy*. And beautiful, both of them. Maybe they were the master's favorites. The taller of the two was black, strikingly dark-skinned, like a runway fashion model. The shorter one was slim, lithe, almost feminine with his elfin face and pierced nipples, blue eyes, and the sort of curly silver-blond hair you almost never saw on boys much over the age of ten or twelve. Beyond them was a slightly older man, mid- or maybe late twenties but kind of hard to tell with how smooth his face was. East Asian and maybe a little taller than Douglas, but with long, long hair—nearly waist-length—that at the moment he was very carefully shampooing. The last man in the line was the tallest of the lot, maybe a full six feet. Hispanic blood in there somewhere, or maybe Italian. Dark eyelashes a mile long. Olive skin. Lean, but also curvy, with a deeply dipping lower back and a plump, pert ass. No wonder the master hadn't paid Douglas the slightest mind. All these men were *stunning*. How was he supposed to even begin to compete with them? It was like putting lipstick on a pig.

And a competition it was, he had no doubt. Not after the way they'd treated him so far.

Well, Nedry had said the master tired of his playthings quickly. Given what likely happened to them after, Douglas didn't want to be next any more than the rest of these men.

"You're a Petrovic, right?" the redhead asked. Douglas paused in his scrubbing, and his eyes were drawn to the constellation of freckles across the bridge of the boy's nose, over his cheekbones, above his bright green eyes. Douglas had the strangest urge to run his tongue across them, see if they had texture, if they tasted as lovely as they looked. Like a sprinkling of cinnamon.

"Yes," he said, a little shiver of pride running through him. "My name's Douglas. What's yours?"

"Not much to look at, considering," the last man said. Italian, definitely. His accent was to die for, even if it was currently dripping with derision. Douglas tried hard not to think about the fact that Nikolai, and now Allen, had bought him as a tagalong to Mat, not for his own merits. Tried hard to remember how often Nikolai had called him his beautiful boy. Nikolai had warmed to him, had loved him, even if he'd underestimated him at first. "You look at him and you look at me, and you tell me why he costs three times as much, huh?"

The black man snorted. "Funny, Bernardo. I look at him, I see a tasty little twink. I look at you, I see Sylvester Stallone with a wax job and an ass like a cheap stripper."

Was that . . . was he *defending* Douglas? Impossible to tell, but Douglas wanted to hope so. More likely, though, that the man would've have defended anyone if it meant getting in his jibe.

"I'm Finn," the redhead said with a quick, nervous smile.

Had he come on Douglas's pillow earlier today?

"Of course Finn wants to stick his cock up your ass," the blond boy said—funny, that, considering he was busy soaping up his partner's ass as he spoke. "Because of you, he's the *old* new guy now."

"At least I've still got balls to slap his ass *with*," Finn snapped, and the blond actually bared his teeth and hissed at Finn like a drama queen. Douglas took a closer look at him, stomach sinking at the implication Finn had made . . . and *holy shit*, yes, he really was missing some vital bits and pieces. Had *Allen* done that to him? Or had he been castrated by his trainer? A punishment, maybe? Or on purpose to give him that pretty soft feminine look? Douglas had a sudden flashback to Nikolai telling him how lucky he was not to be a custom job. That castration was relatively common when it came to boys like him. He shuddered, tried to hide it. Didn't want to offend anyone. Didn't want these men to be any more hostile to him than they were already.

Finn was prattling on, completely unawares, lathering shampoo through his bright red hair. "Although it's true I *am* relieved not to be the new guy anymore. Don't forget to douche, Douglas." He gave a nod to the metal enema nozzle hanging from the showerhead, then took his own down in demonstration. "You get shit on anybody's dick and that's pretty much an automatic demotion. Miss Prissy over there is Ashley, by the way." Miss Prissy being the blond, castrated boy. "And his boyfriend's Cory. Don't let the Ball-less Wonder fool you; he can top like a master, I've seen it. Just—" Finn paused to duck his head under the stream, rinsed the shampoo away and grabbed the conditioner "—not in here. Not with another slave. Or you'll end up losing more than just your berries."

So then why was Cory's cock currently halfway down Ashley's throat? Finn must've caught his confusion, because he followed Douglas's line of sight and said, "Ah. Yeah, that's cool. Just no penetration. The master doesn't mind sharing our mouths, but he gets particular about our asses."

"And occasionally our cocks," the Asian guy put in. "But if he wants to play that way, you'll know it. Because you'll have a goddamn padlock on your junk for a fucking month, not that I'm bitter or anything."

"Next time don't get a boner looking at his wife where he can see you, Henry," Cory said, then groaned and fell back against the tiles. "Shit, Ash, hurry up. Clock's ticking."

Douglas worked conditioner through his hair and snuck a long peek at Cory's cock disappearing again and again into Ashley's mouth. No finesse at all. Ashley wasn't even using his tongue, and his lips were too slack, and he wasn't sucking nearly enough. No wonder it was taking so long.

Bernardo tossed Douglas a knowing leer and took his half-hard cock in his hand, jutting it toward Douglas. "I hear that's why you cost so much. Best-trained mouths in the world, Nikolai's boys."

Best-trained *everything*, Douglas wanted to say. To defend his master's honor, his master's reputation. But these men were just slaves, like him. What they thought didn't matter.

Except . . . his life would probably be a lot easier here if they liked him, wanted to help him. Stopped leaving jizz on his pillow. He could serve the master better if they told him how. And he only had one thing to barter for their kindness with.

He cast Bernardo a crooked smile, licked his lips. "Why don't I let you be the judge of that?"

"Shit," Bernardo said. Not *yes*, but not *no*, either, and now his cock was fully erect, dark with blood. Douglas lowered himself to his knees and shuffled forward on the slick tiles, and suddenly the entire room was quiet but for the sound of running water, even Ashley's sucking and Cory's moaning fading away. They were all watching him. Expectant. Waiting. The tension made his belly flutter with nerves—did they not do this for each other all the time?—but he knew what he was doing here. Knew he could impress them all.

Bernardo's hand fell away from his cock when Douglas settled on his haunches before him. Douglas pressed his nose into that smooth groin, buried it between Bernardo's balls and sniffed. He smelled, and tasted, of fine soap. He was big, bigger than Douglas, bigger than Nikolai by at least an inch, not so fat at the head but very wide down the shaft. Douglas swallowed him right down like it was nothing. No teasing, no choking, no moving. Just held him there in his throat, blocking off his own air, letting Bernardo acclimate to the slick muscled warmth.

Bernardo's hands sank into Douglas's hair, still slimy with conditioner, and he moaned.

That's right. Let me show you how sweet I can be. I can be your sweet thing, and all you have to do is let me. Accept me.

The hands in his hair tightened, and Bernardo growled, "Come *on*, Petrovic," and Douglas took that as his cue to start moving. He wasn't here to tease or torture the man, after all; he was here to make friends. So he pulled all the way back to the tip, swirled his tongue around it once and then pressed the flat of his tongue hard against the shaft as he dove back in, one hand fondling expertly at Bernardo's balls, forefinger and thumb of the other hand gripping tight around the base of the shaft and making short little twisting strokes as he sucked. Everything Ashley had been doing wrong, he set out to do as right as right could be.

"Oh, *fuck* yeah," Bernardo groaned, fingers flexing and relaxing and flexing again in Douglas's hair. "Such a pretty fucking mouth you have, Douglas. So good. So fucking *good*."

Douglas let his eyes close—this wasn't a master, he didn't have to look at the man if he didn't want to—and let the praise wash over him in a warm rush. Hummed his pleasure, knowing how it would transfer and become Bernardo's pleasure too. Pressed his head up into those stroking hands without breaking his rhythm and pretended, just for a moment, that it was Nikolai petting his hair, Nikolai showering him with compliments and affection. But then he felt the rush of fluid under the skin of the cock in his mouth and the balls in his hand draw up, and he turned all his focus to making the impending orgasm as mind-bending as it could be, and then Bernardo was shooting into his mouth with a shout that literally reverberated off the tiled walls, and he tasted different than Nikolai but Douglas lapped him up anyway, sucked and stroked him through it until Bernardo's thighs quivered and the hands in his hair nudged him away.

"Fuck," Bernardo said, shell-shocked.

"Me next," Henry said, flipping his long hair back over his shoulders. His cock wasn't as big as Bernardo's, but it had a wicked leftward curve. He waggled it at Douglas obscenely.

"Sorry, pal," Ashley said, though he didn't sound sorry at all. He must've finished with Cory at some point during the two whole minutes it'd taken Douglas to make Bernardo blow. "No time. Douglas still hasn't cleaned his slutty little cunt out."

And with that, he grabbed Douglas by the arm and hauled him standing, then shoved him up against the tiles. Cory moved in on the other side of him, keeping him pinned while Ashley shoved the shower shot nozzle up his ass and started the water flow. Too fast. Too hot. Douglas groaned miserably, and the nascent erection he'd gotten sucking Bernardo flagged in a heartbeat, but he didn't struggle. Maybe if he suffered this well, he'd earn their respect.

"Don't be so rough with him," Finn whined, but there wasn't a lot of heart in it.

Yes, Douglas decided as a cramp rolled through his abdomen, Finn had definitely come on his pillow. He hadn't necessarily wanted to, but he'd done it anyway.

"Shut up, Finn. You want me to plug up your pussy next? I could put the two of you right next to each other, kill two birds with one stone."

Finn said nothing, but the way he turned his back on the scene spoke plenty loud. He picked up his own shower shot, turned on a slow trickle of water, tested the temperature, and washed himself.

Finished while Cory and Ashley still had Douglas pressed to the tiles, his gut cramping viciously, surely starting to swell. The others finished as well, one by one, water shutting off, shower emptying out. They obviously weren't *supposed* to do more than douche. Wasn't stopping Cory and Ashley from enema-ing out Douglas's fucking brainpan. God, it hurt.

Maybe he shouldn't have sucked off Bernardo after all. Maybe he'd insulted Ashley somehow. Or made it seem like he was here to compete and win, rather than just survive long enough to go home to his Master.

"Please," he moaned against the tiles. "Please, please stop. I'll do anything. I'm sorry. Please."

Ashley jerked the shower shot, shoving it a little higher up Douglas's ass. "What, Petrovic didn't teach you how to take a little pain without crying like a spoiled baby? All his boys are so fucking *soft*."

Hah, wait until you meet my brother, Douglas wanted to say, but if he opened his mouth again, he really *would* cry. He'd screwed up somehow, made an enemy *already*, and the other boys were supposed to be helping him, not *torturing* him, and . . .

"Ah, leave it, Ash," Cory said, letting up on Douglas's shoulder. "You've scared him bad enough for one day. And we gotta get ready. Come on, baby, and I'll rim you a little before I lube you up."

Ashley was up and gone so fast, it took Douglas a second to even realize he was alone. He tugged out the shower shot with a shaking hand, squeezed his cheeks together as hard as he could and waddled over to the nearest toilet, and finally let go. Let himself have one single sob of relief—any more than that, and his eyes might still be bloodshot when the time came to look good for his master.

By the time he'd toweled off and left the bathroom, the other boys were all in various stages of dress. Except Ashley, who Cory was lubing with what looked like a mini turkey baster. Mini or no, it was a *lot* of lube. But then, the master had said he wanted Douglas sloppy wet. Hopefully it wouldn't leak out and stain his panties, though.

Finn, when he spotted Douglas, came and took him by the arm. "Here, I'll show you the ropes," he said. "So here's the deal. We're all on call all night. We get up at three, make sure we're ready at four, and then at five o'clock service starts. Sometimes, when master's having a party, we all go down to dinner together. Sometimes he just requests a couple of us, sometimes none at all. Sometimes you spend the night with him, or one of his friends or clients. Sometimes you get to come back here. Basically, you have to be ready for anything. Here." He handed Douglas his own mini turkey baster full of lube. "Sorry, it's really gross. But you have to do it, so just get it over with. Go deep. And whatever you do, don't, you know, *push* once it's in. Otherwise it gets all over everything, and you don't want to see what happens if the master catches you leaking on the furniture."

Douglas wasn't going to cry again, and he wasn't going to balk, not in front of them. He took the baster and went to his bed, lay down and spread his legs wide. The others were watching him again. Finn with nervous concern, Henry with vague disinterest, and Bernardo with obvious hunger. Cory and Ashley were quick to join them. All watching as Douglas pressed the tip of the syringe against his hole and slowly shoved it inside himself, taking inch after inch until the bulb at the end was nestled in the crack of his ass. He gave it a squeeze. Winced as the cold, viscous lube flooded inside him.

"Where's his plug?" Ashley asked.

"I—I've got it right here," Finn mumbled. "I can help him if you want, you don't need to waste your time. I can do it."

"Waste my time? How could it possibly be a waste of my time to help make sure the poor little new kid is ready for his master?" Ashley smirked, his pretty cherubic face contorting into something twisted and awful. He snatched the plug from Finn's hands. Stainless steel. Fat and heavy-looking. "Ready to have your pussy plugged, new kid?"

Ashley sounded downright mean, but Douglas wasn't afraid of him, not even after what he'd done in the shower. Nikolai had taught him how not to be afraid of *anything* but failing his master. He was a Petrovic, damn it. He'd show Ashley what Petrovics were made of.

So he got up onto his elbows and knees and thrust his ass in the air, then reached back with both hands and spread himself. He *squelched*. Ew.

Well, at least the plug would keep all that lube in.

He'd clearly stolen some of the wind from Ashley's sails, because the boy said nothing else. Just stepped up behind him and jammed the plug into Douglas's waiting ass. Douglas winced, but he stayed silent. And by the look on Ashley's face when he stood up again and turned to him, staying silent counted as a win.

You'll have to do better than that.

Douglas's chest puffed up, and he turned from Ashley like the boy wasn't even of consequence. "What's next, Finn?" he asked cheerfully.

Finn showed him the closets—shared clothes (women's lingerie, mostly) separated by size—and then the makeup tables at the far side of the room. They didn't all necessarily pretend to be women (though that happened sometimes, Finn explained), but they all definitely dressed like them: lace and panties and stockings, corsets or bras or tiny little tops. Cory put on nothing but a garter belt and sheer stockings, the bright red satin a perfect complement to his dark skin, and topped off his "outfit" with a fluffy white bunny tail plug. Douglas wondered about Cory's cock hanging out, and boy did it *hang*—it didn't seem like the sort of thing Allen had any interest in seeing—but Finn assured him it was fine. Ashley, on the other hand, wore what looked to be a little girl's dress, pale blue and knee-length with puffy sleeves and a sweet, bouncy crinoline. His makeup accentuated his soft, childish features, bringing out his femininity so strongly he probably could've passed for a young woman. Finn's makeup was just the opposite: bold eyeliner and sparkly green eye shadow designed to highlight the sweep of his temples, the sharpness of his cheekbones, and all those freckles.

Douglas didn't know what to wear or how best to paint his own face, and while Finn might've been inclined to help him, the other boys clearly wouldn't tolerate that, so he was left to his own devices. What he'd had on yesterday hadn't worked, so he went for something softer today—a sky blue baby-doll top and matching miniskirt, bobby socks and saddle shoes. He eschewed lipstick for a bubblegum pink gloss, and he skipped the eye makeup entirely, except for a subtle sweep of blue mascara. For blush he went nearly natural, brushing on the faintest wisps of color, as if he were really blushing.

Ashley glared at him the entire time. When Douglas finally met his eyes and tried to offer him a smile, the boy said, "That's *my* skirt."

Cory gave him a nudge. "It's the *master's* skirt. Just calm your tits, okay?"

At least that made Ashley turn his glare on Cory instead. Someone wasn't getting a blowjob in the shower tomorrow.

Well, maybe Douglas would just have to step in, then, and show Cory how it was *really* done.

CHAPTER FOUR

T he clock on Allen's office wall read 4:03 when Allen stood from his desk and left the room. Mat was hanging limp and sweaty in Jason's latest rigging—face-down, knees bent and arms tied at the small of his back, the ropes mercifully more a cradle than a rack this time—and gave up fighting sleep the moment the fucker was gone. Who'd have ever thought holding still all day could wear you out so much?

Jason came in just a minute later, brushed the wads of paper and a single banana peel off Mat's back, and began to untie him.

"Thanks," Mat murmured as he carefully lowered his feet to the ground, too tired to muster anything more.

Jason's strong hands massaged a cramping thigh. "I'm sure you'll be glad to hear that's it for the day. Well, at least in here."

Hard to believe he'd only been hanging here for six or eight hours. Felt like forever. "Yeah," he said. Jason untied his arms, massaged his wrists. Nice as that felt, Mat wished he'd hurry up. "I gotta piss so bad my back teeth are floating." Hardly seemed fair that he was simultaneously thirsty enough to *drink* the fucking piss.

"I'll take you in a minute. Let's just finish getting you out of this. Can you walk, do you think?"

Mat nodded. His body might not want to, but he'd fucking *make* it work if it meant getting out of here.

Done untying him, Jason slung an arm around his waist and led him down the back stairs to the slave floor. Nudged him into a bathroom and said, "You have half an hour. Get very clean. Holler if you need help."

Mat emptied his bladder with an aching pleasure that bordered on pain, then stuck his head beneath the sink faucet and drank until he couldn't anymore. The shower was glorious, endless hot water and perfect pressure, slowly easing the worst of the aches in his overtaxed muscles. He almost gave in and eased himself onto the floor, but frankly, he worried he wouldn't be able to get up again. He hadn't been this sore since the day after his last dose of the serum.

He finally roused himself enough to wash his body and hair, reluctantly used the shower shot hanging beside the knobs, and then stayed under the stream, head down and eyes closed, until Jason knocked on the door and called, "Time's up!" Mat shut the water off with a sigh, toweled dry, and came back out to meet Jason, who was holding a pair of padded black leather cuffs in his hands.

Mat sighed again and stuck his hands out. He could fight the guy, but what was the point? Especially given how responsible Jason seemed to be for his comfort and safety here.

"You're all set," Jason said once he'd buckled the cuffs on snugly and then locked them with little brass Master locks. "No clothes or anything needed. Follow me. You can eat, and then you're on duty for the rest of the evening."

Jason led him into an unassuming dining room taken up almost entirely by an empty trestle table. Presumably, this was where all the slaves ate, though maybe Mat's schedule didn't mesh with everyone else's. A young woman in an old-fashioned scullery uniform appeared and dropped a plate and cup in front of him, and then disappeared again.

The cup was just water, and the food was serviceable, if not exactly up to Jeremy's standards. Healthy enough, though, and Mat was hungry enough not to care terribly what it tasted like. He ate it all, faster than he probably should've, worried Jason might pull him away at any moment.

Jason let him finish, though, before bringing him back up to the main floor, then through a warren of narrow slave corridors and out a little door to . . . outside?

The sun was low in the sky, but it was still intolerably bright to Mat's eyes, and he flinched, raising his cuffed hands to his face. Once he'd adjusted, he realized he was on the beach. A beautiful, sandy beach, the kind of beach he'd have loved to vacation on but could never afford to.

Now he never would, because it would always remind him of *this*.

Jason led him barefoot through the sand, out to a wood-planked area where a bunch of tables and chairs and a barbecue had been set up, and off to one side, two tall posts in the sand. With chains dangling from the tops of them.

"What's going to happen to me?" he asked, eyeing up the chains, and it was all he could do not to dig his heels into the sand. Enough. Enough of being tied. Enough suffering. He wanted to lie down and sleep.

"Don't know. Sorry. Whatever gets Allen off, or gets off the people he's sucking up to tonight."

"People he's sucking up to?"

They were close now. The shadow of the posts stretched out across the sand at Mat's feet. Jason maneuvered him between them and gestured for him to raise his arms above his head. He was facing the ocean, the waves washing up on shore thirty or forty feet distant. And there, off near where the horizon fell into the sea, a smudge against the darkening sky . . . Was that land?

"Yeah. Clients. Underworld connections. Guy wants to be the Godfather or something. You'll get used to the constant ass-licking parties . . . if you survive that long."

More like, if I stick around this hellhole that long. The sun was setting somewhere to his back. Which meant that the land—and yes, yes, he was sure of it now—was to the east. Given the weather and the time of year and the fact that they hadn't flown out of the States, that had to be a part of Louisiana, or the west coast of Florida. Or maybe one of the islands in the Keys, or the Caribbean. Or fucking Cuba. Whatever. If he could swim there . . .

Jason attached his cuffs to the chains dangling from the posts, stretching his arms out in a taut Y above his head. Well, at least the cuffs were comfortable, as those things went. And his feet were free. He rested his head on one arm, watched the waves wash in and out. Maybe he could sleep standing up. Maybe he'd need to learn to.

At least it was beautiful here. Maybe he'd give in to his exhaustion, just standing here looking at the sunset, and die.

No. I'm going to be free. I'm earning my freedom, even if I have to swim to fucking Cuba. I'm not fucking dying here, I'm not.

Jason wandered off. Left unsupervised, Mat tested his bonds. It quickly became apparent he wasn't going anywhere; the cuffs were sturdy, locked, the posts anchored deep in the sand, maybe even in concrete foundations. And he felt so weak—sore and tired and underfed and ill-rested. Struggling awoke a thousand aches. This wasn't a battle he could win. He gave it up; Nikolai had taught him that much, at least—or maybe it was Coach Darryl who had, back in another lifetime. Bide his time. Strategically retreat. Regroup. Too bad he couldn't figure out when to *fight*.

He drifted awhile, flotsam on the tide, until the sound of voices came to him over the waves.

He roused himself enough to look behind him. At first it was just men and women in uniforms—someone firing up the barbecue, someone lighting tiki torches, someone straightening the table settings, someone pouring drinks into fluted glasses on silver trays. Such an incongruous scene—formally dressed, white-gloved footmen on the fucking *beach*, mingling with cooks and scullery maids in costumes that would've been equally formal if not for how revealing they were, how low-cut the skirts and tops, and how obvious it was that they were wearing nothing underneath them.

More voices, then, and oh, these must be the "proper" pleasure slaves—half a dozen beautiful men in various stages of cross-dress, spreading out across the beach and draping themselves over chairs, blankets, an empty hammock. Mat couldn't help it: he strained and twisted to see if he could spot Dougie among them. And yep, there he was, at the back of the pack walking hand in hand with a redheaded boy who guided him to a lounge chair, sat down, and draped him over his lap in what must have been meant as a sexy, inviting pose. And then he reached down, his palm smoothing over Dougie's thigh, and hiked up his ridiculous little skirt to show the lower curve of his ass.

Mat looked away. He'd confirmed Dougie was still alive, still in one piece. That was all he needed to see. He wouldn't watch people use him. Wouldn't watch Dougie begging to *be* used.

God, was there anything left of the person Dougie had been? Was he even worth saving anymore?

Stop it. No more thinking. Just . . . be.

He hung there.

"And this here is the new purchase I told you about. Can't let him run free like the rest of these little whores. He'd probably try to kill us all and then swim to shore." Allen's voice. Mat jerked in his bonds and let out a growl, not sure if he was genuinely angry anymore or just putting on a good show. He was starting to worry that staying angry took more energy than he had to give.

"My, he's . . . fierce." Fingernails trailed down his back; he lurched away and lashed out with his foot, glancing off what felt like someone's shin. Not a direct hit, but enough force to make the woman shout and the hand go away.

A split-second of deep satisfaction, followed by a split-second of equally deep fear. He'd hurt a master. Allen would hurt him back several times over. He twisted in his bonds, looked over his shoulder, hoping to gauge the mood, brace himself for how bad it'd be . . .

But the woman was *laughing*. Sitting in the sand in her evening gown, flat on her ass with both hands clutched to her shin, and laughing. The man bending down to help her up—her husband?—looked a lot less amused, but he wasn't the one who mattered. Allen mattered. And Allen looked pleased.

Right. Showing off his rabid dog. Maybe if he was rabid enough, put on a good enough show, he'd escape the evening more or less unscathed. He bared his teeth at the woman and drawled, "Oops." Hell, maybe this would actually be kind of fun, if it meant getting to fuck around with these people without punishment.

"Got to watch out for that one," Allen said with a laugh. "I warned you."

"Consider me warned!" the woman trilled back, a distinct note of arousal in her voice. "Does he heel to you, though? Can you play with him like you do the others?"

"Of course," Allen said, meeting Mat's eyes with an unmistakable silent command—*Don't make me look like a fool, boy*. Allen held his gaze for just a moment, then circled around to Mat's front and grabbed him by the chin. Mat fought the grip just enough for show, but didn't try to kick Allen. Not even when Allen grabbed his cock and balls in one fist and squeezed. "Bark, Dog," Allen ordered, and his hand tightened so painfully on Mat's junk that Mat had no real choice but to make a sound.

He nearly followed it up with *Get off me, you fucker*, but bit his tongue. Insulting Allen in front of his guests right now didn't seem like the smartest play.

But then why was Allen frowning at him?

Before he could figure that out, Allen let him go and stepped back. "Anyway," he said to his guests, "feel free to try your luck. Even his cunt's got teeth, though."

My cunt? Fuck you. Don't fucking call it that.

Allen stepped back a bit then, but the guests stayed close—the married couple, and two other middle-aged men in summer formalwear, incongruously barefoot in the sand, fancy pants rolled up around their ankles. They circled him just out of kicking range, whispering and chuckling to themselves. A couple others drifted over, drinks in hand, either attracted by the pack of wolves or the prey at its center. What was Mat supposed to do here? He couldn't fight them all, not with his hands bound above his head, his soft bits so vulnerable and exposed. But if he *didn't* fight, then how would that make Allen look in their eyes? Like a fool and a liar, and no way that'd end well for him. Why couldn't the man have pulled him aside and told him how to play this? Nikolai would have. Nikolai would have said, "Verbally abuse them, but don't injure them," or "Look scary, but don't speak." He'd have laid out rules and guidelines to follow. He was still a tyrant and a fucking asshole and Mat still hated him, but at least with him Mat had known what to do to protect his hide. With Allen, he was flying blind.

"I'll break your fucking legs," he tried, meeting each of their eyes in turn and lashing out with his foot at the one nearest him. Still too far away to actually hit, but maybe he could intimidate them away before anyone had to hit anyone—him included. And it put on a good show, right? His eyes met Allen's for just a second, and he saw amusement there, approval.

The man he'd kicked at froze, apparently weighing the truth of Mat's words. After a moment of contemplation, he passed his wine glass off to the guy standing next to him, then unbuckled his belt. *That* was his plan? Waving his cock in Mat's face from four feet away?

... Or not. He pulled the belt from its loops and grasped it by the buckle. He wasn't freeing his cock; he was making a weapon.

Great.

The guy lashed out, and Mat turned his hip and drew his knee up, nearly ducking out of the way. The tongue of the belt just grazed him, a stinging lick that quickly faded. The wolf pack seemed to find this funny. More importantly, so did Allen. So defending himself was okay then. Fortunately, no one else was following suit and removing their belts. Just watching. The guy dared a single step closer and struck again. Mat counterstruck; the belt lashed across his flank, but his foot drove into the fucker's hip. Definitely a point for Mat; Belt Guy stumbled back three or four steps and went sprawling on his ass in the sand.

Allen was grinning like the fucking Joker, and he wasn't the only one. The woman Mat had knocked over before whooped once and clapped her hands. Like she thought this was a game of how-many-assholes-can-the-dog-knock-over. She turned her smile from the guy in the sand back to Mat. Slid her arm around her husband's waist and said to Mat, "You should fuck me while my husband watches. Would you like that?"

Mat spat at her.

She seemed utterly unperturbed. "Or maybe a dog sandwich? You fuck me while my husband fucks you?"

"Or you could fuck off," Mat growled.

She laughed again, and then her eyes darted over Mat's shoulder, and Mat had just enough time to realize that Belt Guy was no longer sprawled in the sand before he felt said belt biting into his shoulder blade. He twisted, grunted. Got distracted just enough that the laughing woman was able to move forward, throwing herself around his legs and immobilizing him with her body. Sitting on his feet, giggling, arms curled around his thighs and legs around his calves like a small child, except for the part where her crotch, panties damp, was grinding up against his ankle. Belt Guy hit him again, square between the shoulders. He barely even noticed.

"Get the fuck off!" he shouted, squirming in her grip. No leverage, though, and she was stronger than she looked. Trophy wife. Probably a gym bunny.

Another lash, this one impossible to ignore, burning across the small of his back. He shouted, writhed, trying to throw off either of these fuckers. The rest of them, sensing it was safe, started closing in. Hands fucking *everywhere*, stroking, pinching, slapping. Someone grabbed his ass cheeks. Someone else rammed fingers up his ass. He shouted again. The bitch grinding against his shin rode his thrashing legs like a fucking cowgirl. Leaned forward and—*oh God*—snatched up the tip of his dick between her teeth. Grinned at him. *Bit down.*

"No!" he shouted, pain so sharp it erased his awareness of all the other mouths and hands on and in him. He didn't dare fucking move. "Please, please. Be careful. *Please.*" Would she really bite the dick off someone else's toy? Could Mat count on that? His eyes darted frantically to Allen, but Allen wasn't watching his face; he was watching where Mat's dick was trapped between the woman's teeth, and he was smiling that same fucking Joker smile, like he'd find this whole thing hilarious no matter how it went. "Fine! I'll fuck you, I will. Get me down. Stop biting me there. Okay? Please!"

"Nobody unties him," Allen barked, even as the woman let go with her teeth and latched on with her lips instead, swiping her tongue over the bite marks. She probably meant it to be soothing, to get him hard, but Christ it hurt—he was too raw, too sensitive now to enjoy any touch at all. Not that he'd ever been remotely interested in a blowjob from a woman anyway, especially one who was doing it against his will.

But his body *was* starting to respond. The pain was fading. The woman knew what she was doing. He started to become aware of the other hands on him again, someone pinching both nipples just the right side of too hard, someone kneading his ass, the fingers pumping in and out of him. The woman was letting her guard down, had unwrapped one arm from around his thighs to pump his shaft in time with the movements of her mouth. He could probably kick his way free now. Headbutt the guy behind him, break his nose. Knee the guy beside him in the groin.

But then what? What would that get him but angry tormentors?

And anyway, how often did *anyone* bother to make him feel good? Sure, she was raping him, but at least it didn't hurt. Maybe he should just . . . let it happen. Let all of it happen. Close his eyes and pretend the fingers in his ass were a groupie's, a good-looking guy with a nice smile coming to him after a fight, fingerfucking him and sucking him, worshipping him, and soon Mat would worship back in return. It felt like an entire other universe. His body relaxed, head drooping to his chest, breathing settling into rhythm with the mouth on his cock, and when the fingers disappeared, he moaned, let his hips chase after them, waited loose and hungry for the cock to follow.

"All right, enough." Allen's voice, shattering Mat's delicate illusion into a million jagged pieces. "Time to eat. The dog has a whipping coming; we'll give you a good show after dinner."

Mat's eyes snapped open, and he caught Allen leveling an ugly glare at him. What had he done wrong? It wasn't as if Allen could've seen into his fantasy, known what he'd been thinking.

He was being good for the guy's guests, wasn't he? Fighting until the fighting was futile and then becoming a good little slut, just like all the others wandering around the party. Just like Dougie. And Allen had gotten petulant and . . . and *bored*.

Had he given up too soon, then? Did Allen want him to keep fighting even long after the fight was lost? Even after he couldn't help but give in to what was being done to him? He supposed that would explain Allen's boredom with him all day, the way he'd just *hung* there, not trying to escape his bonds after it'd become clear he couldn't, not taking the opportunity to fight Jason when he'd been untied and repositioned. He'd thought he'd been preserving his strength, protecting his ass, not pushing Allen too far. But maybe, all this time, he hadn't been pushing Allen far *enough*.

And now it was too late. Allen was halfway across the beach already, heading to the tables to eat, and maybe Mat could shout something at him, but Allen probably wouldn't hear it over the chatter and the pounding of the surf, or he might hear it and just not give a fuck anymore. And honestly, Mat had no idea what to say.

He pulled his mind from thoughts of the nastiness still to come tonight and stared out over the ocean. The sun had set completely, but the beach was lit up bright, and light from a hundred torches glittered off the waves. Way out in the distance—about three miles, if he remembered correctly how far the eye could see across the ocean (he could swim that far, surely he could swim that far)—the dark shape in the distance was now dotted with tiny little specks of lights like stars. So, definitely land of some kind. He kept his eyes on it, let his mind drift, pulling away from his aching body. God, he could sleep for a week if only Allen would let him.

But that would never happen, so he stole his hour or whatever it was here, the smell of roasting meat wafting from the barbecue pit making his mouth water and his stomach growl, the sounds of chatter and merriment—at least some of which came at the hands and mouths and asses of eager pleasure slaves (*don't think about Dougie don't think about Dougie*) pushing him even further out toward the fringes of normal existence. His back hurt where the belt had struck him. His wrists and elbows and shoulders—and frankly every other muscle and joint in his body—throbbed dully to the beat of his heart. Sand gritted against the healing brand on the sole of his foot. He couldn't seem to escape this—escape any of it—no matter how hard he tried. No matter how long he stared out at the tiny dots of light across dark water or closed his eyes and focused on the roar of the surf.

After supper, they came for him.

A whole crowd surrounded him, holding their after-dinner drinks, flush with arousal and excitement. Mat caught sight of Dougie on his knees in the sand, a beer bottle wedged up his ass and a cock wedged down his throat. When Mat looked away, it was to find Allen standing directly in front of him. Allen took Mat's face in both hands, holding him still, keeping him from breaking eye contact, even though in his exhaustion Mat wished he could just bow his head in defeat.

"Ready for your whipping, Dog?"

Mat clamped down on the urge to beg. It wouldn't change things. It would only make Allen angry. "Would it matter if I said no?"

Allen huffed out a laugh for the crowd—*Can you believe this guy?* His guests tittered back at him. Enjoying themselves, all of them.

It emboldened Mat a little. This was the right path. It wouldn't stop things, but it might make them gentler. And when the pain came, he could fake it, like Nikolai had taught him, make it look worse than it really was. "I have some suggestions on where you could shove your whip. I bet your guests would really enjoy that."

"Horny, are you, Dog? Needing something up your ass that badly? I'm sure one of my guests could help with that once we're done here. Or maybe you'd prefer to get your cock in someone else's ass instead? I'm sure your brother would find it much more satisfying than a cold, hard beer bottle."

That was one piece of bait Mat wasn't willing to rise to. Didn't know *how* to rise to, to be honest. He was about six hundred percent sure that Allen wasn't kidding, either. Pretend not to care, that's what Nikolai had said. Pretend not to care, and he'll lose interest in using Dougie against you.

If only he still *had* to pretend. It seemed a lifetime ago that he'd been in that tiny cramped cell at Madame's, so desperate to keep Dougie safe, protect him from pain, that he'd offered himself up over and over again. Screamed until his lungs were hoarse.

He wasn't screaming now.

Allen stepped back, seemingly unperturbed by Mat's lack of response. Spoke to someone over Mat's left shoulder. "Whenever you're ready. I think thirty to start?"

Silence for a long moment. Then a too-casual, "You sure, boss?"

Jason. What was this guy, Allen's pet torturer? He just kept a guy on staff to tie and beat people? Didn't do his own dirty work? Clearly Allen had more money than he knew what to do with.

More to the point, thank God for Jason and his scruples. The guy might be a rapist and work for a worse one, but at least he had a *line*.

"Am I ever not sure?" Allen replied smoothly, voice artificially calm. But even Mat, who barely knew him, could hear the cold threat beneath it. The concealed rage boiling beneath the surface.

Another pause, just a moment too long to be respectful. "You got it, boss," Jason said.

No hesitation after that. The whip cracked down.

Mat smothered a scream, jerked so hard in his bonds he thought he was going to break his damn wrists.

"One," Allen said smugly. He licked his lips.

Again, and Mat had just enough time between hearing the crack and feeling the fire bloom like a fucking backdraft against his shoulders to tense every muscle in his body. This time he did scream, no point holding it back—Allen wanted to hear it, after all, and keeping it caged took energy he didn't have. Energy he'd need just to keep his feet under him. He let his head hang, squeezed his eyes shut as Allen said, "Ah, there's the sound I like." Opened them just in time to see Allen reach down and palm his groin. "More. Give him more."

The third strike landed just below the second, and Mat screamed again for Allen, of course he did, felt wetness building in his eyes. Ten percent—this was just ten percent of what he had coming, *to start with*. He couldn't . . . no fucking way. Was it too early to beg yet? Would that disgust Allen or turn him on even more?

Didn't matter. He was desperate enough already to try.

"Please, master," he whispered. Loud enough only for Allen to hear, in case Allen didn't want his guests knowing how quickly his rabid dog had broken.

Allen grabbed Mat's hanging chin, wrenched his head up. Held his gaze as a long, slow sneer spread across his lips. Then he tossed Mat's head to one side and stepped back. "Again," he called.

Disgust, then.

Fuck that. How was he supposed to win here if talking back didn't work, and neither did begging? He had to be missing something. *Had* to be. Allen just wasn't that smar—

Another strike knocked the thought—all thought—from his head. And another, and another. He lost count. Lost track of the screams, the tears, the awed murmurs from the crowd. Held back the begging words as long as he could—Allen didn't want to hear them, they'd only make things worse—but eventually he lost track of even that, lacked the strength to keep them at bay. Lost track of Allen's counting, of time, of everything but the agony in his back, gathered and writhing there like the collective pain of the serum focused in a single place.

It took him several long moments to even realize the whipping had stopped. Slowly, sound filtered in through the pain. Quiet arguing—angry whispers near his head. He tried to lift it, to see who he'd pissed off this time, but he couldn't. Couldn't even get his feet beneath him.

". . . many times I have to tell you, boss. You lay fresh stripes over open wounds, he's gonna scar. He's already bleeding. You want to keep torturing him, be my guest, rub salt on him, fuck him, put weights on his balls, but the whip's out."

"You forget your fucking place," Allen snarled back, at a whisper as well. "I fucking own you, Ja—"

"I am not some piece of ass you bought at a black market auction, *Allen*. Let's not forget you dragged me into your sick shit with a lie and the only power you have over me is mutually assured destruction. I'm still a free fucking man." No more whispering. Jason was shouting now. Shouting on Mat's behalf. Protecting him. "I'm telling you no. I'm telling you I won't fucking whip him even one more time."

The silence that followed was loaded, dangerous. Mat tensed, afraid. Shit was bad enough. He didn't need Allen getting angrier than he already was.

"Final answer?" Allen asked. That artificial calm again. Mat's already roiling stomach flipped.

"Final answer," Jason replied, not a trace of fear in his tone.

The gunshot was so close that it made Mat's ears ring. When the boom faded, the first sound he heard was a woman screaming.

Wait. Not a woman. Dougie. And he was the only one.

Were Allen's friends and the other slaves so used to this kind of violence? The thought made him retch. So did the blood on his foot, hot and thick. He forced himself to lift it off the ground, muscles screaming in protest. A little river of blood oozed across the sand, pooling in the depression his foot had left.

"Then you're of no further use to me," Allen said to Jason's corpse. He tucked his gun back wherever it'd come from, calmly retrieved the whip from Jason's slack hand, and then straightened his jacket. "Shall we resume, then, friends?"

The crowd all cheered, shouting encouragement. Mat didn't hear their words; he was too busy learning the sound a body made as it was dragged by the legs through sand. He couldn't tear his eyes away from the hole in Jason's head. The smeary trail of blood being left behind him. At least it was nighttime. He suspected it all looked so much less threatening by firelight than it would have in full sun.

And then he heard the crack of the whip, and his shouted "No!" turned into an ugly scream as the lash split the skin of his back. Hot blood streaked down his clammy body and he moaned. Wished, for the first time, for the bit gag. He was gritting his teeth together so hard he wouldn't be surprised if they shattered.

Another strike. Another. Another. He was falling under again, drowning in agony and his mind didn't even have the decency to shut down, let him pass the fuck out, too many years of training to stay on his feet no matter what because the floor was dangerous, the floor was where you lost to the guys who were bigger than you, and out cold meant no bonus check to take home to Dougie, and Allen had already shown him that he didn't brook begging, but Mat couldn't stop himself, he *couldn't*, and he sobbed, "*Please*, master! Please, I'm sorry, I'll do anything, *please!*"

Allen stopped.

Time was weird for a while, and then somehow Allen was in front of Mat, right up in his face, bloodied whip coiled in his hand. He pushed up Mat's chin with the handle, made Mat meet his eyes.

"What did you say, Dog?"

He couldn't remember the exact words, didn't have the energy for them anyway, but he'd begged, he knew he'd begged, and he'd do it again in a heartbeat. For whatever reason, it'd worked this time. Maybe it'd work again. "Please, Master," he gritted out. Panting, half-unconscious. "Mercy."

"What's that?" Allen cupped a hand theatrically to one ear, leaned in a little closer. "I'm the stronger man?"

A seed of realization took root in Mat's head. He wasn't quite sure what it would flower into yet, but he sensed it was important. He tried to nod, but it felt more like a spasm than anything.

The whip handle jerked under his chin. Allen's eyes bored into his. He spoke loudly enough for the whole beach to hear: "The big bad dog wants to bow at his master's feet? Worship there?"

Mat nod-spasmed again.

Allen leaned in close, intimate like he was about to kiss Mat, and whispered into his ear, "Say it."

The whip handle fell away, and Mat swallowed, swallowed again, trying to work up enough saliva to answer. Forced the words "Yes, master," through his scream-shredded vocal chords.

But that wasn't good enough for Allen. "Yes *what*, Dog?"

"I want to worship at my master's feet," Mat said, and as the words came out, that seed of realization started to sprout leaves. Mat could see the shape of it now. So close . . . so close. If only he could get his head to clear.

Allen nodded over Mat's shoulder, and then there were hands on Mat's arms and more hands on his waist, lifting him up and *oh God please don't touch my back please don't*, and then his hands were free and he was hunched over in the bloody sand, trembling and moaning on his elbows and knees. Allen's feet came into his field of vision, sandy dress shoes inches from his nose.

"Show me," Allen said, and Mat didn't hesitate, craned his neck out and licked the grit from Allen's shoes. Licked them until they shone. Allen preened above him. The crowd applauded.

And that was when Mat understood, the seed in his mind taking full bloom: It wasn't about fighting too much or too little, begging too early or too late. It wasn't even about finding that mythical balance he'd been groping so blindly for all day. No, it was about *Allen*. About Allen's insecurities, Allen's ego, Allen's need to be the big man, special, in ultimate control. Licking sand and tears from Allen's shoe, Mat realized he could break all he wanted, beg all he wanted, and earn reprieve . . . but only if he begged *for Allen*. Not for Allen's guests, not for Allen's hired help; after all, if he let just anyone reduce him to this, then he was merely *a* rabid dog, not *Allen's* rabid dog. And Allen hated that. Allen wanted to be special. Be the only one who could tame the beast.

Well, Mat thought, nearly as blindsided by the relief of having solved this puzzle as he had been by the first shock of pain from the whip, *I can work with that. Thank fucking God, I can work with that.* The joy of his revelation was so fucking incandescent—or maybe he was just so high from adrenaline and endorphins—that he laughed aloud.

Laughed, and passed out face-first in the sand.

EPISODE 13: THE HOUSE ALWAYS WINS

CHAPTER
ONE

A llen's beach party went on well into the night. Men and women passed Douglas around and played with him, but he went from body to body in a daze, unable to shake the memory of watching a man die. He didn't understand how any of them could, but there they all were, drinking and chatting and laughing and fucking like murder was a normal part of any well-planned event.

What could he do about it, though? Nothing, except be a good boy and make his time here as smooth as possible so he could go home to Nikolai again, where all this would be nothing but a bad memory. A terrible, terrible memory.

He lay half-insensate in a lounge chair beneath a flickering torch, staring out at the ocean as someone's bare foot nudged his spent cock. Whoever was touching him didn't seem to want anything further from him or mind that he wasn't engaging. When the foot traveled up his torso and nudged at his lips, he parted them without thinking. Tasted salt and sand and an echo of shoe leather. The foot went away. So, he thought, did the owner. Uniformed slaves buzzed around him, cleaning up and waiting on the last of the straggling guests. Nobody else bothered him, and he was glad. Tired, so tired. It was the same horrible downswing as after his coming-out party, but this time he was too numb to cry it out. There was nobody here to hold him, anyway. Even Finn seemed to be gone. Entertaining an overnight guest, probably.

Douglas found himself both pitying and envying him. Pitying him because he was probably as exhausted as Douglas, envying him for the attention he was no doubt receiving now. Douglas had once thought himself beautiful and desirable—Nikolai had made him feel that way—but now he felt . . . disposable. Worthless. Practically an appliance, for all any of these people noticed him, to be used and passed around, valued only for a pair of hot holes and his capacity to keep his brother to heel. And he hadn't actually managed that tonight, had he? The master had had to whip the bastard.

No, not had to. Wanted *to.*

Douglas shuddered.

A body blocked the torchlight, and he shuddered again. Contained himself. Made himself smile and slide to his knees. But then he glanced up, and it was just Nedry—who might as well have been a master for all his imperial posture and the sneering derision on his face. Maybe Douglas should offer to suck his cock.

"I don't need you anymore tonight. Go to bed."

I *don't need you.* As if Nedry owned him and not Allen. God, what a tool.

Still . . . bed. Shower. Maybe a real meal too—people had fed him morsels all night, but it wasn't enough. He smiled up at Nedry, and this time it was real. "Thank you, sir." He rose to his feet. Remembered his posture as he walked away; there were still guests here to see him, after all.

"Hey," Nedry called softly after him. "Get sand in the hallway and I'll have you beaten."

Lovely. Back turned to Nedry, Douglas scowled, and mumbled a few choice words about having *Nedry* beaten. Why was everyone so awful here? Except for Finn, they were all a bunch of scheming, miserable bullies, and even Finn's kindness only extended so far. Soon enough he'd forget his own time as the new boy and join in on Douglas's abuse.

Now he really did want to cry.

But he sucked it up. Slapped the soles of his feet to knock the sand off and slipped through the slaves' door into the dark network of halls that would lead him to his bed. Eventually. If he could find the way.

Luckily, after what seemed like ten hours of aimless wandering, he did. The room's lights were out, and he could hear slow breathing. Obviously a couple of the others had returned already, though he couldn't tell who. Sleeping. Yes, he wanted that too. He stumbled in the direction of his bed. He was so tired at this point that if they'd come on his pillow again, he'd probably sleep in it without complaint. But the pillow was dry, and no sooner had he lain down than he was asleep.

Not for long, though. He woke to someone straddling his chest and a thumb rubbing at his lips.

He groaned softly and twisted under the weight, trying to force his eyes open. Force himself into service again, though his body felt like it was made of lead and every fuckable part of him ached.

"You asleep, baby?" someone murmured from above him. Not a master. One of the other slaves. Henry, he thought. All around them, slow breathing let him know that the others were still asleep, getting their well-deserved rest. Everyone but Douglas.

Still, it didn't matter if he was half-asleep or not, if he deserved rest or not. Someone wanted his service.

"Henry?" He rubbed his eyes, cracked a yawn. Yes, definitely Henry, long braid hanging heavy over one shoulder and down his chest, the ends tickling Douglas's throat and Henry's own cock, full and heavy. It wasn't Douglas's job to service the other boys . . . was it?

"Come on, sweetie, just a quick suck. You're so pretty, and the master's guests teased me all night." His thumb swept across Douglas's lips, a gentle caress, almost a lover's touch. "You won't tease me, will you, sweetie? Nikolai's boys would never do that. Too perfect, every one of you."

God, it had been so long since someone had complimented him, made him feel—not good, this wasn't good—but wanted, at least. Henry wanted him. Wanted his pretty mouth, his perfectly trained mouth, a testament to Nikolai's skill. And he was being so kind about it too, although Douglas doubted if he'd stay kind for long if he was refused.

Douglas swallowed nervously. "I won't tease you."

"Of course you won't."

Henry's cock was already so close to Douglas's mouth that all he needed to do was lean forward and glide inside, moaning the moan of a desperate man. Douglas kept his promise, didn't tease. Worked, in fact, to get him off as quickly as he could. Not that he was in a rush to end this, even though his jaw was sore and his head was fuzzy with fatigue—not now that Henry's fingers were stroking through his hair and an endless stream of praise was falling from Henry's mouth—but Henry was clearly desperate to get it over with, find his release. Douglas took him deep into his throat, slid both hands around

Henry's ass, fingers prodding tentatively at his crack. Douglas didn't know if he'd be too sore to enjoy being penetrated, but the moment his fingers brushed close, Henry rose up off his heels with a breathy, "Oh yeah, sweetie, just like that," and a moaned, "God, so perfect, you're so good, *touch* me." So Douglas slid one finger inside, then two, then three. They went in easy; Henry was loose and slick. Half a dozen strokes later, he was tight and spasming, clenching around Douglas's fingers and shooting down his throat.

He kissed Douglas after, and stroked his face. It felt good to be touched, never mind that he'd had to buy this affection with his body. If it meant not feeling so alone, he'd suck every cock here.

When the bed shifted with a new weight, Douglas realized he might end up doing exactly that.

Mat woke to the stink of shit. Shit, and hay, and animal, and maybe . . . leather? But the shit was definitely the most urgent.

Scratch that. The pain was more urgent than any of it. Jesus fuck, his *back*.

He rolled onto his side with a low groan, feeling every inch of scraping hay on his flayed skin.

Hay?

That got his eyes to open. Which was when everything started making sense: He was in a barn. Lying on a pile of clean hay, half on top of what he assumed was a horse blanket, half on the hay itself. Naked. Tacky all over with God knew what. Daylight streaming through a high window skewered right through his eyeballs to the back of his skull. He was burning with thirst. Sore. Abso-fucking-lutely miserable.

Well, at least he wasn't tied up. And he wasn't sharing his stall with any horses, though he could hear their soft nickering through the wooden walls to his left and right.

What the fuck was he *doing* here, though?

And was there a way out?

And if there was, could he make it? It wasn't like he was in any fucking condition to swim to the mainland.

But he had to try. Fuck it, he had to. He owed it to himself, even if he died partway. At least he'd be free of this fucking hell.

He rolled back onto his stomach, had to use both hands to push himself into a tottering, half-upright position. Scabs across his back split and oozed, and he couldn't help but moan. Didn't stop him, though. He clambered to his knees. Planted one foot in the hay—

"Are you awake, then?" a voice called. Cultured British accent, just like Nedry, but definitely not Nedry.

Shit. So much for his escape attempt. He could stay quiet, maybe? Wait until Mr. Bean went away?

But no. Key in a lock, and the stable door was swinging open, and a beautiful brown-skinned young man, lean and strong and naked but for a tiny pair of cargo shorts like he'd come right out of the *Blue Lagoon*, walked in and did a double take. "Hey, hey, no, you shouldn't be moving, what are you doing?" He hustled inside the stall, pausing only to shut and lock the door behind him, then crouched down beside Mat, gentle but insistent hands on his shoulders. "Here, lie down, please, you'll hurt yourself."

Mat collapsed back to his belly beneath the barrage of concern, vaguely stunned, letting the man's words wash over him in their almost musical British lilt.

"Good, that's good, you stay right there, and I'll get you some water, all right? Name's Reginald, by the way. And you're Mathias."

Yeah, thanks, I know my own name. Seemed rude to say that, though. The kid was obviously a talker, maybe one of those nervous types, jittery around the edges, uncomfortable with silence. Seemed nice enough, though. Mat didn't want to be a dick to him.

Reginald left, came back a minute later with an armful of supplies and the promised water, in one of those reusable plastic bottles with a pull top like a straw. Mat rose up on one elbow and gulped down half of it in a single breath, then lay back down, panting, waiting for the agony in his back to settle. Reginald, meanwhile, was arranging water and cloth and disinfectant and some kind of ointment in a jar that smelled strongly herbal.

"I'm not a doctor," he said as he worked, offering it up without apology. "Just used to dealing with injuries. And keeping the master's horses fit, of course; polo can be a rough game for beast as well as rider. Although before this, you know, when I was, um . . . Yeah. My experience was all with livestock—um, animals."

Mat barked out a laugh. "You're in luck then, because apparently I'm a dog. Woof woof."

Which of course immediately reminded him of Dougie, of that horrible video feed back at Nikolai's, and suddenly Mat was heaving the water right back up.

Once he was done, and had finished the rest of the bottle of water to replace what he'd lost, he realized that Reginald might have a fancy British name and a fancy British accent, but he certainly didn't have a fancy British vocabulary. "Where are you from?" he asked.

Reginald guided him to lie down on his stomach on the horse blanket. "Jersey," he replied. "Snooty rich little town called Tewksbury. Worked on a horse farm my whole life."

For privileged, rich white folks with no concerns for child labor laws or brown people, he didn't say, but Mat heard it anyway. Reginald dipped a cloth in the water bowl, wrung it out, started washing Mat's back. *Ow. Fuck.* Distraction time.

"So then why—" Double ow. Christ, this was worse than the morning after losing on points at the end of three rounds.

Reginald chuckled softly, moved his eyes in a way that might've involved rolling them without actually doing anything he could be accused of. "You have a lot to learn yet about the master, I see." He was silent a moment, his hands quick and gentle on Mat's back. "He's . . . How do I say this . . . Well, the people I used to work for back in Jersey would call him new money. And he wants to be old money." Another silent moment, so stark against Reginald's prior chattiness. Reginald looked to the right, the left, behind him—checking for others who might overhear? "Except my old bosses actually *had* class. Master Allen thinks class means making everyone act like his wife's family back in England. Earls or something, I don't know." He returned his focus to Mat's back. "Anyway, you want to get ahead around here? You learn the bloody accent and you take the stupid name and you act like you've got culture. But you're one of Nikolai's boys, aren't you? You should have the culture thing down pat."

One of Nikolai's boys. The way he said it with such reverence and jealousy made Mat want to throw up all over again. "You got the wrong guy," he said instead. "Dougie—my brother—got trained. I only got beaten into submission."

"Beaten into submission by Nikolai Petrovic is better than drugged into the same by some back alley trainer," Reginald snapped back. "At least you've got the prestige going for you."

"And you?" Mat asked gently.

"One minute I'm working less than minimum wage for rich assholes, next I'm working for nothing for rich assholes. At least here I know where my next meal's coming from." He tossed the cloth in the bowl, water stained pink now, and picked up a dry one to blot Mat's back with. "It's no different, I suppose. Keep your mouth shut, work hard, do what you're told. Don't stick your head out, and no one will lop it off."

"That's it? You don't wanna . . . escape?"

Disinfectant now. It stole Mat's breath for a moment. Reginald said nothing either until he was done. Then, "I like the horses." The pause that followed was downright uncomfortable, though Reginald's hands kept at their task, smearing ointment on Mat's back. "My old boss had my parents deported when I was seventeen. I don't know where they are now. I have no family, no friends, no education. Just another migrant worker for rich folks to spit on. If I got out of here, what would I do?" Before Mat could even think of how to answer, Reginald added, "Besides, nobody notices me much out here. The master almost never beats me; the other slaves don't harass me. And I learned my lesson a long time ago about wanting things I can't have. You must've also, no? One of Nikolai's boys?"

Nikolai again, like he was some kind of fucking *god* to these people or something. Mat huffed into his folded arms. "Yeah, not so much."

"Well." Reginald stood, wiped his hands on a rag, started gathering up his supplies. "I guess that's why I'm stuck taking care of you right now, huh. Try not to reopen those cuts again, okay? I'll bring you some food later."

And despite the fact that he was friendly, and despite the fact that Mat had made *his* desire for freedom pretty clear, when Reginald left, he still locked the door behind him.

Word got around. Douglas found himself pushed into corners, grabbed by the shoulders. A touch, a gaze—all of it leading to him on his knees at someone else's feet, buying more scraps of acceptance. He hadn't minded being put into frequent service with Nikolai, but here, it was almost constant, and never with anyone he felt affection for. And though it did earn him a little bit of kindness from his fellow slaves, it didn't earn him the one thing he wanted most of all: his master's approval. In fact, his master hardly seemed to pay him any mind at all, though he was plenty popular with the master's guests—a new toy and all that, he supposed. He served them well, determined to do Nikolai proud, to make his *master* proud even if it took forever.

It hadn't seemed to happen yet, though. He went from party to party, from afternoon drinks on the beach to beer and pool in the downstairs rec room—or rather, the "smoking room," according to Nedry—to intimate late-evening dinners with eight courses and Douglas's ass for dessert. Three days passed, then four, then five. He settled into his routine, tried to never let himself *be* routine (never be *boring*, Nikolai had warned). But nothing changed.

Until Penelope.

It was another dinner party. Another night of Douglas slinking around the long formal table, offering sexual services and taking dainty bites of food in return. Allen's guests liked that. Liked being able to reach out and touch him, like you would a marble statue, or a friendly dog.

And there, on Allen's left side, was Penelope. So perfect in her trim black dress and pearls, her blonde hair swept up to bare sculpted arms and shoulders. Not beautiful by birth, maybe, but by care and discipline and attentiveness. And when she looked at Douglas, she didn't look through him like Allen did. Didn't scowl. Didn't leer.

She smiled.

Douglas shimmied over to her on his hands and knees, holding eye contact all the way around the table, smiling every promise he knew how to give. She looked amused, enticed, curious, open. She let her knees fall apart as he drew near, and he slotted himself between them, rubbed his cheek up against her inner thigh right above the top of her silk stocking. She wasn't wearing any underwear. She stroked his face with a carefully manicured hand—he saw the wedding ring nestled against an engagement ring whose diamond was big enough to buy another slave—and urged his head toward her pussy.

Douglas was well on his way to coaxing her first orgasm from her when he heard the master's voice above and beside him: "Enjoying the new pet, darling?"

Oh god. He froze, gripped by choking fear. This was *Allen's* wife? She'd only arrived here this afternoon, and Douglas had just assumed . . .

"I was until a moment ago," she replied in a crisp English accent, slightly tinged by her (no doubt fading) arousal and what Douglas cautiously hoped was amusement.

"Oh, well," Allen said, and Douglas couldn't tell if the injury in his voice was sincere or not. "By all means, don't let me keep you."

"You already have." She sniffed and pushed Douglas out from under her dress. "But you can make it up to me. Let me have him? Tonight?"

"I spoil you, you know."

From this new vantage point, Douglas could see everyone else at the table watching their happy hosts play at the perfect couple. An act? Douglas wasn't sure. In his old life, he'd have thought anyone who kept a stable of sex slaves probably didn't have much of a marriage. Now he wasn't so sure.

Penelope leaned sideways and kissed Allen—a sweet, familiar little peck that he returned with equal affection—and said, "Nonsense. Nothing's too good for the eldest daughter of an earl."

"So you keep reminding me," Allen said, still smiling. He waved a hand at Douglas, dismissive. "Of course you can have him."

Which was how he ended up spending the night in Penelope's bedroom. *Just* Penelope's; in aristocratic British tradition, she and Allen each had their own, she explained along the way, as if she thought Douglas might need reassuring that his own master wouldn't interrupt them. On the one hand, ridiculous. Yet on the other? Strangely soothing.

Her room was predictably British-manor fancy, feminine and gauzy and yet weighty somehow, with its heavy antique furniture and silk-papered walls. She took him by the hand and led him inside, stopped just before the four-poster bed, and turned her back to him.

"Unzip me?" she asked in that perfect, proper accent of hers. *Asked*, not ordered. Polite, maybe, but Douglas didn't doubt it was an order all the same.

"My pleasure, Mistress," he murmured, crowding up behind her as close as he dared, pulling down the zipper as slowly as he thought she'd let him. Unwrapping her like a gift. Making sure she felt treasured. Strange, but in a way she *did* feel special. He was so rarely with women. And she seemed so gentle. Kind. Reminded him of Nikolai a little, maybe.

He finished unzipping and reached up, leaned in, hands hovering over the thin straps on her shoulders and lips a hair's width from the nape of her neck. She smelled sweet, like roses. "May I, Mistress?" he whispered, breath tickling the fine hairs at her nape.

"It's all right, love. But go have a shower first, while I change into something more comfortable. My husband might like you prettied up, but I don't. My bathroom's just through that door on the left. Come back a man for me."

A man. Not a dog, not a boy, not the woman his master wished to make him—wished he were attracted to?

A man.

Douglas's heart squeezed, and he nodded. Padded off to the shower.

When he returned—clean, fresh, new, a man—she was lying on her bed, clothed in a silky lilac chemise and matching panties.

He wanted her, he realized. Really, truly wanted her. Not to please her, but to please himself. He hadn't realized he was still capable of such a thing. Dangerous feelings, totally inappropriate for a slave, but he couldn't help it, and he wasn't sure he wanted to. His bare cock thickened at the sight of her. He stopped a few feet from the bed, wishing he could take himself in hand, stroke himself, show her what she'd done to him. Instead, he waited for instructions.

"Much better," she said with a sweet smile, looking his body up and down. He felt lean and rangy when she looked at him. Not pretty at all. "What's your name, boy?"

"Douglas, Mistress."

"Penny will be fine, Douglas."

He nodded once. "Penny." Rolled the name around on his tongue. It felt strange, too informal. But it was what she wanted. It made her happy. He grinned at her, genuine and light. "A beautiful name for a beautiful woman."

"You flatter, Douglas. I like that. What a well-mannered boy you are. Tell me, have you been with a woman before?"

He lied. He didn't know why he did it, but it seemed . . . right, somehow. Like it was what she wanted—needed—to hear. "No, Penny. Never."

And in a way, it wasn't a lie anyway. *Dougie* had had sex with women, but *Douglas* had only ever been with men. He was a new person now. New for Nikolai, new for her. Pure.

She squirmed a little in delight, her pretty hands fisting the sheets of her bed. "I do so enjoy being a young man's first."

I know. I understand. Nikolai had given him that, that power. He'd been so awkward around women before. Found them so impenetrable. Now it all made sense.

"How old are you, love?" she asked.

He knew the answer she wanted to hear. "Seventeen. But eighteen, soon."

That turned her sweet smile predatory, every inch the mistress she was. She spread her legs, leaned forward and patted the bed between her thighs. "Well, what say you come here, young man, and I'll teach you things Nikolai never could."

Douglas went.

And Penny kept her promise.

Three days later, Mat woke up feeling strong enough to make a break for it when Reginald came. The question was whether or not he should. He had no idea where Dougie was—heck, no idea where *either* of them were. Didn't know if he was ready yet to swim three miles across open ocean or if he was merely impatient enough to *think* he was. Didn't particularly want to hurt Reginald, either, who'd been nothing but kind to him, bringing him food and water and tending his wounds and talking with him like he mattered. Like he was a real person and not some rich fucker's sex toy. Whipping boy. Whatever.

Which meant . . . maybe he could turn Reginald to his side? The man wasn't brainwashed, not like Dougie was. Just beaten down enough to realize the futility of fighting. But Mat would wager that Reginald had never met anyone like him in a place like this. Had never been faced with the possibility that fighting might *not* be futile. Proposing anything to Reginald would be a risk—he could tattle, send Mat right back to that whipping post. But was it a risk worth taking? Maybe. Just maybe.

Mat climbed to his feet, stretched gingerly. His back twinged pretty loudly, but even the deepest of the whip cuts had sealed over and weren't breaking open again as he moved. Nothing must've been that deep after all—just felt like it. He was still fit. It'd hurt, but he could swim. And, let's face it, staying here would probably end up hurting more.

Definitely a risk worth taking, then. If he cowered forever, he'd end up like Reginald, just another broken slave who nobody had bothered to put back together again, never able to find the courage to disobey or escape. He had to do it. For himself, but for Reginald too, who was a good guy who deserved to know there were options and hope.

And for Dougie. Always for Dougie, no matter how lost he might be right now.

So he sat, and he plotted, and he waited. Reginald would be here soon. He'd be ready.

CHAPTER
TWO

Penny kept a close eye on Douglas after that first night. The other boys clearly resented him for it, throwing him dirty looks each time he settled at her feet, but under the gentle, loving attentions of his mistress, their scorn hurt him less. And he could still pacify them easily enough, putting his hands and mouth to good use while they washed and groomed each afternoon. The cruel little tricks had mostly stopped; none of them wanted to risk losing the privilege of coming down his throat, he supposed. He didn't even feel lonely anymore, not really. How could he, when his every waking moment was spent sucking or fucking or licking, or—when Penny was feeling particularly sated—snuggling against warm, soft breasts? Even better, Penny valued him for more than sex. Like Nikolai, she asked for Byron and Keats, for back rubs and foot massages, for cuddles and laughs. Douglas wanted it all. Wanted her. He worried sometimes that the master would mind, be angry, but Allen didn't seem to care as long as Douglas kept Penny happy.

He kept her happy a *lot*. Three, four times a night. Even five once. Every night so far this week. If this was to be his fate until Nikolai came to fetch him, well, he could get used to it. He could be happy here.

Not, he realized, that his happiness should matter. But it did, somehow, it did. A frightening thought. One he knew he should find a way to push aside. But it was such a little thing, wasn't it? Not even asked for, or sought after, or taken. Just . . . there. And surely Penny preferred him happy anyway? It was all right. It had to be all right, because he didn't know how to stop it. How to deny himself these feelings. Not even the other boys could squeeze it out of him.

Even if he did miss Nikolai terribly. Even if he would rather be there than here. Rather be there than *anywhere*. In that cozy mountain home where nobody begrudged him his happiness as long as he didn't let it interfere with his duties. Where being happy wasn't dangerous. Where being happy made his master happy, too.

Where he *had* a master. A real one, and not just a man whose money had bought his body.

Mat had thought he was ready—had totally, completely convinced himself he was ready—and yet when Reginald arrived, he just . . .

Froze.

Didn't make a run for it. Didn't say a word. Sat still while Reginald checked his wounds, and mumbled thanks when Reginald gave him food. Watched Reginald turn, leave, lock the door behind him again. Realized his opportunity had passed. Realized his heart, for some reason, was pounding.

Realized, several minutes later, that he was a fucking coward.

No. Just not strong enough yet. Not healed enough. I wouldn't make it.

Or so he tried to tell himself, but he knew better. What he needed to gather was courage, not strength. He hated to admit it, but maybe Allen had whipped it right out of him. Or maybe he was just tired. Worn down. Needing a fucking break. Not willing to risk blowing what would likely be his one and only chance.

And so what if he *did* need a break? He'd damn well earned it. He could take another day—it wouldn't make any fucking difference to him or to his perfect little puppet of a brother. Maybe even two days. Any more than that, he might be pulled from the stables; they wouldn't leave him here once he was healed enough to beat again.

So fine. He'd let himself have his moment. Let himself be afraid for a little while longer, let himself cower in relative safety. As long as he was ready to go all in when the moment came.

And he would be. Maybe he wasn't right now, but he *would* be.

Two days. Mat gave himself exactly two more days of doing nothing but eating and sleeping and letting opportunities pass him by. The break did him good. Indulging his needs, his fears, his inner child did him better. He woke on the third day feeling strong, sure of purpose. Knowing Reggie might rat him out, but that he also might say yes. Might help Mat with his escape and save himself, too.

When Reggie arrived with breakfast, Mat was ready.

Reggie must've sensed something was up, because he froze halfway to Mat's hay bed, dropped the plate he was carrying, and tried to run. But Mat was faster and shot out a hand, catching Reggie by the wrist.

The guy whimpered and went limp, falling to his knees.

Well trained. Mat had fooled himself into thinking Reggie was stronger than Dougie, still had more of himself left, but he didn't, not at all. Or maybe he did, but was utterly willing to shed it all at the first hint of trouble.

Mat let him go. "I'm sorry," he said. "I didn't mean to scare you. But look, don't leave yet. I need to talk to you."

Reggie narrowed his eyes. "Are you sure you want to?" he asked, a little weary.

"Want to? Not really." So much easier to curl up and do nothing again, let himself slip back into the helpless funk that'd defined his last few days. "But I need to." This was it. No going back now. Mat swallowed. "I want to get the fuck out of here. I want you to help me. And I want you to come with me."

"I already told you there's nothing out there—"

"Look, I know you've convinced yourself that freedom wasn't much better than this, but I can't believe that. And who says you have to go back to where you came from? Come with me. Come with me and my brother. We don't have much, but what we have, we'll share."

Could he really promise that? Yes, in exchange for his and Dougie's lives, he definitely could. He'd promise the fucking moon.

But Mat's promises obviously meant nothing to Reggie. He was shaking his head, backing toward the door—slowly, slowly, like he feared Mat might pounce and hurt him. A not-unfounded fear, perhaps—hadn't Mat been contemplating doing exactly that not so long ago? "No. *You* look. We're on a fucking *island*, man. Miles out to fucking *sea*. Even if you could . . ." He closed his eyes, shook his head, opened his eyes again. "Even if you could get away from the estate, what then? There's only two places the surf won't smash your ass against the shore, and one's the beach the master entertains on and the other's the harbor." Useful information, that—did Reggie even realize he was giving Mat ammo? He didn't seem to, judging by his current state of agitation. "What are you going to do, steal a boat out from under the guards' noses? And let's say you do get your ass to the mainland, what then? They'd fucking hunt you. Not the master, the Cartel. They have people for that. Bounty hunters. They'd hunt you down like a dog, and they'd send you back to your trainer for 'reeducation'—which is a nice way of saying they'd break you so fucking bad there'd be nothing left of you to put together, not even two tiny pieces. There is no escaping from this, Mat. This is your life. This is your life, and this is my life, and this is your brother's life, and you need accept it."

Tears were slipping down Reggie's cheeks. Genuine grief, maybe, at speaking a truth so painful, at cutting his own hope down to the roots. But he wouldn't cry over nothing, which meant that somewhere, somehow, buried way deep down, he still had to have some hope left.

Well, Mat could work with that. It might take a while, and maybe he'd have that luxury of time and maybe he wouldn't, but it was the best option he had right now, so he needed to suck it up and accept *that* much, at least.

"Hey." He reached out slowly, palm open, and when Reggie only shrank back instead of pulling away, Mat cupped his shoulder. "Hey, it's okay. I get it. I know shit's been awful for you, I know you've thought about breaking free as much as I have, and I know you must've found it as futile as I did when I tried to escape from Nikolai's. But you know what they call me, man? Back at—" Now it was *his* turn to blink back tears. Fucking sneak attack. He sniffed once, shoved it away. "Back at home, in the ring? Stonewall, man. They call me *Stonewall*. You know why?"

Reggie rolled his eyes, but he didn't shake off Mat's hand. "Let me guess. Because you were unbreakable?"

Ha, I fucking wish. "Because I never let anyone knock me over for long. I'd get back up. I *always* get back up. An immovable fucking force, you get me?" Reggie said nothing. "Give me some time, okay? If you trust me, I promise I'll get you out of here, and I won't let them hunt you down, and I won't let anyone hurt you ever again."

Reggie held his gaze for a long moment, and then, at last, ducked out from beneath Mat's hand. "Yeah," he said, gesturing at Mat's torso. "Just like you didn't let them hurt you. I have chores to do. Excuse me."

He turned and left the stall. Mat stayed where he was like a good dog as the door locked firmly behind him.

It wasn't a surprise that when Reggie returned next, he stopped in the doorway without meeting Mat's eyes and said, "Get up. I'm bringing you back to the house."

Mat glowered at him from his bed of hay. Couldn't help it. The fear and betrayal and disappointment all churned and curdled inside him, and Reggie was damn lucky a glower was all he got.

Not that Reggie appreciated that fact, because he scowled. "Oh, don't give me that fucking look, Mat. What did you really expect? You had to know it was gonna be a fucking cold day in hell before I said yes to suicide. No, *worse* than suicide."

The trembling hit first, then the tears. He'd foolishly gone and let himself hope, hadn't he? Just like Reggie had, for that single fleeting moment, when they'd talked yesterday. Reggie had been so *nice* to him, after all. Still had his head on more or less straight. Unlike Mat. He'd been stupid. *Stupid.* "How could you? I thought— I thought—"

"I don't know what you thought, Mat, but before you finish that sentence, you should know I didn't rat you out. I'm not going along with your stupid plans, but I'm not going to get you in shit either. All I said when Nedry asked was that you were back on your feet. I don't know what that makes me to you now, but my conscience is clear. So get up, you're going back to the house. *Don't* bring up escaping with me—or anyone else here—ever again. Those house boys, they see you as a threat; they'd throw you to the wolves in a hot fucking second. You won't get lucky twice."

Mat nodded, because if he opened his mouth, he knew he'd scream. He made to stand. *No. Lunge. Knock him out. Run. Do it. Do it before they drag you back inside. Last chance, last chance.*

He must've let it show on his face, because Reggie took a step back, hand on the door as if ready to slam it in Mat's face. "It's broad daylight, you know." It sounded like he was aiming for condescension there, but his voice was shaking. Mat couldn't even be bothered to feel like a dick for frightening the guy, not anymore. "There's people everywhere."

"I know," Mat said, and stood slowly, regretting the lost opportunity even as he let it go. "I won't hurt you, Reggie." Then, in case he could leverage it later, "Thank you for not ratting me out. I appreciate it, I really do. I'm sorry I snapped at you; that wasn't fair. I was upset."

"Uh huh," Reggie said, shoulders up. He backed into the hall, gesturing for Mat to lead the way.

Mat knew he'd lost. Had Nikolai taught him that, or had his coach? He couldn't remember anymore. As much as he tried to compartmentalize it, this experience was a part of him now. If—no, *when*—he got out, he'd be a different man. Better off than Dougie, but how much so, really? And if Allen had any more time with him, would there be anything left of him anyway?

Maybe it would be easier to give up, like Reggie had. Maybe eventually Allen would get bored of him and send him off to do manual labor like Reggie.

But when they reached the house, and he saw Allen standing there, hands behind his back, looming like the petty tyrant he was, *smirking*, Mat knew there was no hope for him here. Suffer. Die. That was what Allen wanted from him.

"Get back to work," Allen said when they reached him, nodding briefly at Reggie. Fucker couldn't say thank you? He probably didn't even remember Reggie's name. Not that Reggie seemed to care; he peeled off with a relieved, perfectly British, "Yes, Master," almost before Allen had finished speaking.

Allen turned his attention on Mat. "Turn around. Show me what I did to you."

So you can jack off on my back? No thanks.

But he did. Of course he did. Stood there, hands balled into fists at his sides, consciously working to stop his shoulders from crawling up to his ears. Gritted his teeth when Allen's fingers probed ungently over the healing wounds on his back.

"But surely you can fight through this," Allen said, as if he'd already had half a conversation in his own head and simply expected Mat to be able to pick up where he'd left off.

"Fight?" Mat asked. Fight who? Why?

"Good thing you've got looks, you fucking moron. Fight. You know, that thing you've been doing nearly all your life, with the fists and the feet and the crowd goes wiiiiiiild." Allen's fingers left Mat's skin. Ten bucks said he was making jazz hands back there.

Mat turned around, plastered on his best smirk, didn't dare let his curiosity—or his nerves—show. "Yeah, I can fight. Put your hands up; I'll show you right now."

Allen smiled. "Oh, I would *love* to hurt you, Dog, but not right now. Now, I need you fit and strong. And let me be clear: let yourself be injured today, and when I send you to the stables to recover, I'll have you make yourself useful there by collecting semen from my stallions."

Oh *God*. Allen looked *way* too excited by that possibility for the collection method to involve anything other than his body as the receptacle. So . . . No losing. Check.

"Ah, you get my meaning. Not so moronic, after all. Or maybe your bashed-up brain still works half the time?"

I'll bash your brain, you filthy fuck.

"Well, no matter, I didn't buy you to think. Go, follow Nedry. He'll get you ready for tonight."

Nedry materialized from God-knew-where, took Mat by the arm, and yanked him toward the door that led to the maze of slave halls. Halls Mat had never been in, not since the first day. Dougie was back there somewhere, surely. He'd have to keep his eyes peeled.

"And, Dog? Put on a good show for my clients, would you? You understand how it is, I'm sure? The more interesting you make it, the bigger the bets."

Bets? Was this a cage match? Like the ones he'd fought in dozens of times before he'd been captured?

Except back then you at least got a cut to bring home to Dougie, and you didn't have to fight with fresh fucking whip wounds all over your back.

Well, he was still taking care of Dougie, in a way. Still keeping them both alive.

He'd just have to put on a good show for Allen's guests. Woof, woof.

Several hours later, showered and carb-loaded and treated to a dessert of two Tylenol, Mat found himself ass naked in the nicest dressing room he'd ever seen—carpet and curtains (no windows, though) and fancy plush chairs and a fucking *fainting couch*, for fuck's sake, all orbiting around a padded table and supply cart in the center. Weird to be in there alone, without his manager to pep-talk him or his coach to rub him down and wrap his hands. At least there *were* wraps; Allen might be expecting him to fight with his dangly bits, well, dangling, but he had half a shot at not breaking his hands if for some reason he needed to punch his opponent in the head.

He wrapped slowly, methodically, extra heavy over the knuckles to make up for the lack of gloves. No tape that he could find, so he tucked the ends in well. Flexed his fingers. Warmed up with the heavy bag in the corner. Sipped some Gatorade. Stretched. His back twinged, but nothing he couldn't fight through—nothing he'd even notice once the fighting began.

He bounced on his toes, went back to feinting around the bag. He missed Coach Darryl—deeply, powerfully, despite not having thought of the man in weeks. Had never realized how *lonely* a dressing room could be. Yet at the same time, how good it could feel to be back in one. Even if he was fighting for some sick fuck's entertainment. Even if he didn't have the faintest idea of who his opponent was, or what the rules would be. Because this was the closest he'd come in months to being home again—in his element, his world. The cage was, ironically enough, a comfort. A kind of violence he understood, that made sense.

He whirled around at the sound of a door opening—the one he'd come through, that led to the maze of slave halls—and an unfamiliar man popped his head in. "You're on in five," he said. Then, without waiting for an acknowledgment, "Need anything?"

Mat ducked around the swinging bag, drove his knee up, followed with a vicious elbow to Allen's imaginary temple. "Who am I fighting?"

"An opponent," the asshole said helpfully.

This time it was *his* imaginary head Mat drove his fist into. "Rules?"

"Don't die."

Was he joking?

"And the master likes your face, so try not to fuck it up."

Mat danced back, rammed his heel into the bag. "C'mere, I'll mess yours up instead."

The guy threw his head back and laughed. Just once, loud and garish. "Save it for the ring, yeah?" Then he slipped back through the door and closed it behind him. Maybe being lonely wasn't so bad, after all. Not if that was the kind of company available to him here.

After that, it all played out surprisingly like a typical fight. Music came on from beyond the second door, the one that presumably led to the ring, some awful grunge rock he'd never have permitted for his entrance at the UFC. Then the second door swung open, and the man standing there waved Mat into a dim hall. Slipped a silk robe around his shoulders. Slapped him once, hard, on the ass. Mat almost roundhouse-kicked him in the face, but honestly, he wasn't looking for the kind of trouble that'd likely bring him, so he went down the hall like a good little slave instead. Lights strobed at the end, just like any arena in Vegas. Someone announced his name—his *real* name, in typically theatrical form: "Mathias. Stoooooooneeeeewall. Caaaaaarmichaellllllll! Weighing in at 173 pounds, fighting for our illustrious host, Allen Smythe-Kennedy!"

Mat hit the arena proper halfway through the announcer's speech, instinctively squared his shoulders and waved to a crowd he couldn't see when a spotlight hit him. Tried not to stumble as he came to a short staircase going *down* to the ring instead of up and realized that the ring wasn't a cage or even a ring proper but a fucking *gladiatorial arena* in miniature, perfectly round and maybe twenty feet wide, complete with sand floor, shoulder-height walls, and seating like theater boxes stacked above them all the way around, four or five rows high—hard to tell exactly with how well lit the ring was and how dim the house was. Unexpectedly, they were indoors; he looked up and saw a tall ceiling, a catwalk, banks of professional-quality theater lights and speakers.

He whirled at a hand on his shoulder, but managed to contain his instinct to strike. Someone pulled his robe off, and the crowd went fucking insane. He resisted the urge to cover himself, stood tall and proud instead, stared out at the audience, took the time to meet what eyes he could see in the gloom. Men in tuxedos, women in cocktail dresses, jewelry glittering in the lights. Uniformed ushers—slaves?—moved through the aisles with trays of drinks. Others slunk around naked or nearly so—the pleasure slaves no doubt, and no doubt Dougie was up there somewhere too, sucking some asshole's cock.

No, don't think about that now. Surest way to let yourself get your ass kicked.

Two or three men weaving in and out of the box seats were carrying tablets instead of trays. They'd lean in close to whisper with someone, exchange information, then move on to the next person. Bookies. The audience was betting on this. Of course they were.

The music changed. Lights strobed at the other end of the arena. Mat turned to watch the staircase, half-expecting a fucking lion on a chain to pop out of the vestibule. Shit, wait . . . Allen wouldn't *really* do that, would he? Mat was a terrible fucking Christian anyway.

He was more relieved than he cared to admit when a man came down the stairs. Just a man. Naked as Mat was, a big guy, not quite as ripped but clearly not a couch potato either. Mat missed his name, but what the fuck did it matter, anyway? He heard two hundred pounds, which meant the guy had a massive twenty-seven pounds on him. That would've been seriously worrisome if he were even half as lean as Mat was, but instead meant he might just be kind of slow on his feet and that Mat would be wise not to let the fight move to the floor.

The music faded to something nondescript with a heavy backbeat. A ref herded them both into the center of the arena. The sand was a layer of fine grit over hardpack, maybe six inches deep atop what was probably a wood or concrete floor—not so much that he could guarantee a cushioned blow on a takedown, but enough to drag at his feet, slow him down, make everything slippery and unsure. His opponent looked equally off-balance, though he held himself like a man who knew how to fight. Confident. Maybe even *over*confident. Street fighter, perhaps? In which case the fight would be over damn fast and he'd need to draw it out to, as Allen had ordered, "make it look good."

The ref had them touch gloves—well, so to speak. Said, "No points. You fight until someone doesn't get up." Added absolutely nothing else—no rules, no *stop at the bell*, no *no hitting below the belt*, nothing. Even the underground fights had had *some* rules. Maybe they just didn't know any better here.

But then the ref backed off and the bell rang, and there was no more time to think about any of it because his opponent was coming at him in a flurry of shouting aggression, and yes, *definitely* overconfident, some bastard mix of tae kwon do and boxing and maybe jujitsu, judging by how eager he seemed to get Mat on the floor. But he fought like an enforcer—like a guy used to beating up shopkeepers and card counters, people who rarely knew how to fight back. Fast hands—he landed two solid hits before Mat had even gotten his arms up—but he left himself open after nearly every strike he threw, and it wasn't long before Mat was battering him back up into a wall.

Of course, that presented its own set of problems. If they couldn't tap out, and couldn't win on points, and Mat had no intention of grappling with a guy almost thirty pounds heavier than him, how was he supposed to end this fight? Knockout probably meant head punch, which was never a great idea under the best of circumstances, but a fucking terrible one without gloves or tape. Allen wanted it to last a while anyway. And no wonder—Mat didn't doubt for a second that he was the beneficiary of all those bets being placed in the stands.

Pressed to the wall now, crowd cheering wildly above them, his opponent wrapped his arms around Mat, pulled him too close to strike effectively. Not that they didn't both try, working elbows and knees against sweat-slick skin, grappling for advantage. The guy was trying to throw Mat off-balance, using the wall for leverage. Might've even succeeded if he'd had clothes to grab onto.

And then the dirty fucker *did* succeed when he grabbed Mat's hair—first foul—and smashed his forehead right into Mat's nose—second. Followed very promptly by a third—a hard knee to the nuts—while Mat was busy being dazed like a fucking idiot by all the blood pouring down his face and the way his head was ringing.

He hit the sand hard, his opponent landing on top of him like a sack of very heavy, pointy rocks, both elbows driving hard into his chest and one knee in his squishy bits. He lay there stunned a moment, spitting out blood and throwing his forearms up to protect his face from a flying fist, but of course that allowed his opponent to show off those jujitsu skills and work him halfway into a compression lock. Fortunately, the guy seemed to forget about Mat's lower half in the midst of his biceps slicer, so Mat was able to plant a heel, leverage from the hip, and land an elbow in the fucker's face. He wanted to play dirty? Yeah, Mat could play dirty too.

Mat scrambled to his feet, forced himself not to hunch over the bruised ribs he'd earned in the fall lest his opponent spot the weakness. His nose had stopped bleeding, probably wasn't broken, but he couldn't say the same for his opponent's, which was dripping gore into the sand. The guy *was* hunched over, elbows and knees. It'd be easy to take him out now—the ref hadn't called on any of the fouls, so Mat didn't think anyone would care if he KOd the guy with a kick to the head—but he wasn't willing to risk killing him, and besides, Allen had said to make it look good. Now that he knew what he was up against, he could win easy any time he wanted to. Just needed to bide his time, play with his food before eating it.

He backed off. Took a few deep breaths. Let the guy climb to his feet. No boos from the crowd. They didn't want it to end yet either.

The guy raised his hands. Flicked blood from his face. Stumbled once, twice. *Now* someone booed. A single stiletto heel flew from out of the stands and hit the guy in the side of the head. He glared at it, spat blood in the direction it'd come from. Seemed to think twice. Bent down to pick it up. For a second, Mat thought the crazy fuck was going to risk hurling it back into the stands, but then he realized . . . *weapon.*

Well, could've been worse. Could've been a knife or something. Maybe he should end this fight before someone *did* throw a knife.

He charged in. Ducked a telegraphed swing with the stiletto, landed a right cross so hard he thought he heard a rib snap. *Fuck.* What now? He backed off, looked for the ref as his opponent hunched over again, dropped to one knee, hand pressed to his side, face twisted into a grimace. Someone should be calling this fucking fight. Why wasn't anyone calling this fucking fight?

"He's not getting back up!" Mat shouted to the stands, since he couldn't see the ref or Allen beyond the blazing ring lights. "Isn't that what you said? Fight until one of us doesn't get back up?"

His only answer was the other stiletto sailing out of the audience and striking him in the chest. He glared at it, disgusted. "Someone gonna help this guy?" he yelled.

Again, no answer. He went over himself. Put a hand on the guy's shoulder, tried to straighten him out a little to see what kind of damage he'd done. "Hey, can you stand?" No answer. "You o—"

Sand in his eyes and a vicious uppercut to his chin sent him stumbling back and landing on his ass. His opponent was on him in a flash, but he was sloppy, uncoordinated. Mat wrapped his legs around the guy, locked his heels to control the guy's hips, forced the guy's head under his arm and got him into a guillotine choke with a minimum of effort. Held him there until the tense body against him stopped struggling. Didn't knock him out, just . . . contained him.

He looked to his audience again. Searching for a ref, or Allen, or hell, some dour-faced Roman asshole in a toga to give the thumbs up or thumbs down. Nothing. "What the hell do you people want from me?" he yelled, finally, out of pure frustration. Was he supposed to fuck the guy like in those MMA-cum-gay-porn videos online? Knock him out?

"Finish him!" Allen roared.

Finish . . . ?

Kill him. They want me to kill him.

Were they fucking *kidding*? His opponent clearly didn't think so; he began to struggle anew, managed a powerful elbow strike to Mat's bruised ribs despite his head still being firmly tucked beneath Mat's armpit and his hips still being locked by Mat's legs. Mat grunted, arms tightening around the guy's neck but only enough to still him again, and growled quietly, "Stop it." Then, louder, to the audience—to Allen—"No."

"No?" Allen called back, and oh God, he didn't sound angry, he sounded *pleased*. "I thought you might say that. Luckily, any trainer of fighting dogs knows how to awaken the bloodlust in even the most uncooperative mutt."

"Fuck you, Allen," Mat called, as mildly conversational as Allen was. A calculated risk—obviously Allen wanted him to be putting on a show, but how much of one? The collective gasp from the crowd seemed more delighted than offended, at least. "I'm not a killer. You can't make me."

Allen laughed, once, too loud even in the high-ceilinged arena. Beneath Mat's armpit, his opponent whimpered, like he knew the argument was already lost. "Only one of you's walking out of that ring. You think your opponent will show you the same courtesy?"

"I think I'm not the one in a submission hold."

"You'll get tired eventually."

"Fuck you, Allen," Mat said again, just as mild as before.

The crowd seemed to appreciate it less this time. Or maybe they just didn't like the lull in the action. Had they known this was a death match? Put their money on who would kill who? How long it would take? By what method? Whether he'd be willing to do it at all? Well, whoever had placed the bet on him refusing to go through with it was about to become very rich. Mat had long ago made peace with the inherent brutality of fighting, but killing another man was one bridge too far. If Allen tried to humiliate or unman him for that, well, so be it. At least he'd still have his honor. And his fucking soul. And if Allen really did try to push his luck, well, there was no way in hell the guy in the headlock was going to be able to put *Mat* down. Not unless someone handed him a fucking gun. And once they did that, there was nothing to keep the guy from shooting off into the fucking audience.

Mat readjusted his grip on his own wrist, which was sweaty and starting to slip. He *was* getting tired, yeah, but the guy beneath him had stopped struggling again, like maybe he really believed they could both get out of this somehow, or at least that he was better off throwing his lot in with the guy who'd refused to kill him than with the guy who'd ordered his death.

This wasn't right, though. Something was off. Allen wasn't monologuing anymore—wasn't saying anything at all, in fact—and the restless murmurs from the crowd were rising to an agitated pitch. Why wasn't anything happening? No way the fucker was just waiting around for him to magically change his mind.

Which was why it came as no surprise when the gate at the top of the stairs Mat had passed through earlier opened, and two massive men came through.

With Dougie between them.

He remembered Nikolai's advice: pretend not to care about him, pretend it doesn't affect you, and they won't bother using him. But that was a hard concept to actualize when he was standing in a fucking gladiatorial arena and they were bringing down poor, helpless Dougie as a piece of meat for the lions to tear apart.

"Fine," Allen said as the two men shoved Dougie out into the sand. "If you're so certain that this man doesn't pose a threat anymore, have your brother fight and kill him in your stead."

No. *No.* Even if by some miracle Dougie was able to hold his own in a bare-knuckle fight with a guy twice his size . . . "You think he's going to kill someone in cold blood?"

Allen scoffed. "No. I think that piece of shit you're cuddling is going to kill *him* in cold blood."

One of the guards unsheathed a Taser from a thigh holster, pointed it straight at Mat while Allen continued his mustache-twirling routine from the stands. "Don't think I can't remove you from the arena, Dog. You're not special. Kill your scummy little bottom, or he kills your precious baby brother. Your choice."

Mat's opponent tensed again, and Mat didn't know if it was because of what Allen had said or because he himself had gone as rigid as a fucking statue and was inadvertently cutting off the guy's air. *Your choice.* Some fucking choice. What the fuck was he supposed to *do*?

His opponent elbowed his bruised rib again, and for a second Mat was fiercely glad of it—*That's right, fucker, make me mad, make this decision easy for me*—but then he got his fucking shit together and channeled the anger into something more productive, slid his forearm and his heels and rolled on top of the guy, pinning him chest to back.

"Tell me," he whispered in his opponent's ear. He applied fresh pressure around the guy's throat, just enough to let him know how fucking serious he was. The guy struggled briefly, but he wasn't going anywhere, not like this. "Who are you? Why are you here? Are you a slave?"

He eased up enough for the guy to respond. "Fuck . . . you," he spat.

God *damn* him. Mat flexed his biceps around the guy's throat, couldn't push down the surge of satisfaction at his strangled cry. "Look, *please*. Give me a fucking reason not to kill you."

"Dead . . . anyway. Allen . . . caught me stealing. Just do it."

Just do it. Like it was that fucking easy to end a life.

"Mat—!"

Mat startled as Dougie came crashing to the sand, skidding to a stop beside him. Someone had shoved him and shoved him hard. Mat's opponent didn't even try to leverage the lapse to his advantage, though he probably could've. If he'd given up on living already, why should Mat care more about the guy's continued existence than he did?

A guard stepped up behind Dougie, Taser aimed square at Mat's back—*but I could roll us fast enough, I could, he'd hit my opponent and the gun only fires once and then nobody would be awake to hurt Dougie*—and Dougie looked at Mat with those stupid big eyes of his, wet with equal parts fear and fury, and his lower lip began to quiver just the tiniest bit like it had when they were younger and he'd hurt himself and tried so hard to be brave while Mat patched him up, and Mat couldn't fucking look at that for another fucking second, he *couldn't*, and what if he couldn't roll the guy fast enough when the Taser fired after all?

No choice at all. Not really.

He closed his eyes. Pressed his lips to the shell of his opponent's ear and said, "Tell me your name." He owed the man that much, at least. Could take that much with him. Carry it. Bear its weight.

"Dean Grassi."

Mat nodded. Repeated it, just to be sure. Pressed his lips back to Dean's ear and whispered, "I'm sorry, Dean. I'm so sorry." Firmed his grip. Squeezed. Just hard enough to cut off blood flow, not to crush or choke. Put him to sleep.

But who was he kidding. It wasn't sleep. Dean was never waking up again.

CHAPTER THREE

Mat had always been a fighter. Always, since childhood, since the first time some shithead kid had tried to pick on him for having the wrong Ninja Turtle on his backpack. And he'd never stopped.

Now, he was a killer. A fighting dog. As vicious and mindless as Allen had promised he'd be.

He measured his time from one fight to the next. He put on a good show and raked in big hauls, so Allen threw him in that pit twice a month, sometimes for one match, on the bad nights for two. A grueling fucking schedule, but what other choice did Mat have? He entered the ring, faced the other man or sometimes men—he didn't know where Allen got them from, and he didn't ask, though he heard rumors of disposable slaves from the meat markets and free men who'd crossed Allen one way or another—and got it over with. Sometimes it was easy, or at least, the other man didn't put up much of a fight. Sometimes Mat only survived by the skin of his teeth. He made it fast when he could, Allen's *Make it look good, Dog* be damned. Tried not to make people suffer. Snapped necks and bashed heads in and crushed throats. Stopped asking their names—he couldn't handle the weight of it, he couldn't, not if he wanted to live—but never stopped counting their deaths. Twelve so far. Twelve souls, maybe innocent, maybe guilty, but *none* deserving the end they found. All for Dougie.

After the fights, he'd be brought up to Allen's room, still covered in blood and gore and sand, and Allen would fuck him with his cock or toys or fists or sometimes all three, as brutal and as merciless the arena fights themselves—except worse because Mat couldn't fight back. And every time, after Allen was finished, he'd tell Mat to keep his mouth shut, to let no one know that Allen had emptied a load inside him or gotten it up for a man in the first place . . . or else.

He didn't need to elaborate on the threat, because Mat already knew.

Or else he'd hurt Dougie.

So much for Nikolai's advice to pretend Dougie meant nothing to him. Especially when Allen calling his bluff could mean Dougie's life.

At least outside of the fights Allen mostly ignored him. Had lost interest in him, or maybe just wanted to keep him fighting fit and so didn't get up to his usual tortures. Mat was bringing in heaps of cash, now. Allen could find someone less useful to whip bloody.

In between, Mat plotted escape. Nothing else mattered, not anymore. He'd have killed himself after that first fight if he'd thought it would change anything, but he knew better. The men Allen threw in the ring with him would end up dead anyway, and Dougie would be lost forever, or worse, just another dog in a bloody fight. And if Mat couldn't escape by dying, then he had to get off the island. Somehow.

But Allen kept him under tight supervision. Whether in the stables under Reggie's care, or in his little spartan cell in the slave halls, or in the gym Allen kept for his sex toys to stay fit, he was always guarded, always locked in. Never got to go anywhere *near* Dougie, and how could he possibly escape alone, leaving Dougie behind, when he knew—*knew*—all the too-horrible-to-contemplate ways in which Allen would take it out of Dougie's hide?

He was trapped now. There was no tricking Allen into believing they weren't close or that Dougie couldn't be used against him, and everything Mat did or planned or even *fantasized* about had to grapple with that single fact.

Service. After so many days of confusion and isolation and bullying and buying affection with sexual favors, Douglas had found his place in the household, and it was right where Nikolai had told him he belonged all along: serving.

It just so happened that it wasn't a master he was serving—as he'd been trained to—but a mistress. He'd become Penelope's boy. Penelope didn't want him to dress as a woman, or wear a massive plug, or keep himself sloppy. She had his hair cut, and she even let him grow back a little bit of body hair. As long as she was in the house, he was at her side. He trailed after her everywhere: listening to her talk, laughing at her jokes, offering sympathy and massages, giving his opinion on her outfits, brushing her hair. She kept up his piano lessons too—she was much, much better than he was, but seemed to take great pleasure in watching him try.

He served her sexually too, of course. Happily. She was the most beautiful woman he'd ever seen, and he didn't know what he'd done to deserve her, but as long as he had her affection, he wouldn't take it for granted. He loved her.

He *loved* her. Differently, but as deeply as he loved Nikolai, and he wouldn't be sorry for it, and he wouldn't let himself think of it as a betrayal, because by serving her, he served Nikolai too. Nikolai wouldn't begrudge him his feelings; he'd be pleased. Pleased to see Douglas serving someone so well, and so intimately, and so thoroughly.

And apparently he was fulfilling his *other* duty to Nikolai merely by existing. If Mat had gotten into any trouble in the last couple of months, Douglas hadn't heard of it. Strange, considering the animal seemed worse now than he'd ever been—feral, vicious, a murderer who ripped others apart with his bare hands. That he'd done it to keep Douglas safe was the only reason Douglas could stomach watching the fights at all. Not that he knew why that should matter.

He spent the fights sitting at Penelope's knee, where she petted his head anxiously and made disgusted noises at the violence. She had to be there, she said, because it was her duty as Allen's wife to be present and support him in this new business venture, even if she didn't understand why it was necessary to make the dogs *kill* each other.

And it was Douglas's duty, in turn, to be present by her feet. Her slave. Hers. Allen had made it official by gifting Douglas to her for her birthday. What should he care if his brother lived or died, killed or didn't kill, in the face of that? The bond between master (or mistress) and slave was so much stronger than the one gleaned by an accident of birth. He knew that now, watching Mat fighting in the ring for his life and feeling almost nothing.

Only almost, *Douglas? You shouldn't be feeling anything at all.*

He nestled tighter to Penny's thigh, and her fingers threaded through his hair. Well, he'd never claimed to be a perfect slave like everyone seemed to think he was—*one of Nikolai's boys*, they'd say with such sneering jealousy. All he could do was try. And then try harder still.

"I'm thirsty, Douglas," Penny said, voice raised over the sounds of punching and grunting and cheering, but still cultured and sweet as ever. She probably wasn't, really—she'd drank all the tea Douglas had made her thirty minutes before the fight, sipping happily at her cup while Douglas carefully layered clear topcoat on her toenails. But she read him well—too well, disconcertingly well, he could hide *nothing* from her—and she'd probably sensed his unease and was giving him an excuse to leave the fight for a minute or three. Well, he wouldn't take it. If she could sit through this, then so could he.

And really, after that first horrifying day, he'd never been shoved into the arena again. What had happened there since that time simply didn't concern him.

"Are you sure you're thirsty, Mistress, or are you just looking for something to occupy your hands? Because I think you'd find having them in my hair while I lick you out would be much more satisfying than holding a boring old glass of water." He winked playfully, one hand curving around her calf to tickle lightly at the back of her knee. Just like always, she squirmed with pleasure.

"You insatiable boy," she said with a laugh, and she was so, so very pleased. It wasn't even the act that really satisfied her. No, it was to feel so desired, that was what she liked best. And who could blame her, when her husband filled their home with boys dressed like girls and passed over the one real woman under his roof? "You're right, I'm not thirsty after all." And as he'd expected, she parted her knees and sank both hands into his hair, guiding him forward.

Like he needed any help with that.

In a bizarre fit of timing, the whole arena erupted in cheers the moment Douglas's tongue made contact with Penny's flesh. Mat must've killed someone again. Whatever. He didn't care. He and Penny were in their wonderful, loving bubble, and he wouldn't let Mat intrude. He moaned softly, kissing her as he went, but her hands on his hair loosened, and her legs closed abruptly around his shoulders, and he knew Mat had intruded anyway. Damn him.

"You know," Penny said, her hand sliding from his hair to the back of his neck, possessive and forceful enough to worry him, "I think I am thirsty after all. Go get me a drink, Douglas. A mimosa, I think. You can make me one in the kitchen."

"Yes, Penny," he said, looking up to see why she'd been so eager to send him away: two men had come into their box, were leaned over the master, whispering. Big men. Armed. Enforcers. Like the men who'd dragged him into the arena seven or eight fights ago, when Mat had first refused to do his duty.

Douglas rose to his feet anyway. *Penny* was his owner now, not Allen. He'd obey her.

He hadn't managed a single step, though, before one of the enforcers darted out a hand and caught his wrist.

"Stay, pup," Allen said, at the same time Penny growled, "He's *mine*, Allen."

"He may be your pet, Penny, but don't forget that you're *my* wife."

"Just because you can't control your feral fucking dog without—"

"*My* wife," Allen repeated. "You had nothing but a name before I came along. The things I give you, I can take away. Including your little lapdog."

"And what good use you've put that name to!" she hissed back. "Betting and blood sports and grown men dressed up like slutty little girls!"

Oh God, this wasn't happening. This couldn't be happening. Allen would take him away. He knew it.

Douglas fell to his knees. The bruiser's grip on his wrist didn't loosen, so he knelt there with one arm twisted into the air. Knelt at his mistress's feet.

"Please, Mistress," he begged. "It's all right. Let me serve him. I don't want to see Mistress and Master fight. Not over me. I—*it*. It's just a slave, it doesn't want to see its master and mistress fight. It's not worth that. Please."

Penny's hands balled into fists. "Now look what you've done, Allen!" And then her voice turned saccharine-sweet, on the verge of tears. "Oh, my poor baby boy. I won't watch. I won't watch."

At that, she turned and fled, leaving Douglas alone with Allen and his two bruisers.

Allen gave him a boot in the ass, narrowly missing the exposed backs of his balls. "Go on then, pup. Go get your dog of a fucking brother in line before I have you both put down."

He didn't know what the master expected him to do. Had been paying more attention to Penny than to the fight, and maybe for that he deserved his uncertainty now, his fear. He didn't dare ask for clarification. Just went along obediently as the bruisers took him out of the stands, down into the backstage, through the hall, and down the stairs to the arena. They opened the gate, shoved him through onto the sands, stepped out behind him.

He just stood there a moment, allowing himself time to take in the scene, make informed choices, not let the master or mistress down.

The first thing he noticed, of course, was Mat. Just . . . sitting in the sand, legs and arms crossed, wearing an expression somewhere between horrified disgust and the kind of belligerence that could only be scoured away with a whip. He had a thin stream of blood trickling down his face from a cut over his left eyebrow, and a red spot on his right flank that would probably be an ugly bruise this time tomorrow. Otherwise untouched. So the first fight hadn't been a rout, but it hadn't been any real challenge, either. Which meant he had no excuse for not being on his feet.

And his opponent? Douglas scanned the arena, followed Mat's gaze, and finally found the other guy, huddled against the wall. Skinny, naked, curled up tight, covered in bruises, including ones around his wrists that Douglas recognized from when he'd been taken all those months—years?—ago. And he was young. Not quite out of his teens, by the looks of him. He still had a little softness in his jaw and cheeks that even Douglas had mostly grown out of. And all the crying he was doing didn't exactly make him look any older.

Great, so, now what?

He knew how these fights were meant to end, of course—someone had to die—but how was he supposed to make that happen?

One of the enforcers approached the cowering, sobbing slave at the far end of the arena and pressed a knife into his hand. The kid didn't want to take it, dropped it as soon as the enforcer let it go. Mat saw it, didn't even seem to care. And why should he; he didn't need a knife to kill anyone—not that kid, not the enforcers.

So why the hell wasn't he *doing* it?

"Last chance, Dog," Allen called from his box in the front row. Douglas felt the other enforcer close in on him, put a hand on his shoulder. Not comfortable. Menacing. He looked up into the box, hoping to see Penny, but she was still gone. Looked back to Mat, who was just *sitting* there, staring into some middle distance, hands loose in his lap now, slowly shaking his head.

Crying, Douglas realized. He was crying.

What the fuck *for*?

"I can't," Mat said. He was staring at his hands, probably wouldn't have been loud enough to hear if the whole damn arena hadn't been holding its breath. "He's just a *kid*. He's—he's fucking innocent, damn it, not like the others. I can't punish him, k-kill him, for something somebody else did."

"His father's a traitor. A rat. This is what we do to rats. We let the dogs have them." No missing that Allen's speech wasn't for Mat's benefit, but for everyone in the crowd. His audience. This could be them—their kids—just as easily as it was *this* kid. *Today you're my guest, but tomorrow you could be my dinner. Choose wisely.*

Even his own wife's treasured pet wasn't immune.

"Do I have to remind you how this goes, Dog? You fight, or your brother does."

"Dougie—" Mat's voice was filled with doubt, but he spoke regardless. "This kid couldn't—*wouldn't* hurt Dougie. And Dougie won't hurt him either."

"Are you so sure about that, Dog? Willing to make a bet on it?"

Mat turned his eyes to Douglas, gave him a long, hard look, gaze fierce and determined and sad all at once through the tears. "Well, if he does . . ." He sniffed once, swiped at a damp cheek with the back of his hand. The first real moment of vulnerability he'd allowed to show in Douglas couldn't even remember how long. It made Douglas feel . . . strange. Unsettled for reasons he couldn't explain. Like some tiny creature gnawing at the center of his gut. So did what Mat said next: "Then I guess he's not that innocent. At least my hands will be clean."

"Fine," Allen said with a shrug. "Restrain the dog and give the pup the knife. Go on, pup, be a good *baby boy* and gut the little bitch."

Penny's nickname for him. A private name, the one she used when he braided her hair, or after they'd made love and he was left spent and worshipping her beautiful body.

The threat was clear. Kill the kid, or else he'd never be Penny's baby boy again.

The crowd roared with boos and cheers—a *lot* of money would no doubt be changing hands in a moment—when an enforcer passed him the knife, and he took it. Held it steady in his hands as the enforcers dragged Mat, unresisting, from the arena.

He could do this. He wasn't a trained fighter, but he knew enough, and his body was strong. The kid was a sniveling wreck. All Douglas had to do was plunge the knife into his throat. There'd be a lot of blood. The crowd would love it.

He held the knife tight, approaching his opponent. No, not his opponent. His . . . his victim. An opponent fought back. An opponent wasn't condemned to death. Dougie didn't want to kill anyone, but it was his duty. Kill this boy. Not his victim, his *duty*. The consummate slave, just as Nikolai had trained him to be. One of Petrovic's boys. Perfect in service.

But Nikolai hadn't trained him to hurt anyone. His *duty* wasn't to kill, was it?

His duty was to please the crowd. His masters. To be a good slave.

And a good slave knew his master's desires better than his master knew for himself. Anticipated. Served to perfection without needing to be asked.

Roger knew Nikolai that well.

And Douglas . . . Douglas knew this crowd. Blood lust wasn't the only kind of lust, and the crying boy was beautiful under the bruises, with his soft body and pert little nose and pouting mouth, his dark hair and blue eyes big like Douglas's own.

And he knew his master, too. At least well enough to know how happy he'd be when every single bet placed here today ended up being wrong—when the outcome to this fight was the one event no one could possibly have anticipated. Allen would make a fortune.

Douglas threw the knife to the sand.

"Thank you," the boy sobbed.

Douglas grabbed him by that filthy hair and yanked. Turned his face up. Kissed him, slow and deep and pornographic, slathering his lips and chin with his tongue. The boy sobbed afresh beneath him, but didn't fight. Went slack in a way Douglas recognized well—*I'll be good, please don't hurt me anymore.*

That was fine. Nikolai had kissed Douglas through his tears, hadn't he? Fucked him through his tears too. Many, many times, no matter how much Douglas had cried and begged and struggled. And that had turned out for the best.

All Douglas had to do was show the boy a better way, show him that once the tears had dried, there would be peace. Joy, even. A new life. A better one.

Life, period.

He tried to be gentle. The boy was cooperating—no need to cause him pain. He kissed down his jaw, nibbled on the shell of his ear. "I won't hurt you," he whispered. The boy nodded ever so slightly, still sobbing. The crowd cheered. "Be good. Do as I say. Let me take care of you."

He didn't wait for a response—it didn't matter anyway, the boy's fate was sealed—just fisted his hair and tugged him to the sand, facedown, knees tucked beneath him, ass conveniently in the air. The cheering grew downright frantic. Maybe the crowd was too rich to care about the money they'd soon be losing on this outcome. Or maybe they thought Douglas still planned to kill the boy after he'd fucked him. Hopefully the first rather than the second.

He stood, kept a hand on the boy's back as he walked around him. Didn't need to, not really—the boy wasn't going anywhere—but Douglas did it more for comfort than control. He remembered all too well from his early training the soothing power of a touch that didn't hurt. How he'd longed for kindness, any kindness. How well he'd responded to it.

He stroked himself with his other hand, achingly hard already, tipping his head back and moaning. He might not have a porn-star dick, but he sure knew how to use it, how to put on a good show for the crowd. That was the most important thing. If he could get *them* on board, then no one would have to die today.

Still stroking himself, he slid the fingers of his other hand down the boy's back, over his tailbone, into his crack. Wasn't too surprised to find him already wet and loose. The boy moaned, hitched a sob—a quick look made it clear he'd been roughly used recently, no blood but plenty of rawness and swelling. There'd be no way to make this good for him. But Douglas would do his best to make it as not-unpleasant as possible. He sucked two fingers into his mouth, slathered spit all over them; the boy was slimy already but more wetness wouldn't hurt. He didn't have to work the boy open, not really; two fingers slid in without resistance, a third with hardly any. He found the boy's prostate. Rubbed. Took his hand off his own cock to give the boy a reach-around. He was soft, of course, and likely would stay that way, but that didn't mean Douglas shouldn't try.

The dimming cheers, however, made it clear pretty quickly that the crowd didn't want happy feel-good sex. He should've known better. They were in an arena, after all—a field of domination, of conquest. Not the time or place for the gentleness Douglas so desperately wished to give.

He took his hands from the boy's body. Dropped to his knees, leaned over the boy. Wrapped a hand around his throat—for show, mostly, but he did pull the boy's head back far enough to whisper, "I'm sorry, this may hurt," into his ear. Also far enough for the crowd to be able to see on his face the pain that Douglas was no doubt about to inflict. Douglas took his cock in his other hand. Lined up. Shoved in.

The boy cried out loudly enough to be heard over the fresh roar of the crowd, and Douglas cringed but kept going, fucking deep and fast, one hand clutching at the boy's hip, the other sliding from his throat into his hair, drawing him up from elbows to hands, keeping his head pulled back. He'd finish fast this way, but he didn't think the crowd would care, and it was all the better for the boy. For him, too. He wanted this over with. It wasn't supposed to be like this, pointlessly cruel. How could the boy learn *anything* this way? How could he learn joy in submission if there was only pain?

Thankfully, Douglas's orgasm built quickly. He knew what he needed to do. Pulled out, yanked the boy around by the hair. Stroked himself to completion, and spilled all over the boy's tearstained, grimacing face. Let go, dropping the kid face-first in the sand, then rose to his own feet. Found Allen in the front row, bowed to him, dropped to his knees in perfect position. "Master," he said, clear and proud. *For you. All for you.*

For a moment, silence reigned. Then Allen stood. "Good show!" he called, applauding. "Well done breeding that sniveling bitch."

And the crowd erupted into cheers.

He thought to bow again, but knelt there instead, head bowed, and let his master bask in all the glory and praise. Like a good slave should.

And he *was* a good slave. For now, at least, his master thought so too, which meant he'd get to see Penny again. And soon. Because fuck Mat—not even his complete and utter disobedience could bring Douglas down. Not anymore.

CHAPTER
FOUR

D ouglas didn't pay much attention to time. It wasn't important to him, didn't matter to his duties as Penny's slave, so he didn't bother with it. He didn't know how long it'd been since they'd been taken, since they'd been sold, since their escape attempt, since their branding, since coming to Allen's, since finding his place at Penny's feet. Sometimes it felt like days or even hours, sometimes it felt like years. All he knew was that he was no longer the boy he'd been a lifetime ago under Mat's dubious care.

But today? Today, he knew it was July fourth. Independence Day. Because Allen was throwing a huge party on his yacht, and Douglas and all the other boys were expected to entertain. Douglas was the only one of the pleasure slaves who didn't have to wear matching women's lingerie printed with the stars and stripes. As the only real boy among them, the only one allowed to be a man, he was splashed with "patriotic body glitter" but nothing else. He felt proud. Strong. Beautiful. And very much desired every time Penny's gaze fell upon him.

He had to be careful not to get any of the red, white, and blue stuff on his mistress's gorgeous red dress, though. He zipped her up with care, setting a tiny kiss between her shoulder blades as he went.

"What do you think?" she asked, lifting the few stray wisps of her hair from her nape so he could do up her diamond and sapphire choker.

"You're the most beautiful woman I've ever seen," Douglas said, not one word of it a lie, and she knew it. She always knew it, because Douglas wasn't some flatterer. Some pandering slave. He loved her. He was her lover. There was no room for doubt about his affection for her, nor hers for him.

She turned and kissed him full on the lips, soft but lingering, more sweetness than heat. "You flatter," she demurred, like she always did. But she knew the truth, and she smiled and blushed, and it made her even more beautiful than before. "But good, because you're the one who bought me all of this."

Well, that was confusing. How? Douglas didn't have money. He certainly hadn't been allowed to accompany her on any of her shopping trips. Well . . . No matter.

She leaned back in, swiped a thumb over Douglas's lips. "I've got some on you," she said.

He caught her thumb gently between his teeth, licked it once, and let it go. "The master will like it." But he wiped it off anyway. Because *she* didn't like it.

"Are we all set, then?"

Douglas cast her a final appraising glance. New dress—the one he'd somehow bought her—a perfect, flattering fit. Hair in a flawless chignon. Makeup nearly invisible, highlighting her elegance. Diamond-studded purse in one hand. Couture shoes shined right down to their red soles. And, most importantly, a genuine smile in place. "Yes, Mistress," he said. He hadn't meant to—she liked it when he called her Penny—but he couldn't help it tonight. She took his breath away. His thoughts. His ability to do anything at all but worship.

He held out an arm, and shivered as she slipped hers through his, bare skin to bare skin, heedless of the glitter. His cock ached, bobbed against his belly as he walked, but that was okay. Let the whole world see what she did to him. How crazy she made him. How perfect she was.

Allen met them at the top of the staircase, unceremoniously shoved Douglas off his wife's arm, and took it for himself instead. But that was okay too. She belonged to Allen as surely as Douglas belonged to her. It was the master's—the *husband's*—prerogative to walk at his wife's side, even if Douglas did feel cold and a little empty walking in their shadow.

They headed down to the docks, the whole way lit by torches and festooned with sparkling decorations, and made a grand entrance on the yacht, whose deck was already full to bursting with Allen's guests. Slaves wove in and out of the crowds, entertaining in their myriad ways. Liquor flowed freely. Music played. The yacht shoved off and motored quietly out to sea as the sun began its slow descent to the horizon. Soon the island was a twinkling dot off in the distance, barely visible, then not there at all. Allen mingled, and Penny mingled, and Douglas followed eagerly behind, the perfect pup at her heels. He ate when she fed him and drank when she tipped her glass to his lips, and laughed and danced and loved the party as much as she clearly did. He was looking forward to watching the fireworks with her, maybe some drunken private time belowdecks.

But all that changed when Allen walked up, grim-faced, and put a hand on her shoulder. "My dear," he said. "It's time."

"Really?" she complained, slurring a little from the wine. She pulled Douglas's head more firmly into her lap.

"Really. So thank the boy for the outfit his body bought you—" that last bit spoken through his gritted teeth "—and send him on his way."

She flapped a hand. "Oh, fine. Spoilsport. Go on, Douglas, but hurry back to me so you don't miss the fireworks."

Douglas was confused, horribly confused, and frightened too, but he nodded. "Of course, Mistress."

Allen took him firmly by the arm, his mouth pressed to Douglas's ear. "The man you're about to see paid a small fortune to secure this meeting, and more than that, he could prove a very useful connection for me if this goes well. So do us a favor and make *sure* it goes well."

"O-of course, Master. Absolutely. You won't be disappointed."

Why was Douglas so frightened? He'd served plenty of the master's guests. It was . . . well, it wasn't always fun or enjoyable, but it was rarely unpleasant or painful, not so long as he remembered why he was doing what he was doing. This time would be no different. He'd serve this man, this useful connection who'd bought Douglas's mistress her beautiful dress, and then he'd return to the party. Maybe he'd even get back in time to see the fireworks.

Allen nodded, though he was still eyeing Douglas with vague suspicion, or maybe doubt. Douglas squared his shoulders, forced the worry from his face. "I promise, Master. Don't worry."

Another nod, and this time Allen handed Douglas off to one of the footmen—currently dressed in white livery with a red bowtie—who led Douglas to a cabin door two decks down.

"Ring the service bell when he's done with you," the footman said, fake-British accent impeccable to Douglas's ear. "I'll come back to fetch you. If you or the master's guest needs it, the key for the shackle is in the mirrored case on the dresser."

Shackle? Was the master's guest going to restrain him? Whatever for? Maybe he got off on it—it wasn't like Douglas hadn't seen his share of kinks since he'd been here, or like he hadn't learned how to fulfill even the strangest fantasies. He'd really prefer not to be bound, but what did it matter what *he* wanted anyway? He'd find a way to make it good without his hands.

"Go on, then." The footman gave him a gentle shove between the shoulder blades, then turned and walked away. Douglas nodded once, mostly for his own benefit. Took a deep breath. Opened the door.

And nearly gave in to the urge to flee right back through it when he saw what was on the other side.

No. Not him again, anything but him again. I can't. I can't.

"I know," Mat said. He sounded choked, like he was trying not to cry. Sitting on a massive bed in artfully ripped jeans and a Metallica T-shirt and a varsity football jacket and a shackle around one ankle. Beside him, someone had laid out a schoolboy's uniform with a tie and cap and knee-high socks.

"But I won't let him hurt you this time, Dougie. I *won't*."

Bullshit. Douglas remembered how much a promise of protection meant from Mat. Remembered oh-so-clearly where that trust had gotten him last time.

Last time, because Douglas *knew* who Allen's important client was. All that was missing were the bunk beds and the baseball bat.

"My name is Douglas," he spat as he yanked on the horrible clothes, red-white-and-blue glitter flying everywhere. He hadn't meant to say anything at all, not to that lying animal—the one who'd *thrown him to the fucking dogs* a mere week ago in the arena—but it seemed he wasn't as well trained as he'd have liked to think. "Just shut the fuck up and do what you're told, and maybe I can get out of this with my ass intact this time."

Mat stood, lurched forward, got lurched right back by the too-short chain on the shackle. "God damn you, Dougie! Don't you realize—" He turned his head, and for a moment Douglas thought he was too much of a coward to keep eye contact, but then he realized Mat was looking at the far wall, at the sliding glass door and the balcony and the blackness of the nighttime ocean beyond it.

"Realize what? That we're in the middle of the fucking ocean? That we have a fucking job to do? That you're going to get us both killed if you don't stop being such a fucking moron? Yeah, I realize perfectly." He sat on the other end of the bed to pull on his kneesocks, Mat watching in stunned silence. "He could be here any second. Stop distracting me." And then the tears started falling. Tears of anger, he told himself, not of fear. "This is all your fault. All of this. Every time I think things are going to get better, you make them worse. You made me run away from Nikolai. You got me sold to Allen. You put me in that death-match ring and almost lost me my mistress. And now, here I am with you, again, about to be—"

Tortured. No two ways around it.

Well, maybe this time, Douglas would throw *Mat* to the dogs. He'd learned that from his big brother, after all, hadn't he?

"I—" Mat hung his head, and his shoulders shook, and Douglas knew he was silently crying. "I can't even argue with you. I can't make you see sense, Dougie. I can't. Not anymore. All I can do . . ." His breath hitched, and he sniffled, wiped his cheeks in that same stomach-fluttering show of vulnerability he'd made in the arena. "All I can do is try to protect you now."

"*Fuck* your protection! I wish you weren't here! I wish you were dead, I wish you'd succeeded in running away! I wish you'd been killed in one of those fucking fights. Because if you were, he'd send me back to Nikolai. I'd be back with Nikolai right now. Not here with you. Back . . ." Douglas stopped speaking as he realized *what* he was saying: If Mat weren't here, if it weren't for Mat, he'd be back with Nikolai. That was the agreement. The one Nikolai and Allen had signed.

He'd be back with Nikolai.

He'd be back.

With Nikolai.

His eyes moved from the shackle around Mat's ankle to the mirrored case on the dresser, the one the footman had told him about. Shaking with adrenaline, he strode over to it, too consumed by his intentions to hear what Mat was saying. He opened the case. Took out the shackle's key. Was this a test? Was the footman laying a trap?

No, Allen wasn't that clever. He wasn't Nikolai. *Nikolai* tested people, constructing schemes and ploys. Allen just . . . pandered. Pandered to men like the one who was coming now, who liked to play father to naughty boys. Who would probably have a hard time fitting a shackle into his fantasies, in which case Allen would give him the means to release Mat—at his own risk, of course—to make the fantasy more real.

Douglas opened the mirrored case, and sure enough, found a key nestled there in the velvet lining. He looked at it, but didn't touch.

If he did this, there'd be no going back.

Did he want to go back?

He loved his mistress—he did—but as long as she was married to Allen, he'd never truly be hers. She could never cherish and protect him the way Nikolai could.

And really, Mat was a terrible slave. Maybe he simply wasn't meant to serve the way Douglas was. Maybe it would be better for everyone, masters and Mat, if he were free and out of everybody's hair. Especially Douglas's.

He snatched up the key and hurried to Mat's side, kneeling at his feet.

"Dougie, what—"

"Shhh. Shut up and listen to me. I'm unlocking the shackle. Don't move. Not until you have a chance to make sure he's *down*. He can't be allowed to alert anyone. He can't be allowed to run or yell or any of it. In fact . . ." He squinted at the glass doors leading to the balcony, where the sky was black-blue except for a ring of pink at the horizon. "The fireworks will be starting soon. It'll be noisy. Everyone will be watching them, even the guards. Nobody will notice if you slip out. We're, I don't know, somewhere east of Florida, Penny said. So swim west. Find the North Star—I know you know how to do that, you taught me. Put it to your right and swim. You'll hit shore eventually."

"Dougie, are you—"

"I said shut up." He shoved the key into the lock. Turned it. This was it. No going back. "I'm not doing this as a favor. I'm not doing this because I love you—I don't even fucking care if you drown at sea." He closed his eyes for a second, testing the truth of that. An image flashed into his mind of Hawaii, Mat and Dad two distant dots in the ocean while Douglas and Mom sunned on the shore. He'd been so scared for them then, even though the guide had said it was perfectly safe, especially for such strong swimmers. His mother had been a little scared too, though she'd tried to hide it. Well, his mother was dead, and so was his father, and so were his one-time feelings for Mat. "I'm doing this so you can get the fuck out of my life."

"Dougie . . ." Mat's eyes ran freely with tears. He did what he was told, though. Didn't stand up, didn't run to the balcony, though he must've been twitching to. He reached out to Douglas instead, clasped his biceps. For whatever reason, Douglas let him. "Come with me."

"Fuck you."

Douglas shook him off, but Mat just grabbed him again. "Dougie . . . *Douglas*. I still love you, I do. No matter what, remember? We can *fix* this. I swear I won't let you down again. This time, I'll cut out the tracking chips. I won't let you drown. *Come with me.*"

Lies. Foolishness and lies, all of it. Douglas couldn't allow himself to fall for it again, be seduced by it again. Too dangerous. "Y-you had your chance."

"I know, I know, I know. But Dougie—*Douglas*, look. You don't understand. That time was a trap, okay? It was a trap Nikolai set. He wanted you to see me fail. He wanted you to stop trusting me, and he succeeded."

Douglas slapped him across the face. "Don't you dare fucking talk about Master that way. Don't you dare lie about him to make yourself look better. Don't you *dare*. Now shut up. He'll be here soon. Remember, if you give the game away too early, he'll alert everyone and we'll both be dead. Do one thing right in your fucking life and just . . . wait until the time is right."

And then he took his place on his knees by the door.

The wait was short, but interminable. Mat had stopped talking at least, but would it kill him to nut the fuck up and shut off the waterworks? It was embarrassing to both of them. Worse, to Nikolai.

The door opened.

"Well, well, well. Look who it is, my boys, my sons. Long time no see!"

"Hello, Daddy," Douglas said, staring at his knees, willing Mat not to get up, not to blow their chances.

"Thought you were free of your old dad, eh? Thought you could run off and be fags together?"

"Yes, Daddy," Douglas said. Mat said nothing at all. At least he didn't make any wrong moves. Any moves at all, as far as Douglas could tell from the corner of his eye.

Dad took off his hat, hung it on a hook by the door. Closed and locked the door behind him. "I had to search a long time to find you two, you know." He shouldered out of his tux jacket, hung that up too. Undid the knot in his bowtie. "Had to track down your ID numbers and your records of sale out of the Cartel's databases. And they don't let just anybody have those. Luckily, Petrovic still owed me a favor after I let him play hero and punch me in the face."

Let him? Huh?

Dad squatted down beside Douglas, grabbed him by the chin, and pulled his head up. Appraising eyes raked over every inch of Douglas's glitter-dusted skin, settled back on his face. "It's one of my biggest regrets, letting him cut our first meeting short, my faggy little boy."

There it was again—*let him*. He *couldn't* be implying . . . No. Nikolai had *never* lied to Douglas. Would *never* trick him like that, *manipulate* him like that. He didn't need to, had never needed to. The truth and his steady, patient love had always been enough.

"But then, how was I supposed to know how special you and your brother were before I met you? How perfect and slutty you are? How strong the bonds between you are? How much suffering you cause each other, making every blow against you ten times as painful?" He dropped Douglas's chin, stood. "You're my perfect sons. I need you. I need to finish what we started."

Already he was unzipping his trousers. Not wasting time with games this time. No story line about being caught masturbating, just finishing where they left off.

"Now, let's get those two slutty brother mouths on my dick, eh? And don't be afraid to share spit while you do it."

Douglas licked his lips and shuffled on his knees until he was nuzzled close to Daddy's legs. He stretched out his tongue, lapping at Daddy's acrid-tasting slit.

"You too, big brother. Come on and get in there."

Did he not know Allen had chained Mat up? Douglas turned to Mat, tried to convey the necessity to wait until the fireworks started.

But he couldn't read Mat's intentions through the heartbreak on his brother's face. No way to know how he'd play this, if he'd ruin everything again like he always did.

The silence stretched. Douglas sucked a little more desperately at Daddy's dick, hoping to keep him distracted. Side-eyed Mat, urging him to listen, not to fuck up.

Finally, *finally*, Mat slid from the bed to his knees with a nearly robotic "Yes, Dad," and shuffled over to join them.

Thank God.

He took the head. Mat took the shaft. A few minutes in, Douglas took Mat's hand in his own, lacing their fingers together. *Make it look brotherly. Make it look like you still love each other. Make him stick around long enough for the fireworks.*

He was surprised when Mat squeezed his hand.

Comforting him? Really? Now?

No, no, no. Douglas wouldn't let him get away with that. Still holding Mat's hand, he turned and kissed him square on the mouth, making sure to shove his tongue deep down Mat's throat. Mat grunted and recoiled like the untrained beast he was, fingers clenching painfully tight around Douglas's, but Daddy lent a helping hand, fisting Mat's hair and holding him in place. Then his cock was there too, shoving up against Mat and Douglas's writhing tongues.

"Oh, that's my boys, that's my boys. Little fag sluts, seducing your daddy."

Somewhere above their heads, Douglas heard the first pop-sizzle-bang of a firework going off.

Mat pulled back, and Douglas winced, expecting the worst, but then Mat said in a husky voice, "Dad, I have an even better idea. Why don't we get a little more comfortable on the bed here? I can ride you while my brother fucks my ass from behind. His dick's so small and my slutty hole is so loose, I bet it won't hurt at all, even next to *your* big cock. You can have both of us at once then."

Douglas smiled and nodded along, breathless with relief.

Another firework, and another. Distant cheers and laughter. Daddy licked his lips, eyes darting back and forth between Mat and Douglas's faces. Oh yes, he *liked* that idea.

He yanked Mat up by the hair—not because he had to, but just because he could—and shoved him ahead of them onto the bed, dragging Douglas behind by one wrist. "Show me that sloppy boy-cunt of yours," he said, and Mat obediently bent over, dropped his jeans, and spread his cheeks with his hands, completely ignoring the still-very-raw-looking whip cuts striping the skin there. Punishment, no doubt, for his refusal in the arena last week.

Douglas turned his eyes from Mat's ass to his face, and oh God, Mat was *grinning*. It wasn't a nice grin, either, not at all. It was like staring into a fucking horror-house jack-o'-lantern.

This wasn't going to end well. For any of them. Why the fuck had he agreed to this? Was it too late to stop it? "Daddy, wait—" he called as another firework shot off somewhere above them, filling the room with hot red light. It made Mat look even more ghoulish.

Too late, too late. Daddy was already settling himself on the bed, legs spread wide, back propped up against two pillows so he could watch when Mat speared himself on his cock. "C'mere, son," he said, tugging Douglas over. "Go on now, do as you're told. Fuck your big brother's ass with that baby-boy prick of yours."

Mat straddled Daddy's thighs, stripped off his shirt at Daddy's urging; Douglas nearly recoiled at the state of his back, but no, fuck it, Mat deserved it and then some. More fireworks went off—the noise was more or less constant now. Douglas climbed up behind Mat, keeping a careful distance. It'd be over soon. One way or the other, it'd be over.

Sooner than he'd expected, actually—it all happened so fast he didn't even *see* it. One second Daddy was stroking his cock, guiding it toward Mat's waiting ass, and the next he was sprawled unconscious and Mat was scrambling off the bed, ransacking the desk for God-knew-what.

The man hadn't even shouted. All their careful timing, and there'd been no noise after all. The thought sent a shiver down Douglas's spine. How close he'd just been to someone so fucking *dangerous* that he could knock a man out in a blink, without a sound.

"*Damn* it," Mat blurted, moving from the desk to a case of bookshelves. "Come on, come on . . ." What was he looking for? He was already unchained, didn't need a key. "Dougie, help me. I need something sharp. A letter opener. *Something*." His eyes landed on the mirrored jewelry box, the one the key had been placed in.

He grabbed it between his hands. "Stand back," he warned. Stood waiting, waiting . . .

A firework sizzled. At the exact moment it exploded overhead, Mat hurled the jewelry box to the ground, where it smashed, fragments of mirror scattering across the floor. He stooped and picked one up, a shard no longer than his thumb, jagged and sharp. Felt around his opposite forearm with the tip of his index finger, probing for the implant. Douglas knew he'd found it when he took a single deep breath, closed his eyes for half a second, and then sliced into his forearm with a grunt. Blood welled up and streaked down to his elbow, spattering to the floor. A short, clean cut, a little digging with the tip of the shard, and then he flicked his wrist and the next droplets of blood included a sparkle of something metallic.

He was still grinning like a maniac when he bent to pick it up—a slimy, blood-and-silver grain of rice between thumb and forefinger. "See?" he said, holding it out to Douglas like some fucking prize. "Only hurt a little." He snatched the bowtie from around Daddy's neck, wrapped it around his wounded forearm and tied it off with his teeth. "Your turn now. I'll be quick, I promise."

"No." Douglas took a step back. "No, I'm not going with you. I'm going back to Nikolai."

"Are you fucking kidding me, Dougie?" Mat tossed his hands up, looking an awful lot like he'd rather be punching someone instead. But he dialed it down when Douglas took another step back. His voice went softer, imploring. "That guy *just* finished telling you how Nikolai tricked us both! How he planned that whole thing with the . . ." He lowered his voice to a horrified whisper, like he was sorry to bring it up, like saying it aloud would bring it back. "The thing with the baseball bat and punching that sicko in the face. And not just that. The escape attempt, too. He meant for it to be that easy. He always knew he was going to bring us back again. He manipulated you. He messed with your head. He messed with both our heads, and you don't need to go back to him. I'll take care of you. I'll fix what he broke, and I'll never let anyone hurt you again, you hear me? Never."

Douglas ground his teeth, balled his own hands into fists. He had to stand there and *breathe* for a minute, because if he opened his mouth, he'd shout and shout and shout, and not even the fireworks still exploding above would be able to hide his fury. "I'm. Not. *Broken*," he growled. "And I'm not *yours* to protect. And last I checked, in this country, people are innocent until proven guilty. You had your chance, Mat, and you blew it. Over, and over, and fucking over. I'm going back to Nikolai, and he'll have his chance too. He'll explain." He *would*. Maybe Douglas wasn't clever enough to see the real truth on his own, but Nikolai would help. He would. He *had* to. "Now go. Go before I change my mind and start screaming."

For a long, leaden moment, Mat stood frozen there. Blinking. Sniffing back those fucking tears again. And then he nodded, grim as Douglas had ever seen him. "If you're going to stay, it has to look like you didn't help me. They need to believe you had no part in this. I have to—"

No warning. He socked Douglas in the nose, the pain of it sending him to his knees.

When Douglas finally looked up, cupping his gushing nose in both hands, Mat was shaking out his hand. "That was to protect you, but you know what? It also kinda felt good. Do what you want. I don't have time to fight with you right now, not if I wanna get out of here, so fine. Stay." His expression crumpled for an instant, then hardened, twice as determined as before. "I'll come back for you. You will be free, Dougie. And eventually, you'll learn how to be *happy* being free again, I promise. I'll help you. I *will*."

He looked so stricken, so deadly serious, that for a second, Douglas . . . almost kind of nearly believed him. Felt that same awful gnawing in his middle again. Shook it away. Turned his head. He couldn't look at Mat looking at him like that.

"But for now, you need to help me. We have to throw him overboard before he wakes up and starts screaming and ruins everything. You get the legs, and I'll get the top half."

No choice. Douglas had never killed anyone, but if this monster was the one he had to start with, he wasn't going to spend much time crying over it. Besides, the guy might not actually drown, right? He swiped uselessly at the blood running down his face and nodded. Took his legs. Helped Mat maneuver him out to the balcony, then over it. *Goodbye and good riddance, "Daddy."* The body hit the water hard, flat on, with a splash drowned out by the sound of the engine and the fireworks overhead, then bobbed off into the darkness, forgotten.

Mat turned, stepped close before Douglas could dart away. For one horrible moment, Douglas knew for certain that Mat was going to throw him overboard too, force him to come along—

But then Mat just seized him in a hug, bone-crushingly tight, kissed his temple, and said, "No matter what."

And then he dove, graceful as ever, into the sea, as fireworks flashed like rainbow bomb blasts above their heads.

EPISODE 14: INDEPENDENCE DAY

CHAPTER ONE

I t was after 10 p.m., and Nate was so tired he was nodding off mid-conversation. Not that it wasn't an amusing story, because it was—it always was with Ty and Zane, and he hadn't seen them outside the office in months. But he was beginning to deeply regret having offered to host Fourth of July celebrations at *his* house. Unfortunately, he was the only one in the whole damn department with a yard big enough to actually put people in. And when it came to free food, nobody even minded the commute into the suburbs.

But he was surprised his neighbors hadn't started to complain yet about all the noise at this late hour. Between the drunken conversation and laughter and the '80s music blasting on the patio, he could hardly hear himself think. Well, at least nobody was shooting their guns into the air . . . you never did know with this crowd.

And all he wanted was to go to bed. The fireworks had ended an hour ago. Why wasn't everyone going home? It wasn't even the fourth, for God's sake—it was the fifth, because apparently the city thought nobody would bother to attend fireworks on a Thursday.

Louise interrupted his internal grousing with a beer to the face. "Here," she said. She popped the top for him, plunked it in his hand. "Smile. Oh, hi boys." She waved to Ty and Zane. "Wasn't expecting to see *you* at the misanthrope table."

Zane, nursing a Coke, smiled and nodded once. Ty saluted her with his beer and said, "Well, we go to the same Gay Agenda meeting every Sunday while everyone else is in church. Would've been rude not to say hi."

Louise just shook her head. Pointed at Ty's lap, where T'Challa was curled contentedly, sleeping, like Nate wished he were doing. Except not in Ty's lap. Well, okay, maybe in Ty's lap—it was, admittedly, a very sexy lap. Except for the part where Zane would murder him slowly and painfully, then resurrect him to do it again. "Is that Nate's cat?" Louise asked.

"He misses those damn evil beasts we were cat-sitting," Zane said.

Ty glared at him. "Well, if someone would let me take him to animal control to look at the kitties . . ."

"You're not setting foot in that fucking place."

But there was no heat in their words or gazes, and Nate found himself laughing. And kind of jealous. The two of them were so comfortable together, like an old married couple. Then again, when Louise grabbed his beer out of his hand, took a swig, and then draped herself across his lap like T'Challa across Ty's, he supposed he and Louise probably looked that way to the outside world too.

"Come on," she said. "Come dance with me." ABBA was playing. She wanted him to dance to *ABBA*? He wasn't that kind of gay.

He grabbed his beer back and gave her the stinkeye. "Can't. I've gotta, um . . ." He waved vaguely with his beer, and just when he thought he'd have to admit that he didn't know how to finish that sentence, his phone vibrated in his pocket.

There really is a God.

"Gotta take this," he said, knocking her off his lap as he stood. He pulled his phone from his pocket, didn't recognize the number. "Hello?"

"Is this Special Agent Nathaniel Johnson?"

Nate's brow immediately firmed up, every ounce of relaxation fleeing his body at once. He strode to the edge of the yard by the fence, waving off Louise as she called after him. "Speaking."

"The Special Agent Nathaniel Johnson responsible for the Carmichael missing persons case?"

"This is he." His stomach clenched; there was generally only one reason to be getting this kind of call this long into a disappearance, especially at this time of night on a holiday weekend. Somebody somewhere had found a body. Professional dread warred with personal grief. He was suddenly not even remotely thankful for the call.

"My name's Detective Ofelia Constanza, with the Boynton Beach Police Department in Florida. I think you might want to hop on a plane tonight, Agent. Mathias Carmichael washed up on City Beach this morning"—Nate's eyes closed, chest tight—"and he's just woken up."

Woken up?

Alive.

He's *alive.*

There really is a God, indeed.

"And the brother?"

"Still missing, but Mathias seems to have a lot to say about that. He's . . . agitated. Knocked a nurse unconscious. Hospital staff had him 5150ed, so he's not going anywhere anytime soon."

"Did he say what happened? Where he's been?"

"Kidnapped," the detective said. "Guy's a mess, but he's alert and oriented."

"All right. I'll be on the first flight out. You staying with him?"

"Yeah, I'll be here all night. Text me your flight info when you have it; we'll send a black-and-white to pick you up at Palm Beach International."

"Good. Thanks, Detective. I'll bring you coffee."

He could hear her weary smile. "I like you."

"Ditto." Because, really, she'd just given him the best news he'd heard in months.

He hung up the phone, smiling for the first time all evening, and walked back over to the table where he'd been hiding before. Ty and Zane were still there, chatting amiably with Louise, who could probably have charmed the pants off both of them if she'd really wanted to. He snagged her arm mid-sentence with a "Sorry, excuse me" aimed at his old friends, and dragged her over the patio and into the house. "Go home. Pack a bag. I'll pick you up in half an hour."

She went from mildly affronted to dead serious in about two-tenths of a second. "What's up, partner?"

"Just heard from a detective down in south Florida. They found Mathias Carmichael."

She stared at him a moment, then raised her eyebrows, prompting, ". . . And?"

Nate's smile grew. "And he's alive."

Four hours later, Nate and Louise were standing in the hallway of a locked psychiatric ward in south Florida, buzzed on coffee and good news, waiting for Detective Constanza to brief them. He handed her the coffee he'd promised her—Starbucks, not the garbage they served in the lobby—and peered through the window into Stonewall's hospital room. He looked asleep. In the chair by his bedside, a man in his early fifties with salt-and-pepper hair was leaning forward over his knees, holding one of Mathias's hands in both of his own.

"Who's that?" Nate asked. It was nearly four in the morning, and on a locked ward; he hadn't expected to see visitors.

"Brother's foster father. Mike . . . something." Constanza flipped through her notepad. "Stacks. Got here a couple hours ago. Lives in Miami."

Nate gazed through the window again. He should go in there. Talk to them both. But he was loath to wake Mathias after all the guy had been through. He'd read Constanza's report on the plane—evidence of months' worth of violent rapes, beatings, restraints. Someone had *whipped* the guy, for fuck's sake, and more than once. Branded him with their fucking initials. No wonder he'd freaked out when he'd woken up in a strange place with strange hands on him.

But Douglas was still missing. And Mathias could help them find him. And if the brother was being treated even a tenth as badly as Mathias clearly had been, then every second counted.

"They drug him?" Louise asked.

Constanza shook her head. "He was insistent. Not even Tylenol. He came in unconscious and stayed that way for almost ten hours, so they got fluids into him, and some antibiotics in case he inhaled any seawater. But he ripped his IV out when he woke up, wouldn't let them put it back. They can hold him against his will for seventy-two hours, but they can't *treat* him against his will without a court order."

Nate took a deep breath, followed it with a swig of coffee. "All right," he said to no one in particular. Looked at Louise. "Ready?"

Louise nodded. Constanza swiped a key card through the lock on the door. The little light turned green. "Careful," she said. "He . . . startles."

Nate nodded, and he and Louise went inside.

CHAPTER TWO

T he guy who walked in next was too damn gorgeous to be legit. Detective Ofelia was pudgy and had a hardened, weary face. The various nurses who came and went were middle-aged or stout or grizzled or carelessly groomed. The doctor had bad acne scars. Mike was ... Mike, except for the part where he looked like he'd aged twenty years since the last time Mat had seen him.

But this guy? This guy was six feet tall and firm-bodied, with high cheekbones and striking hazel eyes that were impossible to miss: so bright against his copper-brown skin. The woman beside him was also too perfect; petite but strong, like a gymnast or a fighter (*or a sex slave*), thick dark hair pulled back into a ponytail, brown eyes almost too big in her delicate face. They couldn't be cops. Couldn't be social workers. Not in this room, not with Mat. It was too fucking convenient. It was too fucking perfect. *They* were too perfect.

And here Mat was fucking restrained, wrists and ankles pinned to the bed by wide leather straps. They'd fucking *restrained* him. He knew it was useless, but he tugged at the straps anyway, weak and exhausted as he was. Couldn't help it. The heart monitor was broadcasting his rising panic for all the fucking world to hear, and Mike was *touching* him, fingers tight around his own, and he couldn't even make *Mike* let go, let alone protect himself from what was coming—

"Easy, easy, they're with me." Detective Ofelia smiled at him like he was some tantruming toddler, and the guy and the woman reached into their pockets—and God, no, there was *no fucking reason* for him to be panicking at that like he was—and pulled out ...

Badges?

No, no, badges meant shit. Badges could be faked. The Cartel would definitely fake them, if they needed to. And they'd have the skills and resources to make them look real, even if Mat were versed enough to know the difference.

"Stay back," Mat barked, his throat still rough. Then, darting his eyes to where Mike's hands lay curled around his own, "Mike . . ."

He didn't have to say anything else; the desperation in his voice was perfectly clear. Mike let go with a guilty little "Sorry."

The man and woman kept their distance, hands up in what they probably figured was an unthreatening posture, fake FBI badges dangling from their fingers.

"I'm Special Agent Nate Johnson, and this is my partner, Special Agent Louise Menendez. We've been on your case for over four months now. We're here to help."

Mat tugged against the restraints again, sat up as much as he could. Fell back, exhausted, a moment later. Stupid fucking body—now was not the time to be giving out on him. "Let me go," he demanded, even if it did come out more like a plea. Mike looked guilty, but nobody moved to unstrap him. "Who owns you? Is it Nikolai? Allen? Does he really think he can drag me back there? I'll fucking kill myself first, you hear me?"

"Mat . . ." Mike, sounding half-pained and half-embarrassed, and God, why was everybody *looking* at him like that? Like he was fucking insane. An object of pity. Fuck that noise. He looked the guy dead in the eye and yelled, "I said who owns you!"

The guy's brows drew down in a convincing mask of confusion, with just a dash of indignation. "I . . . *what*? Nobody. *Nobody* owns me. I work for the FBI, in the DC bureau, under Assistant Director Pileggi." He turned to a nurse, who'd presumably been drawn by the commotion, and asked, "Is he lucid? I think . . . he seems to think I'm a *slave*."

The guy sounded as offended as Mat felt at being talked about like he wasn't lying right fucking here.

"Yes, I'm fucking *lucid*," he said at the same time the nurse said, "He's alert and oriented, has been since he woke up. No sign of hallucinations. But he *needs his rest*," she added pointedly. "So perhaps you should come back tomorrow."

"A young man's life is at risk," the guy—Johnson, was it?—replied.

Mike stood, like maybe he was planning to put himself between Johnson and Mat, and said, "Look, maybe you should just—" at the same time Mat said, "I don't *think* you're a slave, I fucking *know* you're a slave, pretty boy."

"Boy, now, is it?"

The woman grabbed the man's arm, pulled him back a step. "Careful, partner." She moved to stand between him and Mat. Mike, looking lost, sat down again. "Sorry about him," the woman said to Mat. "He gets touchy sometimes. Let's start again, huh? My name's Louise. I'm here to help you find your brother. But to do that, I need to know where you've been for the last eleven months. Think you can talk to me about it?"

Eleven months. Jesus.

"You fucking know where my brother's been. You fucking know."

"Mat," Mike said, and reached to touch him but then thought the better of it. "Mat, buddy, you've got to calm down. These people are here to help you."

What if they are? What if they're telling the truth? Dougie . . .

One more useless, exhausting tug at his restraints. "Show me your feet, then. I'm not saying a word until I see your feet. Both of you."

A long, awkward pause, and then Agent Johnson said, "All right," clearly trying to put his anger away but not quite succeeding. He lifted his leg, showing off one shiny black shoe.

"Your bare fucking feet," Mat shouted.

Johnson's hesitation—as good as refusal—was all Mat needed to know; he turned to Mike, gave up all pretense and outright begged: "You gotta let me out, man, you don't understand. Please, *please*, for *Dougie*, let me out of these damn—"

"Hey." Soft, gentle. The woman.

"I'm sorry, Mat," Mike said, actually a little choked up about it. He looked devastated, and Mat felt terrible even putting him in that position. But he needed out. *Needed* it.

He turned back to the woman. She'd moved a step closer, was reaching out to put a hand on Mat's shoulder. He jerked away, and she pulled her arm back, looking sheepish. "Hey, look, it's okay. I get it, you need to see for yourself. No brand. See?"

She bent down, unlaced both shoes, toed them off. Took her socks off and straightened up. Elbowed her partner in the side, which seemed to get him moving; he bent down to do the same. While Johnson was untying, Louise lifted one foot, effortlessly balancing, and waved it toward him, baring the sole. The blank, unmarked sole.

"Now the right one," he said. The incessant beeping of the heart monitor had slowed, and he no longer tasted dirty metal in the back of his throat. She switched feet, exposed her right sole and waited patiently while he looked. No brand on either foot. He turned his gaze to Johnson. "Now you."

Johnson didn't balance quite as gracefully as Louise did, and he looked grumpy about it, but there was no brand on his right foot, and no brand on his left either.

Mat . . . actually kind of didn't know how to feel about that. Relieved, sure. But just because they weren't slaves didn't mean they weren't bounty hunters. Still, he *wanted* to believe they could help him. *Needed* to, quite frankly. Because he couldn't spend the rest of his fucking life freaking out every time he saw a pretty face. And if he was going to get Dougie free, he'd need help.

"Sorry." He rubbed his face against his shoulder, wishing he could rub his eyes. "You have to understand," he explained carefully, trying to get the rage and fear out of his voice. "The people who took my brother and me . . . they'll be looking. They might even already know where I am. I took the chip out, but that doesn't mean shit, I don't think. They've got people. People in the government. They're powerful."

The looks on the two agents' perfect faces told him he sounded completely crazy. Of course, of course. Chips, agency spies. Add in a little talk of the apocalypse, and it was the kind of shit homeless people on street corners raged about.

He blew out a noisy breath, consciously made himself stop struggling, tried to calm the fucking beeping of the heart monitor. "Look. I know how crazy all this sounds, believe me, I *know*. But you saw my chart, yeah? You saw—" He had to stop, swallow. His eyes stung. He turned to Mike, asked, "Could you, um. Could you maybe go get a cup of coffee or something? You've been sitting up all night."

Mike nodded, stood. "Sure, buddy." He kind of sounded like he wanted to cry too. He leaned in, like maybe he was going to ruffle Mat's hair or kiss his forehead or something, but stopped himself, wincing, when Mat cringed. What the fuck was wrong with him, shying away like some stray fucking dog? This was *Mike*. And Mat hadn't exactly been a wilting flower these last eleven months, so why now?

"Sorry," he murmured, cheeks heating, but Mike just nodded, said, "Don't apologize. I'll be back in a little while."

Mat waited until he was gone, the door closed behind him, before speaking again. "You're investigating a missing persons case. You must've seen your share of sex trafficking in the past. I've spent eleven months—" That fucking tightness in his throat again. Jesus fuck, he was *not* going to break down crying over this. Not fucking now. "*Eleven months* being raped and tortured and fought like a fucking dog, and the evidence of every second of that is all over my body. I haven't seen my chart, but I know what's written on it. I know what the doctor found. My back. My body. My . . . my ass. So why is it so hard for you to believe me?"

"We believe you," Louise insisted.

Even Johnson's face had softened, like maybe he realized he'd been hasty to judge. He nodded. Rubbed at the back of his neck with one hand, then put them both out, open, in front of him, and stepped forward. Reached for Mat's wrist. "I'm sorry," he said, and then said it again, stepping back, when Mat tensed at the proximity. Johnson sounded like he really meant it, too. "Just . . . what Louise said. I get a little . . . touchy sometimes." He flashed a lightning-quick grin, guilty, apologetic, a little fierce. "Although I think a little touchiness is justified, don't you?" Mat didn't bother to reply. Johnson cleared his throat, his hands inching toward the restraint on Mat's left wrist again. "So, um, how about I untie you, and you don't punch me in the head"—another quicksilver smile, like what Mat had done to that poor nurse was funny, or . . . no, just self-deprecating, that's all—"and you can tell us all about what happened to you and your brother so we can help bring him home."

CHAPTER
THREE

"**Y**ou can't do this!" Penny shrieked, throwing herself between Douglas and her husband.

Although fat lot of good it did *now*.

Now that Douglas was doubled over on his knees, broken hands tied behind his back, choking on the blood running from his nose into his throat.

"I can do whatever I fucking like." No sophistication in Allen's voice now.

"He's my pet. You *gave* him to me!"

"And you're my wife. What's yours is mine, and what gifts I give you, I can fucking take back." He lashed forward, snatching the necklace at Penny's throat and giving it a hard yank until it snapped, the strand hanging limply from his hand. "Whenever I fucking want. What are you going to do, call the police? You think property law applies here?"

"I'm a Smythe! Lady Penelope Smythe! You can't—"

He lashed out again, this time to slap her. Douglas lurched as hard as she did, wishing he could protect her somehow. But he couldn't even protect himself. He was just a slave. Just a slave.

"You're a broke old horse-faced bitch. Now shut your stupid fucking hole and go make yourself useful. Oversee the fucking staff if you don't want any of the precious shit I bought you getting left behind."

Slaves were swarming everywhere, loading crates and luggage onto the yacht, but Penny ignored them, flung herself on the bed, hand pressed to her reddened cheek, sobbing. Douglas didn't blame her.

Especially not now that he and Allen were face-to-face.

"You helped him escape, didn't you, cunt? You thought once he was gone, you'd go back to your trainer, and since the dog refused to die, you helped him run."

Douglas sucked back a throatful of blood, too afraid to spit it out anywhere near Allen. "I swear, I swear, Master, I swear I didn't. He knocked me out. He knocked me out and when I came to, he and your guest were gone."

Allen sunk his hand into Douglas's hair, tugging hard enough to rip some free of his scalp. "Don't lie to me, you filthy little bitch. I should cut your fucking balls off. I should cut your tongue out. I should break out all your teeth. I should throw acid in your pretty fucking face." Douglas moaned, half-convinced he might tremble apart and save Allen the trouble of ripping him to pieces. "But I still need you mostly intact to make sure Petrovic finds and returns your feral fucking brother and doesn't just take all my cash and run."

"Let me help you, Master," he begged. Sobbing helplessly, couldn't stop. He hurt so much. Was so afraid. Why hadn't he seen this coming? "Please, I know him, I know him. I know where he'll go, Master, I can help you, let me help you."

"Oh, you'll help me, my pretty little whore." Allen's voice was pleased, so cruelly pleased. He pulled his cell phone from his pocket and held it up in front of Douglas. "Now smile for the camera."

Selected and stalked. Taken in the middle of the night by a group of thugs. Raped and transported. Examined and microchipped by a doctor. Filmed, for some purpose. Auctioned on a massive stage to an audience full of people in masks. Transported again. Taken in by a man who called himself a "trainer": Nikolai Petrovic who was camped out somewhere in the mountains of southwest Virginia, or maybe Tennessee, Mat thought. Nate would run the name, not that he expected to find anything. This operation was way too sophisticated for that.

Raped and tortured by Petrovic in the name of "training." Made to do unspeakable things, things that Mat couldn't even vocalize, that even hearing the poor guy talk *around* made Nate sick to his stomach. Signed like a piece of art with a branding iron. Sold on to Allen Smythe-Kennedy.

Now that was a name Nate knew: some ultra-rich scumbag already on the Most Wanted list, but for shit like racketeering, intimidation, and gambling rings, not human trafficking. Had a house on some private island in the tropics, according to Mat. While there, Mat and his brother were sexually abused and tortured some more. Mat forced to fight to the death—that took some time to get out; the poor guy broke down for ten solid minutes while recounting how he'd been forced to do Smythe-Kennedy's dirty work. Asked if he'd go to jail for it. Sounded like maybe he thought he deserved to. Nate told him no and fucking meant it. Would never let that happen, no matter what.

Mat sniffed back his tears and carried on. There were other slaves, too. At least a dozen people in captivity at Smythe-Kennedy's place. More at Petrovic's, namely a guy Mat called Roger. *Hundreds* moving through the auction houses. Mathias had first names and aliases for his fellow victims, mostly, and one full name: Dean Grassi, who was dead.

Bounty hunters to track escapees. Multiple auction houses, though Mat had only seen the one. Trainers. Procurers. Guys who made it look like their victims were dead or had fled on their own. Louise scribbled furiously in her jotter, writing down everything they'd want to follow up on before the interview transcript would be ready.

Whatever this was, it was huge, and it was organized.

It was almost too fucking crazy to be true, except Mat's body was his evidence. Mat's unwavering story. Mat's gut-wrenching tears. Nate had been doing this job long enough to know bullshit when he saw it, and not one word of this—not *one*—was bullshit.

One glance at Louise told him she didn't think so either.

It was nearly 7 a.m. when he turned off the recorder and said, as gently as he could, "Why don't you get some rest."

Mat rearranged the blanket at his shoulders, tucking himself in completely, but shook his head. "Slept all day. Not tired."

Now *that* was bullshit—the bags under his eyes and the way his chin kept dipping toward his chest made that perfectly clear. But fuck, if Nate had been through even half of what Mat had been through, he was pretty sure he'd never sleep again. The nightmares must be unreal. Not to mention that his brother was still out there somewhere, and Smythe-Kennedy was probably *pissed*.

Mat shifted beneath the blanket, restless. "Will you get me out of here? I need to leave; they won't let me leave."

Nate was halfway to patting his arm before he remembered that touching this guy was probably the worst possible fucking thing he could do. He nodded instead, covering his awkwardness. "Yeah, but you gotta rest up, man. You're no good to your brother if you run yourself into the ground."

Mat's eyes hardened. "I'm *fine*."

"You're—" Nate stopped himself again, shook his head. Mat didn't need reminding of how damaged his body was. He was living inside it. Different tack, then. "The docs said there might be serious side effects from seawater inhalation. Just . . . stay here, all right? Just one day. You've been carrying all this shit for so long I know you've probably forgotten how to let someone else take care of you for a change, but you need to. You know you do. Take the antibiotics and let them give you the damn pain meds and get some sleep. My partner and I, we'll stay right here, okay? We won't let anything happen."

Mat's gaze raked over Nate, then Louise, who was sitting in the chair Mike had vacated; Mat hadn't let him come back into the room. She gave him a little acknowledging nod.

"And look, I'll get on the phone right now, and start setting things into motion. Look into the names you gave me. See what we can dig up. It's going to take some time to make arrangements for you anyway, so—"

"Wait, what? What arrangements?"

"You said there are bounty hunters, right?" Mat nodded. "So they're gonna be after *you*, right?" Mat nodded again. "Which means you're not safe. You can't be out there alone. And I hate to break this to you so bluntly, but you don't have a house to go back to anyway. The cops thought you ran to Mexico; the bank foreclosed almost four months ago."

For a moment Mat just stared at him, lips parted slightly, then blinked hard. Blinked again. Turned his face away. He'd sweated and bled for that house—literally. To find it gone after all he'd been through must've been a huge blow.

"I'm sorry," Nate said, feeling stupidly inadequate even as he said it.

"Yeah," Mat said, voice tight.

"So if you just . . . Stay here and get better while we work all this out, okay?"

"Yeah," Mat said again, face still turned away. Something about him in profile made Nate's breath catch—he was fierce, beautiful, even more so for the vulnerability he was showing now, something Nate had never even seen a hint of in him before. He felt a little dirty thinking about it, given the circumstances, but as he watched Mat's eyelashes flutter, too fast, over those gorgeous blue eyes, he couldn't quite seem to help it.

"Guess I've gotten good at waiting anyway," Mat added.

As he excused himself into the hall to make his phone calls, Nate tried not to think about how exactly Mat had earned that patience.

CHAPTER FOUR

They'd believed him.

Mat told himself that was half the battle already won. They hadn't dismissed him as some raving paranoid schizo to be forcibly medicated.

They'd believed him.

They'd taken notes, written down names, were now making phone calls, running checks in their databases.

And Mat was . . . lying on his back in a hospital bed. His still-very-fucking-sore back, not that that was any excuse for just . . . *sitting* here.

But God, he was tired. Felt like he'd swum ten miles. Maybe he had. It seemed kind of like a fever dream now. He remembered hitting the water hard, remembered the taste of salt, the burn of it in his throat and lungs and on open wounds, finding the North Star and then swimming, and swimming, and swimming, not sure if he'd ever reach land. And then he remembered being face-first in the sand, some woman telling her kids "not to bother that homeless man." And then she must have seen him, actually *seen* him, his bloodied back and bruised body and his nakedness, and she . . . hadn't freaked out. Just the opposite, actually: she'd calmly sent her children down the beach and knelt with him in the sand while she called an ambulance.

He wondered where she was now. Seemed strange, to think of such a normal family, a normal mom and normal kids on a normal July Fourth weekend trip to the beach, coming into contact with the horrible mirror-world reality he'd been living in.

She'd wanted to touch him, too: bit her lip and fingered the edges of the healing wounds on his back, as if she couldn't believe they were real, that this wasn't some kind of sick scam or movie set. And then, when he'd whimpered—whimpered!—she'd gone all motherly and touched him again, the same way his mom used to, brushing the tips of her fingers across the hair on his brow, sweeping her knuckles over his temple.

He'd cried—so much fucking *crying* today, Jesus Christ—and that had only made her touch him more, try harder to comfort him, until he'd gathered the saliva to beg, "Please don't," and then she'd squatted there awkwardly, looking ashamed, until the paramedics and the police had arrived.

The paramedics had touched him, the doctors, the nurses, the orderlies who'd strapped him down. Mike had touched him. Even Agent Johnson had reached out once or twice.

But he was free now. He was *free*. And he didn't have to let *anyone* touch him anymore if he didn't want them to.

Except for the part where, actually, he kind of *did* want them to. He *wanted* to take comfort from that kind woman, the paramedics, the nurses. From Mike—the man was practically family, for God's sake. He needed it; he knew he did. Desperately. Craved it like he'd craved the water no one would let him have until the doctors had checked him over.

So why couldn't he bear it now? After all he'd borne already? It seemed so *stupid*.

And here was another nurse, coming in no doubt to check his vitals, his wounds, *touch* him again. The sun had risen. Morning rounds would follow soon. More doctors with it.

He needed to get out of here. Before he hurt someone again. Before they locked him up again and wouldn't let him go.

The nurse hesitated at the door, her eyes wide and her jaw stiff. "His restraints are off," she stated, uneasy.

"Yes," Johnson replied, not looking up from whatever he was typing on his laptop. "I took them off."

"Did Dr. MacKay say he could be out of his restraints?"

Johnson looked up sharply. "Frankly? I don't give a shit. He was upset before. He's calm now. The door's already locked, and my partner and I are armed. He isn't going anywhere and he isn't hurting anyone. He's been through a significant trauma and the last thing he needs is to be tied down to a bed, all right? If Dr. MacKay has a problem with that, you send him to me."

The fucking heart monitor betrayed Mat's thoughts on the subject once again, but in truth, he wasn't sure if he was freaking out about the thought of being tied down again, or swooning a little over just how forcefully Agent Johnson was defending his right *not* to be. Probably both. He licked chapped lips, turned to the nurse, and tried to look harmless. "I was out of it before, when I hit that poor woman. I'm so sorry. I didn't know where I was, and I thought . . ." Whoa, no going down that road, not if he could help it. He cleared his throat, blinked a little too much. "Anyway, I know now, okay? I'm not going to hurt anybody. You don't need to restrain me again." He lifted his left arm, turned it palm-up. "You can even put the IV back in. I won't fight you."

She seemed to relent at that, shoulders untensing as she walked over to a cabinet by the sink and rummaged for a fresh IV kit. She ignored his outstretched arm, though, went around the bed, and nodded at the right arm. "You were so dehydrated when you came in, we blew every vein in that arm. Have to use the dominant one instead."

Looking apologetic, she pushed over the blanket just far enough to expose his arm. Took his hand ever-so-gently, turned it palm-down. He shuddered, closed his eyes. He could do this. The pads of her fingers moved in firm, clinical circles over the top of his hand, searching.

"Little pinch," she warned, and then a prick, the pain almost invisible after all he'd been through. He didn't watch her hook up the tubing. Didn't stop her when she injected something into the port that eased his aches and left him too muzzy to be nervous about how helpless he'd suddenly become. He slept.

He *dreamed*.

He thought he might've woken up screaming. No more muzziness. The pain was back, but he didn't care. Someone's hands were on his shoulders, holding him down, and he wasn't going through this again, he *wouldn't*—

"Mat! Hey, hey! It's me. Eyes on me, Carmichael, come on."

". . . Coach?"

Yeah, those hands felt awfully familiar, and he went loose and easy beneath them, let them position him like he always had. Opened his eyes to Coach Darryl's lined face, blessedly familiar pinched lips and worried squint and receding hairline, and oh my God he couldn't remember the last time he'd seen something so beautiful and familiar and *safe*. He reached up with both hands—Coach Darryl let him, could read his body well enough to know he wasn't freaking anymore—grabbed the man by the face, pulled him down, and kissed him square on the forehead.

Realized, halfway through, what he was doing. That he was *okay* with it. Was still okay with it even when Coach Darryl pulled him into a hug, never mind his raw back or cracked ribs, never mind the hands on him, the strong, constricting arms. He squeezed right back. Took the permission he'd been given, buried his face in the man's neck, and just . . . let himself go. Strange, that a man who'd spent the last twelve years shouting "Suck it up, Carmichael!" was now patting him on the back and rocking him as he sobbed. Stranger still that Mat didn't feel the least bit awkward about it. Not even with Agent Johnson sitting in the corner, typing away on his laptop and pretending not to listen.

Mat wound down after a while, exhausted again, and the creeping horror of hands on his body began to seep back in. Coach Darryl must've felt him tense, because he let Mat go but didn't go away, instead sat on the bed by Mat's hip and handed him a tissue and a cup of water and held his gaze. No pity, no sickly sympathy, no disgust at the thought of what Mat had been through; just the same steady strength he'd always exuded, the same no-nonsense no-excuses sense of authority. Mat blew his nose and drank his water under that scrutinizing gaze, found he could bear it because Coach Darryl wasn't seeing what everyone else seemed to see: a victim, or a body to be used. No, he saw the same fighter he'd always seen. It made Mat feel . . . well, not strong, exactly, but maybe less hopeless.

"We'll get him back," Coach Darryl said. Reading Mat as well as he always had. No doubt, no hesitation.

"Yeah," Mat croaked, because he wasn't gonna fucking cry again, and because when Coach Darryl said it, Mat believed it.

"You tell me what you need, Mat. I'm here for you."

Mat nodded. "I know." But he didn't know what to say to the other part. Didn't know what he needed. Doubted it was something anyone could give to him, anyway.

Wait, no, there was one thing: "I need to get out of here."

The look Coach Darryl gave him could've withered a whole field of flowers. "You need to *heal*. I know you, Carmichael; none of this bullshit. You're not fighting before you're ready."

Mat winced. Yeah, he should've seen *that* coming.

Coach Darryl looked utterly unapologetic. "I brought you something," he said. Stood from the bed, retrieved a canvas grocery bag from the empty chair where Mike had held vigil. "I sent him home," Coach Darryl said to Mat's unasked question. "Or to a hotel, rather. He needed sleep. He'll be back after dinner." Mat nodded, took the bag from Coach Darryl's outstretched hand. His favorite gym clothes—an old pair of royal blue Adidas track pants and an even older gray hoodie, worn so soft he slept in them sometimes. He must've left them at the gym before he—

"Thanks," he said, throat tightening again. He cleared it, swallowed, squeezed his eyes shut. Jesus Christ, this bullshit was getting old fast. Why couldn't he get a fucking hold on himself?

"There's more," Coach Darryl said, gesturing at the bag.

Mat pulled the hoodie out to see what lay beneath it.

Contraband. All his old favorites from his brief period of rebelliousness as a teenager, the ones Coach Darryl made such a show of tossing in the trash if he ever found them in the bottom of Mat's bag or locker. Funyuns, of course, even though he was pretty sure everyone else suddenly realized how disgusting they were the day they turned eighteen. A slice of honest-to-God apple pie, in a Tupperware container; he'd bet a hundred bucks it was homemade. A Cadbury egg—where'd Coach Darryl get that in July? And a bottle of Dominion Root Beer, still cold, that must've been harder to find this far outside the DC metro area than the Easter candy in summer.

"Thanks," he said again. Barely even managed to get it out this time, the tears were so close. He grabbed the apple pie and the root beer; Coach Darryl wheeled the little over-bed table within reach and unscrewed the cap off the root beer bottle for him, sparing him the embarrassment of having to admit that he probably couldn't do it himself right now.

"Don't make yourself sick," Coach Darryl said. "That nurse scares me."

Mat's laugh was sudden and unexpected, hurt his ribs and unstoppered the dam that'd been holding the tears back, but it was wonderful, too; he couldn't remember the last time he'd laughed without bitterness or anger or outright hatred, and suddenly he felt so giddy he wanted to hug the guy again. But he smiled instead, a little sheepish—*sorry I'm so fucking crazy right now*—wiped his eyes on his blanket, and dug into his apple pie.

Holy *Christ*, was that ever good. He groaned, and Coach Darryl grinned. His diet had been so strictly regulated for so long, voluntarily when he was free, and then as just one more aspect of the obsessive control he'd lived under in captivity. Felt so good to choose for himself what to eat again. Felt even better to know somebody cared enough about him to give him this. And not in a creepy expects-all-kinds-of-sick-ass-things-in-return kind of way, like Nikolai might've. No, Coach Darryl didn't want anything from him but for him to get better. Be happy. Probably wouldn't even care if he never fought again.

Which was good, because—

Mat shuddered, the pie going sour in his mouth. Fourteen men. God help him, he'd killed *fourteen men* with his bare fucking hands.

"Mat?"

He looked up, forced himself to swallow the bite of pie, chased it down with a swig of root beer. Coach Darryl was giving him that steady, assessing look again. Missing nothing. Didn't ask if he was okay—it was a stupid fucking question. Just waited him out.

"'S'nothing," Mat finally said. Pushed the memories away. He'd gotten good at that lately. Only way to live with himself. He slid an apple slice from between the crusts with the tines of his fork. Plastic, just like at Allen's, at Nikolai's. Guess the nurses didn't trust him any more than his captors had.

And why should they. He'd killed fourteen men.

He pushed the pie away. "Just not that hungry, I guess. Thanks, though."

"Maybe later," Coach Darryl said, snapping the lid back on the container and placing it carefully back in the grocery bag, eyes on Mat the whole time. Letting him have his excuse, but also letting him know he *knew* it was an excuse. Which, frankly, was about six thousand times more permissive than the guy usually was. But still not pity—not from him. Thank God. Mat couldn't fucking handle that. Didn't deserve it anyway.

I don't even know their names.

He'd stopped asking after the first. After Dean. Couldn't bear it.

"Maybe you should get some sleep," Coach Darryl said.

Mat broke eye contact, couldn't stand it anymore. Tugged his blanket up to his neck, carefully covering both shoulders. He wished he could put on the clothes Coach Darryl had brought him, but there were tubes and wires fucking everywhere. "Yeah, maybe."

"I'll just stay here, then." Coach Darryl settled himself in the empty bedside chair with a magazine.

Mat licked his lips, nodded, grateful the man hadn't posed it as a question Mat would have to figure out how to answer, trapped as he was between feeling stupidly needy and too exposed. "Yeah, okay," he said. Then added, softly, "Thanks. You know, for everything."

Coach Darryl's smile was quick and too tight, like Mat wasn't the only one trying to hold back a tidal wave of sentimentality. "Go to sleep, Mat," he said, reaching out and smoothing a hand over Mat's blanket-covered shoulder.

"Yes, Coach," Mat murmured, and closed his eyes.

CHAPTER FIVE

Nate got six solid hours of quiet in which to work after Coach Darryl Dickson arrived. Mathias yielded to him like a boy to his father, pliant and trusting, and finally slept for a good long stretch, not even stirring when the nurses came to check on him. Coach Dickson didn't leave the room, not once, not even for coffee or to take a piss. Just sat in the chair pretending to read a *Sports Illustrated*, eyes watchful on Mat over the tops of the pages. Nate sat across the room, resisting the urge to interrupt the man's meditation for any reason, valid or otherwise—he did have some questions he wanted to ask him about the case, and under better circumstances, he would've been fanboying all over the guy. But for now he let him be, and read through all the electronic case files they had about every name Mat had dropped or hinted at, while Louise caught some sleep in an on-call room for the long days to come.

Too much of what he needed was still in a dusty file somewhere, though. He'd have to go back to DC soon. Sitting around in some cramped hospital room with a laptop balanced on his knees and unbearably slow public wi-fi wasn't going to cut it, and the longer Mat stayed here, the more likely it was that one of the people he said were after him would actually be able to track him down—if they hadn't already. AD Pileggi had managed to kill any new media coverage, had kept Mat's *name* out of the papers. But there'd been one story on the local news and in a couple small papers about a John Doe washing up naked and beaten and giving beachgoers a scare. It might have been okay without the naked-and-beaten part, but that was a massive flag for anyone keeping an eye out for him. And sure, the FBI could maybe use that to their advantage, but Nate wasn't about to go dangling Mat as bait if he could help it. The man had suffered enough already. More than enough.

Just as he was thinking he really needed to get Mat out of here—quietly move him to another hospital, ideally—Mat woke up and insisted on the same.

"I need to leave," he said before Nate had even realized he'd regained consciousness. He had no idea who Mat was talking to. Maybe no one. It was almost like he was continuing on with a conversation that'd started in his head, or maybe the dream he'd woken from.

Nate closed his computer and stood at the same time Coach Dickson closed his magazine and leaned forward over Mat's bed.

Mat met Coach Dickson's eyes. "I need to get out of here. We need to go. I get that you think I'm hurt or whatever, but every minute I'm lying here in this bed and you two are sitting here staring at me is another minute Dougie's alone with a complete sociopath." He scrubbed his hands over his head. "I shouldn't have left him. I should have tried harder to convince him. I should have thrown him fucking overboard—"

Coach Dickson dropped a heavy hand on Mat's chest, pushing him back to the bed, and for a second Nate was *sure* there'd be violence. The heart monitor was beeping like crazy, but Mat . . . just kind of went ragdoll beneath the man's touch, shut up, and flopped back without fighting.

Huh.

"Assessment," Coach Dickson said, calm and not-quite-stern, hand still resting on Mat's chest but no longer holding him there—didn't need to, Mat wasn't fighting.

Mat closed his eyes, took a deep breath. Another. Seemed to be centering himself, or maybe thinking. "Okay, yeah," he said. Licked his lips, which didn't seem quite as cracked as they'd been last night. "Headache; not serious. Back hurts; also not serious. Ribs maybe a problem—could you move your hand?" Coach Dickson slid it to Mat's shoulder but didn't remove it. Didn't apologize either. This was a routine, had to be. No way they hadn't done this a million times before, this self-check, evaluating his fitness to continue. "Tired but not sleepy, sore as hell but nothing sprained." A pause, tongue darting across those lips again—Nate's eyes were drawn to it in a way that left him feeling decidedly lecherous. "That's it." Another pause, eyes tightening a moment. "Yeah. That's it. I'm fine. I swear." Unsaid but heard: *I've been through* so *much worse lately. I can deal.*

Coach Dickson pulled his hand back. "Okay." He turned to Nate, features a little hard, daring him to argue. "Agent Johnson here will get a doctor to release you into his custody now."

Nate knew he should probably kick up some kind of stink about the fact that Coach Dickson was a visitor and not in charge of those kinds of decisions or of Nate's case, but he totally agreed with the guy's plan of action, and frankly, anyone able to bring a little calm and solace to Mat right now was okay in his book. Nate wasn't the kind of egotistical hothead to get into power struggles like that anyway.

He texted Louise to wake her, and less than a minute later, she was there. Nate turned to her the moment she'd shut the door behind her. "Any word on a local safe house?" he asked.

"I slept well, thank you for asking. You ready to move, then? I got us a nice little motel room the local LEOs like to use. Couple of uniforms are gonna meet us there and stay on the door. But sorry, it's not as close to Disney as I know you were hoping for." She winked.

Nobody laughed, of course, but Nate admired her for trying, and he pasted on a tight, watery smile in an attempt to show it. "But not us. Mat and me." Because no way he was leaving Mat alone with anyone he didn't personally know and trust with his life. Not with how insidious Mat was making this Cartel out to be. "You're taking the first flight back to DC and getting to work on the leads Mat's given us."

Louise bristled, but didn't argue. She did grab Nate by the elbow. "That flight may need to wait," she murmured, and then spoke louder for Mat's benefit. "We're gonna go find you a nurse now, kid." She dragged Nate into the hall. "Before I go, I'm going to have a talk with a lady who's been sitting in the waiting room down the hall for going on twelve hours now. See who she's visiting, if you catch my meaning."

Nate's shoulders and hands tensed. Yeah, he caught her meaning. They couldn't be too careful when it came to observers and bystanders; any stranger who came into contact with Mat—especially one who'd been lurking nearby for so long—could pose a threat, could be a part of or working for the organization responsible for Mat's abduction.

Or she could legitimately be someone waiting on a family member in the hospital. But in that case, it was worth interviewing her to see if she'd seen or heard anything suspicious.

Mat was right to be uneasy about being in the hospital. Even if there wasn't a mole, there were too many people coming and going. Too many chances for people to blab about the curious new patient. Too hard to keep Mat safe. The guy wasn't just a star witness in what was turning out to be a massive case; he was also a human being in need, one who almost everyone in this world had turned from.

It made Nate wonder how many *Fled to Mexico* files he'd set aside, how many men and women and maybe even children like Mat he'd failed to rescue in the process.

The guilt ate at him, but the logical part of his mind was busy teasing that fact apart. The people who'd taken Mat had *known*. Known who to take and when, and how to make sure the case got the least amount of attention possible. How to clean up behind themselves, cover what few tracks remained. Nobody had questioned Mat and Dougie's case. Nobody had looked into it further. Nobody but Nate, and not because he was some kind of super cop, but because of his personal connection. If Nate hadn't recognized Mathias Carmichael, missing person, as Mat "Stonewall" Carmichael . . .

Mat still would have escaped. He's weak now, but he's no damsel in distress. He saved his own damn self, and you need to give him credit for that.

"Partner?" Louise snapped her fingers near his face, and he blinked, realized he'd been standing in the hallway like an idiot, staring into some middle distance. "Maybe you need a rest."

"Can't," he replied. "You know I can't. I feel responsible for this. We should have been following this disappearance from the first second it was reported. Maybe we could have found them before Mat had to go through what he did. Maybe we could have—"

"Come on, Nate. Don't talk like that, you know it doesn't do any good. He's here now, he's safe, and he's going to help us bust this sick ring wide open. Here and now. That's what matters. The brother's still out there. Who knows how many other people are still out there." God, he *knew* that, he didn't need her to tell him that. She reached up, gave his arm a squeeze. "You've been to this rodeo enough to know that running yourself into the ground isn't going to help anyone. Sound familiar?"

Okay, point. He'd said the same thing to Mat just this morning.

Louise raised a wry eyebrow. "Great. So take your own advice, huh? I'm going to go have a chat with Miss Suspicious in the waiting room. You're going to grab a couple uniforms—I vetted everyone at the hospital six ways from Sunday this morning—and take Mat back to the motel. Where *you will sleep* while the uniforms stand guard. For at least three hours. There'll be two guys outside too, okay?" She pulled out her phone, poked at it for a few seconds. "I've just emailed you the names, photos, and badge numbers of every officer I vetted. You will let them handle guard duty for a little while. I'll call you when I get back to DC. And here." She reached into her pocket, handed him a flash drive. "That's everything Detective Constanza got out of the witnesses from the beach. And don't give me that look—nobody saw a fucking thing or I'd have given it to you earlier." She planted fingertips on his chest and gave him a gentle shove. "Now go."

She turned and left for the waiting room, and Nate mumbled "Yes ma'am" to her retreating form, then went to track down a doctor so they could leave.

It took more arguing than he cared for. And paperwork. Always so fucking much paperwork. Mat dressed in the bathroom while Nate filled out forms. Coach Dickson stood guard at the door, offered Mat a hand he didn't take when he came out of the bathroom, looking stiff and uncomfortable and oddly vulnerable. Maybe it was the injuries. Or maybe it was the weirdness of being dressed for the first time in eleven months.

They left out the back, rather than through the lobby. Coach Dickson escorted them to the waiting cruiser, looking ready to snap the neck of anyone who came within ten feet of them. Nate, just as paranoid, checked the profiles Louise had sent him against the uniforms in the car. Even still, Coach Dickson insisted on coming with them to the motel.

"We've got it under control, Coach, I promise."

Coach Dickson's squint said pretty clearly what he thought Nate's promises were worth. "Mat's still in danger?"

"Well . . . I mean, we don't actually *know*—"

"But you've set up a safe house. You've got four officers standing watch. You're obviously fairly certain."

Nate reluctantly nodded. Mat stepped around him and climbed into the backseat, shut the door behind him. He looked relieved to be sitting down, to be away from the tension.

"Then I'm not leaving him alone. You could use another set of hands and eyes. I may be getting old, but my hands are still better than most."

And didn't he know it. "You have to get your own room," Nate said.

"Fine."

"And for God's sake, stay out of the way if shit goes down."

"Fine," Coach Dickson said again. Nate decided to pretend he wasn't lying through his teeth. Truth was, Mat wasn't the only one who felt safer with the guy watching his back.

CHAPTER
SIX

M at fiddled with the little strip of tape stuck to the back of his hand, trying not to panic at the sensation of the seat belt across his chest and hips.

It's just a seat belt. You can hit the clip and get it off you anytime. You're in control of this. It's just a seat belt. It's just a seat belt.

But the more he tried to calm himself down, the more his heart rate ratcheted up. He pulled the shoulder strap around his back and put his head between his knees.

Coach Darryl's hand hovered over the center of his back—he could feel it there, through the distance, through the hoodie—but didn't touch. Finally the hand dropped on his shoulder, above the whip marks. Gave a gentle squeeze.

"I don't get it," he moaned, hands fisted at his temples, face pressed to his lap, every ounce of focus on that warm, solid, grounding hand. "I don't . . . I managed this shit for eleven months—*eleven months*! I was okay, I held it together, I didn't . . . ." The hand squeezed again, thumb rubbing little circles down his arm. "And now I'm not even *there* anymore, no one's gonna . . . gonna . . . anymore, and suddenly I'm—" He lurched upright, slammed the heel of his hand into the barrier separating the front seats from the back.

"You get it. You think you don't, but you do. You needed to be strong back then, just to survive. Now you're not in survival mode, and everything's catching up to you. Same as how you're more tired after the fight than when you're still throwing punches, even if it's only ten seconds to the bell. You don't feel any pain in the ring. It all just builds and builds and lets itself out the next day. Your body knows when to let you feel tired and hurt, and when you can't afford to."

Mat rubbed his hand, blinked down at his lap, feeling the urge to cry again and absolutely fucking *refusing* to give in to it. "Yeah, well, it sucks."

Coach Darryl laughed, a single dry chuckle, and nudged Mat's shoulder with his own. "You and easy never did get along very well, kid."

Mat nodded sulkily, glanced out the metal-mesh-covered window and watched palm trees and suburban sprawl go by. He was sick of cages. Wanted out. Even if this one was supposedly keeping him safe.

Coach Darryl nudged his shoulder again. "Look, we'll be at the motel soon. Run you a hot bath, get you a nice meal. How about a steak? I could go for a steak. Or we could order a pizza covered with every edible animal known to man."

"Yeah, sure," Mat said, only half-listening. He wondered what Dougie would get to eat today. Probably nothing—no way Allen wasn't punishing him for Mat's escape.

"We'll find him," Coach Darryl said.

Maybe. Maybe not. But all Mat could think was that he never should have lost him in the first place.

Mat disappeared into the bathroom as soon as they were settled in the motel room. Nate heard the water running. Didn't blame the guy at all.

Coach Dickson—*Please, call me Darryl*, he'd said—rented the adjacent room and then headed out for food. The motel was old and shabby, but it was clean, and it had great wi-fi, and most importantly, there were guards, and they weren't in that fucking hospital anymore. Nate felt like he could finally relax, a little. Sat down on the end of one bed and undid his tie. He turned on the TV, half for noise and half to make sure no one was talking about this on the local news. Satisfied the media blackout was safely in place, he finally got his laptop out.

An email from Louise, of course. The woman in the lobby had been a bust—her story checked out, or at least, the (unfortunately deeply unconscious) patient she was here to see *was* a patient here who did live in the same apartment complex she did, so they couldn't exactly hold her. They *could* follow her, though; Louise had let her go and put a tail on her, promised to let him know the instant anything came of it.

Next was more info on the names Mat had given them. He'd discovered this morning that the girl Leslie, who Mat had mentioned as being a fellow prisoner at the auction, matched the description of Leslie Prince: a missing person's case filed around the same time Mat and Dougie had first been reported missing, but there wasn't much else in her electronic records. No concerned coaches or foster parents for her, just a notice from one of those activist organizations that kept tabs on high-risk sex workers. She'd been eighteen when she'd been taken. Would be nineteen now, if she was still alive. Grew up in group homes, shunted around until she'd aged out of the system. Another person fallen through the cracks, and Nate couldn't help but feel partially responsible for that. It was cruel pragmatism, choosing which cases to pursue, and which to leave open and unsolved.

Mat's other name had turned up a criminal record for some underworld lowlife. Multiple counts of assault and intimidation. He'd been in and out of jail twice already. No huge loss. Louise had dug a little deeper for him, though, uncovered some connections that might be useful. Seemed Dean Grassi had worked for Ruggero Napolitano who was a known associate of Allen Smythe-Kennedy. Shame nobody knew where Napolitano was right now.

Through the closed (and locked, he had no doubt) bathroom door, he heard the water shut off. A few small splashes as Mat settled into his bath. Nate looked up from his computer screen and listened for a moment. Just to make sure he was okay, didn't fall and hit his head or something. He could almost picture it, Mat stripping that protective layer of clothing away, sinking down into blissfully hot water for the first time in God knew how long, leaning back with a sigh and closing his eyes, taut muscles relaxing as water lapped at his chin . . .

Shit. What the fuck are you doing, *Nate? Thinking about a sexual assault survivor like that.*

He was getting a really fucking inappropriate erection—that's what he was doing. Jesus, this was bad. God forbid he ever did that in sight of Mat. When had he become such a terrible fucking person?

Focus.

He needed coffee. Correction; he needed *sleep.* But not yet, not with Dougie still out there and Mat still so raw. For all he knew, the guy would rabbit on him the second he closed his eyes.

He paged back to Leslie Prince's files, the juvenile record Louise had dug up, searching for . . . fuck, *anything*. This was the stage in a case when he needed to let his eyes unfocus and his mind wander, seeking out connections you could only see in your peripheral vision.

Group homes. Mat had talked about that. More than once.

They hadn't been after Mat; they'd been after Dougie. Mat had just been collateral damage . . .

Nate lurched up from the bed, nearly knocking his laptop to the floor before he caught it and set it aside. Grabbed his phone. Called Louise.

She answered on the first ring: "Hey, partner."

"We need to go to West Virginia."

Pause. "West Virginia? You just sent me to DC."

He raked a hand through his hair, paced over to the kitchenette and started rummaging around the cabinets for coffee filters. "I know, I know, but look. The connection is there, not Florida, not in some dusty file archive in DC."

Another pause, slightly longer than the last. He found the filters. Popped one in a machine that looked older than he was. "Nate, the local LEOs interviewed everybody and their mother when those boys went missing—including everyone who knew them from their old hometown. *You* interviewed everybody and their mothers and their aunts and uncles and cousins when you followed up. What could you possibly be expecting to find now?"

Coffee. Coffee would be nice. There didn't seem to be any; he'd have to go get some. "Yeah, but we didn't know what we were looking *for*. Now we do. Think about it. Anecdotal evidence suggests every single person taken by the Cartel was a loner—no family, few friends, group home kids, foster kids, orphans. *Someone's* gotta be giving the Cartel their targets. Social worker, administrator, I don't know, but they have access to the databases."

He could practically hear her nodding. "Okay. Yeah. So maybe they know what happens to the kids and maybe they don't, but whoever's passing on the intel has to be passing it to *someone*. A contact."

"Right, right." He ran his hand through his hair again, paced back toward the window, peeked out the drawn curtains. One of the uniforms in the cruiser parked out front caught his eye, nodded, then tilted his head to where Darryl was pulling up in his own car. Nate gave the uniform a nod, and a few seconds later, Darryl was coming through the door with a bucket-sized coffee and a pizza box. Nate flashed him a tight smile and returned to his train of thought. "And that contact may lead us to the procurers, who can lead us to the auction houses, who can lead us to the trainers, and both houses and trainers must keep records of who they've bought and sold, and to whom. We know Nikolai does, at least. We just have to figure out who the leak is."

"Leaks, plural," Louise corrected. "Mat and Dougie were snatched in Vegas, but Dougie's records aren't in the Vegas system; he left foster care in West Virginia. That other guy, the one Mat talked about, Reginald? Mat said Reginald was snatched in Jersey. That's two separate family services databases—that we know of. I'm sure there are more."

Maybe all over the country. Maybe even all over the world.

"Okay, I'll start pulling financials and criminal records on everyone who worked at the office Dougie cycled through during his time there. Hell, they might even keep track of who accesses records and when. If they do, I'll see if there's any suspicious activity there, anyone accessing his file multiple times or accessing it recently. You figure out what to do with Mat, pack up all your files, and get your ass on a plane. I'll meet you there as soon as I can."

"Right. See you." Nate hung up the phone, heart practically vibrating in his chest. Darryl was watching him from the kitchenette, drinking his massive coffee, eyebrows raised. Nate didn't think he could spare the patience to explain the plan right now, so he didn't. Luckily, Darryl seemed satisfied to wait.

Adrenaline coursed through Nate in steady waves, and he couldn't seem to get a grip on it. The last thing he wanted to do right now was get the rest he'd originally been planning. He could sleep on the plane. But who was he kidding, he probably wouldn't be able to sleep there, either. His thoughts were running a hundred miles a minute, practically shorting out his brain. Fight-or-flight response, and Nate wanted to *fight*. He was ready and raring to go. As soon as Mat got out of the tub.

Mat . . . had been in there a really long time, hadn't he?

And Nate hadn't heard any splashing since he'd first—

Oh, shit.

He jumped to his feet, making it to the bathroom door in two long, determined strides. He knocked. "Mat, you okay in there?"

No answer.

"Mat! You okay in there?"

Darryl put his coffee down, strode up behind Nate close enough to crowd him, for Nate to feel his tension. "Hey, Carmichael!" Darryl called. Banged on the door with a loose fist. "Answer me, kid, come on!"

Nothing. Now his heart was pounding so loud he could feel it in his temples and hear it in his ears. Darryl didn't look any calmer—in fact, he looked ready to kick the door down. There were no windows in the bathroom, which meant nobody could've gotten in to hurt Mat, but that didn't mean Mat hadn't hurt himself. Or just passed out and drowned.

"I'm coming in, Mat," Darryl called. Stood back. Nate recognized that stance—he was about to wreck the door.

Nate risked a hand on his arm and a "Whoa, whoa, I got this, no need to knock the place down. I'm worried too, man, but just give me a sec."

He hurried over to his suitcase, grabbed his lockpick set. Felt Darryl's eyes boring into him the whole time. The bathroom lock only had two pins. He had it open in about five seconds.

"They teach you that at FBI school?" Darryl asked as he shoved by Nate to get inside.

Nate followed behind him, steeling himself for what they might find. "My mother, actually." He narrowed his eyes. "She's the white one, before you get the wrong idea."

Darryl grunted, and then the whole conversation disappeared from Nate's mind, because he was in the bathroom and there was Mat, lying in the tub, naked, staring blankly at the ceiling.

"Mat?" Nate prompted, terrified of what might happen next, but then Mat's eyes slowly rolled over to him, taking him in but not really reacting. He didn't sit up. Didn't try to cover himself. Just floated on his back in the water, completely on display.

And despite Nate's earlier fantasy, nothing could have been less erotic than what he was seeing now. Mat seemed barely present, not relaxed so much as clinging to the edge of consciousness. He was just as muscular and lean as Nate had imagined, and better endowed, but it was hard to appreciate any of it when the evidence of his ordeal was written all over his body. Mottled bruising across his ribcage. Bite marks at his thighs, belly, and neck. Handprint bruises on his hips. The stitched-up wound on his arm from where he'd dug out his tracker with a shard of glass. Cuts and welts on his flanks that took Nate a minute to realize must've come from the whip wrapping around. He'd seen the photos the doctors had taken for evidence, but this . . . *This* . . .

Darryl shoved past him with a growl and scooped Mat out of the water like a child. That seemed to snap Mat out of whatever funk he was in—he shouted, kicked. The bathroom was too small for three grown men at the best of times, and his foot connected hard enough with Nate's chest to send him stumbling halfway out the door.

Nate stayed there a moment, palm pressed to the throbbing ache, and let Darryl handle it. Mat was still shouting, fighting dirty, going for eyes and groin and kneecaps, but there was no strength left in that body, and Darryl clearly knew its moves well—he had Mat on the floor in about three seconds, wrapped up in a bear hug back to chest, wrists in his hands, legs trapped beneath his own. Was whispering something in his ear Nate couldn't hear, didn't want to anyway—too private, all of this was way too fucking private—and at last Mat stilled, went slack in the man's arms, dropped his chin to his chest and closed his eyes.

Nate got his shit together long enough to drape a towel over the poor guy's lap. Not that he seemed to notice or care that he was naked in front of a stranger, but then, why the hell would he? He'd spent eleven months naked in front of strangers.

Mat looked up when the towel touched his lap. Nate's hand accidentally brushed his chest—he was freezing, shivering; the water had long gone cold.

"Coach?" Mat asked. He didn't bother to look behind him to confirm who was holding him. Nate bet he knew that body almost as well as his own, after all the time they'd spent training together.

"Yeah, Mat." Darryl sounded choked. Didn't say anything else. His grip eased on Mat's wrists, but he didn't let go, didn't unlock his legs.

Mat blinked, the confusion falling from his face at last, thank fuck. Guy was dangerous to everyone—himself included—when he was out of his head like that. "I fell asleep, and then I was . . ." He looked around, helpless. Freed one wrist from Darryl's grasp without resistance and pulled up the towel, covering as much of himself as he could, like he'd finally realized he was on display. Nate handed him another one. ". . . somewhere else," he finished, like he was mortified, loath to admit it. His gaze dropped to Darryl's other hand, then to Darryl's legs slung around Mat's own. "I . . . Did I hurt anyone?"

Darryl looked to Nate, who shook his head, even though he'd probably have a spectacular bruise on his chest come morning. "No, Mat."

Mat's eyes closed a moment, and he swallowed, clearly relieved. "Let me up, please." No missing the desperation in that request. Darryl let go immediately. Mat clung to his towels as he staggered to his feet, didn't accept Nate's outstretched hand, used the toilet and Darryl's shoulder instead. He grabbed his clothes piled on the vanity, shuffled past Nate into the bedroom, and Jesus, his *back*. The wounds were a week old, well on their way to healing, but it was far too easy to imagine how torturous getting them must've been, dozens and dozens of crisscrossing welts and lacerations. Nate had to force himself to stop staring, give Mat his privacy while the guy pulled on some clothes. Darryl was still sitting on the floor, looking about as dazed as Mat had when they'd found him.

"Darryl?" Nate tried. He wasn't going anywhere near the guy, not while he was blinking into the middle distance like that. One kick to the chest was enough for today.

Darryl's eyes dragged up to his. There was a long, very uncomfortable pause. Finally, Darryl said, soft and distracted, "I have to go." Climbed to his feet. Walked out the bathroom door, past Mat on the bed pulling socks on, and right out the motel room. Took off down the street at a hard run.

Yeah. Nate didn't blame him at all.

Except, of course, now he was the one stuck with the twitchy PTSD victim he barely knew at all, who also happened to be able to kill a man with, like, one finger.

Great.

And he still had to make arrangements to get to West Virginia. He hesitated between Mat and his computer, wanting to help the guy but not knowing how.

Best way is to get to West Virginia and crack this case.

"You, uh . . ." He scrubbed a hand through his hair, made himself meet Mat's eyes. Or try to, anyway; Mat was staring pretty resolutely at his socked foot, crossed over his opposite knee. "You with us?"

"Yes," Mat snapped, his *fuck you* silent but well heard. "I'm fine. Stop looking at me like that." He ran out of things to fiddle with on his sock, put his foot down, stood. "Where are my damn shoes? I need to go for a run."

Was he *kidding*? "Mat . . ."

Mat's glare held such physical weight that Nate found himself stumbling back a step.

"Look man, you know you can't be out there right now, people are *looking* for you, it's not safe."

"So, what, I'm *your* prisoner now?"

"That's not—"

"Should I strip for you, Master?" Mat spun around, put his back to Nate and threw his arms out like a supplicant, shouted over his shoulder. "Wanna tie me down and fuck me? I hear I give real good head—lots of practice, you know."

"Jesus," Nate said, and somehow he was stuck in the very strange, very paradoxical state of blushing and feeling like all the blood was draining from his face at the same time. "Jesus, Mat. Mathias. Mr. Carmichael. No."

"Don't you ever say that name," Mat snarled.

He didn't need to specify; right at the beginning, Mat had made it clear that "Mathias" was a no-go. And like a fucking callous moron, Nate had forgotten. He'd just wanted to put some boundaries between them, let Mat know this was a professional relationship, nothing personal, nothing sexual.

God, what if I did look at him like . . . He'd thought he'd been so careful, but maybe . . .

Nate sat—well, collapsed, more like—on the end of the bed. Still wary, eyes never leaving Nate, Mat sat down on the edge of the other one. "I'm sorry, Mat," Nate said. "I'm sorry. As experienced as I am, even I'm feeling ten steps behind with all this. There's no road map. No manual. Well, there is, sort of, for survivors of rape and human trafficking, we go through sensitivity training, but—" He licked his lips, tried to tamp down on the word-vomit. "With you it's different. I don't know if you know this, but I knew you, before. I'm a fanboy. I went to every one of your fights within a day's drive of DC. Even flew out to Vegas once. Went to after-parties hoping to bump into you. Never got up the balls to talk to you, but God, I wanted to."

"And now look at me." Mat's voice was ragged. "Not gonna have any fanboys now, am I? Not like this."

Mat ducked his head, and Nate hunched down until he caught his eyes again. "Honestly? I see now you're about a thousand times stronger than I ever realized. But that's not the point I'm trying to make here, Mat. I just mean . . ." Now it was Nate's turn to look away. "You're not just a case to me. I'm looking at you as an agent, and I'm looking at you as that starstruck guy, and . . . And now that there's real evidence to follow and others willing to get involved, I should probably take myself off the case because it's too damn personal for me, but I *can't*. Maybe it's egotistical, but I know I'm the best guy for the job, lack of professional distance or no. I'm not trusting you to anyone else."

He felt Mat's stare boring into his bowed head, worked up the courage to stop talking to his hands and meet Mat's eyes. The intensity there, the focus, made it physically hard to breathe. But he saw no judgment. No accusations. He pushed on.

"I already hate myself for not getting you out of there. I can't take any more risks. I'm sorry if it feels like I'm keeping you prisoner, but I'm trying to do right by you. Better late than never, right?" He huffed. "And I'm sorry if you kind of . . . caught on to that lack of distance. I'm sorry if I ever gave you the wrong impression, if I ever looked at you wrong or made you feel—"

"No." Mat was still looking right at him, not a trace of hesitation. "You didn't. I'm sorry I said those things about you. Honestly, you and Mike and Coach Darryl are the first people in almost a year who have looked at me as anything other than a piece of meat or a body to be used and abused. You look at me and you think you're acting starstruck, but to me you look like you're seeing a damn *person*. And if I . . . if I lash out, I promise, it's not *you* I'm angry at."

"Okay," Nate said. Sucked in a big breath, blew it back out. Forced himself to maintain eye contact. "But that wasn't the only reason I'm apologizing. It's also because I . . . I wasn't just looking for an autograph, when I wanted to talk to you all those times. I wanted to . . . In the interest of transparency, I mean, I wanted to ask you out. Home. With me." His cheeks heated, but with luck, Mat wouldn't be able to tell. "I had a crush on you. A part of me that's lagging behind on all this still does, and I don't want to make things any more difficult for you than they already are, so if that makes you uncomfortable, if you want someone else to take over, if you want Louise to stay with you instead, whatever you want, you just say the word, okay?"

Mat sat silent a long moment, shoulders hunched in a little, arms curled around his middle. Had he been like that before Nate had opened his big mouth, or had Nate stepped in it even deeper than he'd realized? "I want . . ." Mat began, eyes on his lap at first but then darting up to meet Nate's, "I want you to help me find my brother."

"And we will, I promise. The Bureau's throwing every resource it has behind cracking this oper—"

"*You*," Mat said, gaze locked on Nate's face. "I want *you* to help me find my brother."

Nate swallowed. Nodded. "I will."

"Good. And look, it's okay. It's okay if there's some part of you that's still attracted to me or whatever. Not that I'm ever going to sleep with you—or anyone—ever again, but . . ." His eyes skidded back to his lap, and he licked his lips again—an unfortunately distracting nervous habit, Nate couldn't help but notice, even despite the conversation they were having. Then Mat curled up a little tighter on himself, and it fucking broke Nate's heart, watching him do that. "Honestly, I'd rather you look at me and still get turned on by that memory, than look at me and see somebody too broken and used up to even contemplate fucking. I'd rather you jerk off to me than curl your nose at me 'cause I'm damaged goods."

"Mat, you're not . . ." Christ, he wished the man would look at him, stop hunching over like that. "You're not used up, and you're *not* broken. You saved yourself. You're gonna save your brother. You just need some time, okay?"

Mat shoved off the bed, still not looking at Nate, made a beeline toward the kitchenette and grabbed a slice of pizza. "Anyway," he said, maybe a little too loudly, opening cabinets to find a plate, "I know you won't hurt me, is all I'm saying. That you don't *want* to. You seem like a really nice guy, Nate. That's good enough for me, okay?"

Nate watched Mat stuff half a slice of meat lover's pizza in his mouth, tried to figure out how to reply. All he could come up with was, "In that case, we're going to West Virginia."

Mat froze mid-chew. Swallowed hard. Dropped the rest of the slice on the plate he'd found and asked, slow and suspicious, "Why?"

"There's nothing left for us here in Florida, and Louise and I both think the key to figuring this whole thing out is to figure out who's feeding information about potential targets to the Cartel and how. We think they've got someone working in family services. Someone going through the files of fosters, looking for ones they can make disappear with a minimum of fuss. We think that's how they found your brother."

"Can't we stay here and let Louise handle that?"

"We can, but there's really nothing left for us to do here. The people who found you on the beach don't know anything, and the longer we stay here, the more likely it becomes that somebody we don't want finding you is gonna track you down."

"But Dougie—"

"Could be halfway around the world right now. Allen's not going to be sitting around waiting for you to lead us to him. He'll be long gone from anywhere near here by now. And I'm sorry to say this, but this whole thing is way bigger than you and Dougie. If I focus on taking out Allen and not the organization as a whole—hitting their infrastructure, taking out some major players—I'll be letting everyone else in captivity down."

"Fine," Mat growled, all his earlier gentleness, his earlier reticence gone. "*You* go hunt down the Cartel. *I'll* go hunt down my brother."

He started toward the door, and Nate hurried to cut him off without needing to touch him, bracing himself for an attack. "Mat, *stop*. Wait." Mat paused within punching distance, glaring, fists curled at his sides. Nate put his hands out, nonthreatening as he could make himself. "Tell me, do you know how many islands there are in the Caribbean?"

"What?"

"Do you?"

The tension in Mat's body didn't ease, but he stayed put as he answered. "No."

"Over seven thousand, Mat. Seven *thousand*. And that's in the Caribbean alone. You don't even know for sure that that's where Allen *is*. Or maybe *was*, now; maybe he panicked and fled when you escaped. You don't know what state you were in when the guards put you in that transport boat. Palm trees? Hot air? Fuck, Mat, that could've been South Carolina, Georgia, Florida, Louisiana. You don't even know what body of water you were in. The Atlantic? The Gulf? And you have no idea how long you were stuck in that hold—only that it was night when they put you there and morning when they pulled you out. You could've been *anywhere*. In case you hadn't noticed, the ocean's *huge*."

Mat's eyes narrowed into slits, but it wasn't anger anymore. It was a wince.

And Nate was sorry for causing that expression, but he couldn't hold back, either, until he was certain Mat understood. "And as for your escape. Do you know how long the boat was in the water before you jumped? How fast it traveled? In which direction? Do you know how long you swam? How far the currents could've carried you? We have *no idea* where to start looking, Mat. You *can't help him* here. We *can* help him in West Virginia."

Mat looked like he'd been punched in the gut. Sagged, then just sort of . . . deflated. Backed up a few steps and sank down onto Nate's bed.

"I'm sorry," Nate said. And God was he ever.

Mat nodded. He'd folded in on himself again, shoulders hunched, arms wrapped around his middle, eyes on his lap. "I just . . . Going back there . . ." He pried one hand from around his waist, gestured broadly.

And Jesus, Nate had been a total fucking moron again, hadn't he. Of *course* Mat didn't want to go back to the place where his whole life had been shattered the first time—where his parents had died, where he'd lost Dougie to foster care. To have your illusions of safety destroyed even *once* was terribly traumatic. But to have it happen twice? And of course the first time would remind him of the second, of that awful night eleven months ago and everything that'd followed. Of all the precious things that had been taken from him both in West Virginia *and* in Vegas.

To have to admit that his old life—everything about it—was over, gone, never retrievable again.

"I know," Nate tried. "I mean, I don't know, but I know. I sympathize with you, but you have to do this. For your brother, and for everybody else. You need to stay strong." Mat nodded, head still bowed, and Nate couldn't stop himself from adding, "But I'm here, you know? To lean on. To help. Whatever you need."

One second of panic where he worried he'd sounded way too . . . what? Intimate? Needy? Pushy? . . . but then Mat's head lifted, and his eyes met Nate's, and he sort of almost smiled, and maybe even looked a little relieved, and was he blushing? He murmured, "Yeah, okay. Thanks," and licked those chapped lips again, and Nate had to look away before he started thinking about things like how they'd feel pressed to his own.

Because if ever it was not the fucking time, that time was now.

CHAPTER
SEVEN

Mike went home to his family after making Mat promise to keep in touch and call if he needed anything at all. Then he and Nate and Coach Darryl headed to the airport, escorted by uniforms, flew under fake names, got picked up by a couple suits in a nondescript sedan, and dropped at a little house in what passed for the suburbs of Greenbrier County that Nate said the local field office used sometimes. Two officers were waiting inside, and just as Nate had with the officers patrolling outside, he checked their faces against images on his phone before letting anyone else in the house.

It was late by the time they got settled in. The kitchen was stocked, so they had dinner—Coach Darryl insisted on staying (even though that meant sleeping on the couch), and one of the uniforms drove him to a local market to get those steaks he'd promised Mat before. He came back with food, beer that Mat couldn't work up the enthusiasm to drink, a bottle of ibuprofen, and—thank God—two shopping bags full of new jeans and shorts and T-shirts and socks and underwear. He didn't really meet Mat's eyes much as he handed them over. Mat tried not to think too hard about what'd changed between them from yesterday to now—about what Coach Darryl had seen, what he knew now, how differently he was looking at Mat. Tried not to think too hard about whether or not it'd last, or if Nikolai and Allen and the rest of them had taken *this* from him too, the one parental figure left in his life, the one person who'd never doubted his ability to tough his way through any and everything.

Maybe Coach Darryl just needed some time, was all.

So Mat left him to it. Ate and changed into his new clothes. Afterward, he was itching to *do something*, but Nate was pretty insistent that they rest and not harass people at bedtime.

Mat had his own bed. His own bed*room*. It was strange to have his own space again. To be able to close a door behind him and know that nobody had the right to barge in.

Barge in and—

He shuddered and shook his head.

Well, there was a baby monitor in here, but he supposed the FBI needed to make sure nobody could climb through the window and snatch him without them noticing. He could live with that. Wasn't like he'd be doing anything he didn't want someone to hear, anyway.

He slept. Didn't think he'd be able to, wasn't really even sure he wanted to, but he passed out pretty much the moment he closed his eyes. If he had nightmares, he didn't remember them upon waking. There was something about knowing that Coach Darryl was just twenty feet away (even if he was guarding Mat like the runt of the litter now, the weakling, a *victim*), that Nate the FBI agent with a gun and a personal stake was just as close, that cops were watching the house inside and out . . . All that maybe chased the bad dreams away. Maybe having a real bed and a door to close did too. And his favorite old clothes to sleep in.

Even if they were the only thing left from his old life. Maybe *especially* because they were the only thing left from his old life.

Somehow, Mat slept clear past lunch. No one had bothered to wake him, and really, why should they have? Nothing he could do, anyway. He was nothing but deadweight. When he came stumbling into the living room, freshly showered and back in his comfy old clothes, he found Louise at her laptop, cup of coffee and his bag of Funyuns resting by her feet on the coffee table.

"Pot's still on," she said, waving toward the kitchen.

Not big on pleasantries, then, huh? But she smiled at him, seemed friendly enough. He headed toward the coffee, suddenly craving it even though he never really drank it. Coach didn't approve of caffeine for his fighters. Speaking of . . . "Where is everyone?" he called, spooning far too much sugar into a mug. He was gonna make himself even more jittery than he already was.

"Nate's been on interviews since nine. Coach took a uniform to make a supply run. If he goes home, he can't come back—might be followed—so I think he's planning to set up camp here for a bit."

Didn't he have to work? Mat wasn't the only fighter he trained— guy would've gone broke years ago if that were the case. He ran a whole gym, for God's sake.

"He said not to worry," Louise called while Mat poured ridiculous quantities of cream into his coffee. He was gonna fucking *enjoy* this shit. "Jenny's covering for him?"

He grabbed his coffee, headed back into the living room. He kind of really wanted to be alone, but he also kind of really didn't. And there was something distinctly . . . nonthreatening about Louise. Maybe because she was a woman. Maybe because she didn't treat him any differently than she probably treated anyone else. "Jenny's his daughter," he said. "She's kicked my ass a time or two; I'm sure she's got things under control."

He sat in an empty armchair, aching everywhere, careful not to lean back. Sipped his coffee. Man, was that ever good. Wished he had a magazine to read or something, then remembered he was allowed to ask for shit like that now. "Is there a paper?"

Louise looked up from her laptop screen. "Huh?"

"You know, like, *USA Today* or something. *Fight! Magazine.* Whatever." Honestly, he'd prefer the paper. Or a laptop. Surely the world had gone on turning while time had stopped for him; he wanted to know what he'd missed. "Or maybe a computer? I just kind of . . ." he shrugged ". . . wanna catch up, you know?"

"No internet," Louise warned. But then she pulled her phone out, fiddled with the screen a second, handed it to him. "We gave Darryl a burner phone. You can ask him to pick something up for you. No names. No saying where you are. Got it?"

He nodded—didn't even *know* where he was. Called. Drank his coffee. Went through a gentle stretching routine while he watched some CNN. Coach Darryl came back a couple hours later with an entire bag full of newspapers and magazines, everything from the *New York Times* to *Rolling Stone* to *Ultimate MMA* to *People*, like maybe he didn't think he knew Mat well enough anymore to be precise about what he'd want to read.

Maybe he really didn't. Maybe Mat *had* changed.

Of course you did. How could you not have after what happened?

As if to prove his own point, he picked up a *Newsweek* and poured another cup of coffee-flavored cream and sugar.

Mat spent most of the next four days doing nothing but sleeping and eating and worrying. He supposed he shouldn't have been surprised by any of that—his body desperately needed the rest, even if his mind kept trying to keep him from it with nightmares and fears about Dougie. Indulging in creature comforts like rich food and a soft bed was pretty much all he could do to console himself. He couldn't help; Nate and Louise wouldn't let him out the damn door. Didn't even want him peering through the blinds on the windows. He was free, sure, but he was still a damn prisoner. And yeah, logically he could tell himself that at least he wasn't being raped or beaten or made to . . . to hurt anyone else, but it was a cold comfort, especially at 3 a.m. when he was stuck watching infomercials instead of taking a good long run after waking up from a panic attack.

He felt even worse for taking up Coach Darryl's time. But truth be told, he didn't argue too hard with Coach Darryl about it. Because the house wasn't all that big, but Mat knew how quiet and empty it'd feel without the man in it. He was already rattling through its halls like a ghost; he couldn't imagine what'd become of him if Coach Darryl left. Maybe he'd learn to walk through walls, then. Be a ghost for real. Maybe that's all hauntings were: just lonely, listless people, terrified and trapped and fading away.

And Mat *was* fading. Circles under his eyes. Ashen skin. Even his irises seemed more gray than blue. He felt like a sweatshirt that had been washed so many times it was colorless and ugly and sad. Not even comfortable or comforting, just . . . used up. His posture was bad. He was even getting flabby—not that anyone but him claimed to see it—probably from all the inactivity and contraband empty calories.

And he was still wearing Nikolai Petrovic's fucking initials on his fucking skin.

The sun wasn't quite shining yet through the closed blinds, but he'd woken an hour ago to the sensation of bones crunching beneath his fists and hot blood and hands on him and then *in* him, and hadn't been able to get back to sleep. Probably wouldn't anymore today, so he threw the covers back and sat up. No need to get dressed—he'd gone to sleep in his favorite hoodie and track pants, and he wasn't planning on wearing anything else today, either. Quietly, careful of the squeaky board near the door, he left his bedroom and headed toward the kitchen. Made a pot of coffee in the dim silence of dawn. No noise, no lights, just another shadow among shadows. Didn't even wake Coach Darryl, who was asleep on the couch in the living room.

Nate had come back from his interviews yesterday with bagels and cinnamon cream cheese for Louise, who was stuck here all day long sifting through crates and crates of financial records and background checks, and claimed that carbs helped her think better. Mat didn't need to think—would prefer not to, in fact—but he did want to feel warm and sated. Months of being lean and hungry and naked and cold, all at the whims of sick masters, and now he half wanted to be fat and stuffed with carbs just to give them the fucking finger. He sliced a bagel with a sharp serrated knife—and that felt good too, comforting, holding power like that in his hands, being *allowed* to—and slathered it with a heart attack's worth of cream cheese while the coffee finished brewing. Loaded cream and sugar into a big mug of the stuff, and took his meal over to the kitchen island. Took the knife, too. Perched on a stool.

Crossing one leg over the other, that was his mistake. Sitting like this, he could see the sole of his bare foot, the one with the shiny scar tissue. The brand. He traced his fingernails over it idly as he stuffed his face. Followed the NP with his fingers like he'd done a thousand times before. It felt fucking wrong, like if he'd woken up one morning with a massive growth on the side of his face. It didn't belong. It didn't feel right, didn't follow the natural lines of him. And it was a stark reminder of his sickness.

I killed fourteen people, he'd told Nate, and Nate had kept his face oh-so-carefully neutral, not a hint of horror or disgust, but Mat knew, he *knew* that he was the man Nikolai had made him, just as surely as Dougie was. Infected. *Diseased*. How else could he have done those horrible things?

You only did what you had to do to save Dougie. Those men were dead anyway. If you hadn't killed them, Allen would've, and you and Dougie besides.

He shook his head, sipped his coffee. Didn't know what to believe, which voice was right. Somehow the knife was in his free hand. Surprisingly well balanced for cheap cutlery. He twirled it once.

Again. Again. Sipped his coffee. Traced the blunt point of the blade over the NP branded into the sole of his foot.

Like a cancer. Cut it out at the source.

It would be easy to do, after already having used a mirror shard to gouge a tracking device from his arm. He knew real pain now, they'd taught him that much. This would be nothing. Just one more cut on the path to freedom.

He spun the knife again in his hand. Took another sip of coffee. Stared at the calligraphy on his foot.

It wouldn't even cost him anything, really. He'd have to spend a few days off his feet, just like after he'd first been marked as Nikolai's creation, but it wasn't like he was doing anything pressing now. He could lie in bed a few days. Nobody would question it. Hell, they didn't even care that he slept thirteen or fourteen hours a day. Didn't care if he woke up at three in the afternoon or went to bed at ten in the morning.

Why not?

He touched the blade to his foot, lining up the edge of it parallel to the first line of the N.

That was when the kitchen lights flicked on.

Mat didn't turn. Too apathetic to jump in fright or care who'd come.

"Mornin'," Coach Darryl greeted, voice slow and careful. "Having a bagel, are you?"

Mat took another swallow of coffee as Coach Darryl poured himself his own cup, black, like always. "Yep."

"You save any cream cheese for the rest of us?"

Mat put his mug down, picked up half his bagel. There really was a lot of cream cheese on it. He took a bite. Said nothing.

Coach Darryl puttered around at the counter for a while. Cabinets opened and closed, then some chopping, then a pan rattling on the stove. Mat nibbled at his bagel. Considered his knife. Coach Darryl hadn't tried to take it from him—that had to mean something, didn't it?

It means he trusts you not to be an idiot.

. . . Or maybe he's afraid you'll stab him if he pisses you off.

No. The first one. Definitely the first one. Right?

He closed his eyes, propped his chin in his hand. He was so tired. Needed more coffee.

"Here." A plate clattered down in front of him, and he opened his eyes to see Coach Darryl sitting on the stool to his right, placing a glass of water beside the omelet he'd just cooked. "Egg whites, onion, broccoli, and tomato with a sprinkling of feta." His old favorite. Coach Darryl grabbed the plate the bagel was on, slid it away from Mat. Mat thought of taking it back, but Coach Darryl looked . . . determined. Maybe even a little pissed. Mat didn't want him to be angry with him. Didn't think he could handle that right now. So he let Coach Darryl take the coffee too. Was surprised when he didn't take the knife along with the rest of the toxic things.

"What is this garbage you're putting in your body, huh?" The words were harsh but the tone was soft. Imploring. Mat realized he was *hurting* Coach Darryl, even if he wasn't quite sure how or why. "What are you doing to yourself?"

Mat shrugged, burning with shame and wanting it fucking gone. "Nothing worse than what other people have done to me already."

"Uh-huh, uh-huh. So to get revenge on them and celebrate your freedom, you're gonna ruin everything you worked for? Talking about cutting off your nose to spite your face."

Or your foot to spite your trainer.

"What's the point? I'm never gonna fight again, I think we both know that. I've crossed a line—they made me cross a line, and there's no going back. No *holding* back. Put me in the octagon again, who knows what I'll do."

Trick question. I know. I'll kill again. Just by instinct, I'll kill.

Or I'll give up. Huddle in a corner like that poor kid I wouldn't touch and cry. Disaster either way.

Coach Darryl didn't try to convince him otherwise. Which made Mat wonder why the fuck he was still *here*. It had made sense, Coach Darryl taking care of him, back when he'd had something to gain by it. But now?

"Do you remember why you started fighting in the first place?" Coach Darryl asked.

Mat shrugged again. "It was fun, I guess?"

"Is that all?"

"Dude, I dunno. I was *five*. I liked it. I was good at it. It made my parents proud, and the other kids jealous, and I felt—"

Oh.

Coach Darryl's lips turned up ever so slightly at the corners. "Yes?" he prompted.

Mat switched the knife to his left hand. Picked up the fork in his right and used it to cut a corner off the omelet. "Powerful," he said to his plate. "It made me feel strong. Confident. Secure."

"And when you started competing, did you do that for your parents? The crowds? Your friends? Or did you do that for *you*?"

His parents hadn't liked the competitions, actually. Thought they were dangerous, that they distracted from his schoolwork. Which, in fairness, they had; he'd ended up a C student with occasional Bs, and had never even considered college. But he'd wanted to do it, and like the good parents they were, they'd supported him.

He'd wanted to do it.

He wanted to do it.

Mat put down the knife and ate his omelet.

CHAPTER
EIGHT

Nothing. They had nothing. Louise had gone over the financials of everybody who'd so much as *breathed* in the vicinity of Dougie's file in the foster system—in both the county *and* the state office—and come up with nothing. Nobody who'd been paying close attention to him, revisiting his file in the weeks and months leading up to his disappearance. Nobody with large unexplained deposits into their bank accounts—or their family's or friends' accounts—that might suggest some kind of payoff. There wasn't even any evidence of frequent, smaller deposits that would signal a more piecemeal payment. Nobody suspicious in the interviews, nobody with a background that might raise an eyebrow.

Nothing.

The only explanation now was that a hacker on the Cartel's payroll was accessing the databases from the outside. And trying to chase down any hacker worth his salt was an exercise in months of futility and delay.

"So we give them some bait," Louise suggested, looking as worn and drawn as Nate felt. He must have made a disapproving face, because she rolled her eyes. "I don't mean we put some poor foster kid in the line of fire, but you know, we make up a fake file, make sure it's nice and attractive to these sickos. No living relatives, nobody to miss them. Make sure the photo is good-looking. Then we get some of the agency computer geeks to write up some kind of code or something to, I don't know, track back on anyone who tries to access the file. Find our hacker that way. I'm sure it's been done before."

Nate scrubbed his hands over his face, trying to ignore the incessant *thwack thwack thwack* of Mat in the corner, jumping the rope Darryl had brought him a couple days back. He was thrilled that Mat no longer seemed to be, well, *wallowing*, for lack of a better word (not, mind you, that he wasn't thoroughly entitled), but this new focus of his was almost scary. From one extreme to another. "And if it works like WikiLeaks? Just some anonymous online drop box where the hacker uploads the information without ever knowing who he's connected with inside the Cartel? What if his payment comes through some Swiss bank account? The trail goes cold, and we're no closer to breaking this thing or finding Mat's brother."

Thwack thwack thwack thwack . . .

"And what if that's not the way it works?" Louise said. "What if the informant meets up with someone from the Cartel in person? What if he gets a signed check? What if he's not a contractor, but actually works within the Cartel itself? Didn't Mat say that one of the men on the procurement team was working off a laptop from the van? Maybe *he's* the hacker. You can't sit there and say this angle's useless without even pursuing it first."

Thwack thwack thwack thwack thwack . . .

She was right. Nate was being impatient, and it was making him sloppy. But how could he *not* be impatient, knowing what was at stake?

He needed to resolve this thing for Mat so the guy could have his fucking life back. For Dougie, too. For *all* the men and women (and, God help him, children) who were trapped in this hell.

Thwack thwack thwack . . .

Jesus, didn't the guy ever get tired?

He was still there in the corner, jumping and jumping and jumping, staring into some middle distance, jaw tight with single-minded determination. Listening to them, probably, but he wasn't intruding upon the conversation. He wasn't letting himself be left out, either. It was why Nate didn't ask him to go to another room so they could concentrate without the incessant noise of the rope and Mat's sneakered feet hitting the floor. Not to mention his heavy breathing.

"All right. We'll set it up in the morning, get an assist from the local field office. And in the meantime, I guess we keep working leads."

Louise was polite enough not to say, *What leads?* Just like he was polite enough not to mention that any organization that'd managed to get this large while still staying this secret for this long would never be foolish enough to scope out new targets while the FBI was on their trail. They'd lay low, get their "product" from international sources—or at least not from fucking West Virginia while he and

Louise were in it—stick to working in places the FBI wouldn't be monitoring.

"Anyway," Louise said, and slapped her thighs. "Since that's all we can do for tonight, I'm hitting the sack. You should too." And then she turned, looking to Mat, completely fearless in the face of his off-putting intensity. "And so should you, Double Dutch. Get some rest before you collapse due to jump-rope-related exhaustion."

But Mat didn't stop until after she'd left the room. In fact, the instant her bedroom door closed, the rope stilled. The *thwack thwack thwack* now sounded only in Nate's ears.

"You going to bed?" Nate asked, gently. Mat should've been exhausted—he'd been going *forever*. His track suit was soaked with sweat, his hair plastered with it. Nate could smell him, strong but not at all unpleasant, even from across the room. Why was he dressed so warmly for such a hard workout?

"No." Mat shook his head. Dropped the rope and strode to Nate's side with rapid, almost possessed steps. Looking every inch the fighter he was, and though Nate was pretty tough himself, it took a concerted effort not to flinch. Mat's tongue flicked out to wet his lips. "If you're setting bait for the Cartel, why not just use me?"

"Not a chance," Nate snapped, and looked away. He started closing manila folders, stuffing them into boxes, anything to avoid looking at Mat, who was standing there breathing so heavily and smelling so much like *man* and full of so much intensity it made Nate's skin prickle.

"Come on. I'm your only lead on this case, and you know it. Use me! You put up that stupid fake file, they're gonna know right away it's a fake. Put me out on the street, and you'll have someone on the inside by the next day."

"Someone on the inside? You mean *you* back to being raped and tortured?" Mat flinched ever so slightly at that, but Nate didn't regret it. Had to be said that way to get through. "That's not me putting 'someone on the inside,' that's being complicit in their crimes. No way. It's not happening."

"They have bounty hunters. Following me. Tracking me down. They want me back. They know I can't be allowed to walk free."

"So if they find you, they'll kill you to silence you, that's what . . . that's what I'd do. You're a liability to them. They'll kill you."

"No." Mat threw down the jump rope, which snapped like a whip. Nate shuddered at the mental image of it carving bloody stripes into Mat's back. "No, look. If they'd wanted me dead, they'd have killed me at the hospital. I'm worth too much money to them. Besides, they know damn well there's no evidence to back up my story, and more than enough evidence to support *me* being the criminal here. They know you won't find anything. Why do you think they're letting you try? So you can disgrace me, and put me back out on the street where they can scoop me up without the law sniffing their assholes while they work."

Nate felt the anger in his throat, felt it burn and rise and try to turn into tears. He slammed his fist on the coffee table, sending papers flying and a paper coffee cup rolling. "You think I don't know how fucking hopeless this is, Mat? You think I don't realize how every fucking lead in this case leads to a dead end? But I'm still fucking here. I've always been here, even when everybody else had given up. Because I can't fucking give up on you, Mat. I can't. I can't. And now you want me to hand you back to them?"

Mat's shoulders slumped. His eyes went soft. His lips parted. When he swallowed, Nate heard it. "I don't want you to give up on me," he said, sitting down on the couch beside Nate, closer than he'd let himself get to anyone who wasn't Coach Darryl since he'd escaped. Nate could feel the heat pouring off him, smell him even stronger now. If he turned, their knees would touch. "And I'm grateful you haven't yet. But hear me out. I know how this works. I was on the inside long enough to hear some things, put some of their business model together. They have a protocol when it comes to people who escape, you know. They have to. They recapture us and bring us back to our trainer for 'reeducation.' We're worth too much to be disposed of, and I know it sounds . . . petty, but none of their egos could handle losing one of us even if we weren't. Allen will want me back, but not until he gets a promise from Nikolai that I won't try to run again."

"I don't see how that's a promise he could make without breaking you. I thought Allen didn't want that."

Mat shrugged. "Allen's wants have changed. Maybe he got bored with his rabid dog, or maybe he just realized it paid better to fight me,

I don't know. But I *do* know he'd do this. And anyway, who's to say it's up to Allen? It might be compulsory. The Cartel will want to protect their interests, too. Allen or no Allen, they won't want me escaping again. To be honest, I don't think it's really ever happened before. From trainers, sure. From auction houses or procurement teams, maybe. But not from the end buyers. We're supposed to be broken and obedient by then. Dougie didn't take the chance to escape, after all." A brief grimace at that, but it quickly hardened into that same bullheaded determination. His tongue flicked out. His eyes were wide and shining, following his train of thought to its mad conclusion. "You put me out on the street, the bounty hunters will be there, and they'll take me straight back to Nikolai."

God, the very *thought* of it made Nate sick. "Mat . . ."

"No, listen, I'm not asking you to give me back and leave me, I'm asking you to put me in there to take them *down*. Follow right behind me. *Fight* with me. If we can crack Nikolai, we can crack the Cartel. He knows who's buying, he knows who's training, he knows who's selling. And not just his own business records, either. There was something this other guy said. The guy who tracked Dougie and me down to Allen's. He said that Nikolai had access to some kind of databases, some record of everyone bought and sold within the Cartel. If we can get that, we can find everyone. Everyone in captivity, you understand? *Everyone*." He reached out, grasped Nate's hand. His palm was sweaty, his grip fierce. He didn't seem to realize he was touching someone of his own volition, and Nate was too afraid to shatter the moment to point it out. "We can save them *all*."

Nate swallowed, swallowed again. Every fucking breath tasted like Mat, like clean sweat and cheap shampoo and raw animal power and human strength. He needed to let go of Mat's hand. Couldn't make himself do it. "At what cost?" he finally asked, his voice tight with emotion.

"No price I haven't already paid," Mat replied, plain and without a shred of fear. "I spent eleven months at their hands, and for what? For *nothing*. A few more hours, a day maybe, to free them all? You and I both know it's the right thing." His hand tightened on Nate's, and his eyes watered over, and for a moment, Nate could practically hear the wailing souls of the fourteen men Mat had been forced to kill, the guilt hung so heavy around him. "The *only* thing," he added. "You have to let me do this."

You've paid more than enough for your imagined sins, he wanted to say. Wanted to cup Mat's face and wipe that one stray tear away with his thumb and lean in to kiss him so gently he'd forget what pain even was. But instead he said, "And what about the cost to me?"

"Wha—"

"What about the cost to me? I'm bound to protect you. You're asking me to go against everything I swore to do when I joined the FBI—and, by the way, to try to convince my partner and my AD and probably an entire SWAT team to do the same while somehow not getting my ass fired. But more than that, I—" He shouldn't be saying this. It was too personal, too honest, too inappropriate, too schoolboy crush. "I can't stand to see you hurt anymore. Not just as an agent, but as a man, you understand? I want you safe." His shoulders slumped with the force of the admission. He dropped his face into his hands.

Was surprised again when Mat's hand cupped his shoulder. More touches from the man who'd kept the whole world—except for one exceptional man—at a safe distance.

How could one person still contain so much bravery and tenderness after being shown such inhuman cruelty? It didn't make sense. Nate reached up, covering Mat's hand with his own—

Mat slipped out of his reach, standing and dancing back, as graceful as the fighter he was. He was panting again. Jaw clenched but eyes incongruously soft, like he was trying very hard to hide the reaction he'd just had. To Nate touching him. *Stupid.* Should've known better than to push.

"Just think about it, okay?" Mat said. "I think you know it's our best—and maybe our only—option. And look, not to pressure you and be an asshole, but the more time you waste fucking around with this fake foster child bullshit, the more time Dougie's still there, on the inside, suffering. You think about that. Tell me how much *that* costs you."

And then he stooped, picked up his discarded jump rope, and left the room.

Mat avoided Nate after that. Told himself it was because he wanted the guy to suffer and stew, but really, it probably had more to do with the fact that he was afraid he might accidentally touch the guy again. He hadn't meant to, the first time. Didn't even know why he'd done it. Nate had just looked so earnest, and caring, and it had been like that time with Roger. Mat had wanted to connect with someone. Someone who wasn't trying to hurt him, even if they weren't exactly helping him, either. The absence of pain wasn't pleasure, but it was still *something*. Was Mat wrong for seeking it out?

If you're gonna freak on the poor guy when he tries to touch you back, then yeah, it is *kind of dickish.*

Of course, Nate was no idiot; he'd figured out that Mat didn't want him around and acted accordingly. Even if Mat did catch him staring sometimes. But it wasn't a creeper-stare, didn't make Mat feel examined or molested or really even uncomfortable. Not like a *slave*, that was the main thing. And Nate would always look away when caught, a faint blush making that perfect copper skin just a little rosier.

Nate kept pretty busy anyway. He and Louise set up their stupid fake-trail file at social services, using some obscure but drop-dead gorgeous male model from Detroit or some shit. Didn't matter, it was never going to work. He was pretty sure they knew that, too—oh, they went through all the steps, got the tech guys involved, built a whole imaginary life for this imaginary kid, but they didn't sound terribly enthusiastic about it getting them any results. And the whole time, Mat sat by, watching the seed he'd planted in Nate's mind—*use me for bait, put me back in there so I can destroy them from the inside*—slowly take root and grow, fed by the frustration of one dead end after another. It was only a matter of time. No need to nag the guy, no need to push him. All he had to do was wait. Take care of himself, get strong again, be ready for when the time came.

Of course, Mat had all the time in the world. Dougie didn't.

But he tried not to think about that. Tried not to think about much of anything, truth be told. Because every time he did . . .

He shuddered. Put down the magazine he was reading, eyed Nate and Louise on the couch in the living room, heads bowed close over a massive pile of papers. Reading was a terrible distraction anyway—he couldn't ever seem to concentrate for more than a few sentences at a time—and he needed a shower. Okay, sure, he'd already taken one today after his workout, and how fucking clichéd was the "rape shower" anyway, and he'd only been *thinking* about it anyhow, nobody had so much as *looked* at him funny in two weeks. Yet here he was, skin fucking crawling, and all the track pants and hoodies in the world couldn't hide him from his memories. So, shower it was.

He'd healed enough for the hot water to relax instead of sting, but he still had this . . . *thing* about being touched, even by his own damn hand. Soaping up and scrubbing down didn't come easy anymore, which was patently fucking ridiculous, but all the *Suck it up, Carmichael*s in the world didn't seem to change that. He pushed through it like he pushed through everything else, but truth be told, he was getting awfully fucking tired of fighting everything all the time. He couldn't rest until this was over, though. Until Dougie was home safe. Until *everyone* was home safe. Maybe then he'd finally stop looking over his shoulder every ten seconds. Jumping at shadows. Feeling phantom hands and mouths and cocks on his skin. Seeing the mangled faces of all those dead men in his dreams.

Or maybe you get to keep that bit forever—nice little party favor to cap off all the "fun" you had in the arena.

Whatever. Didn't matter. *Ending* this mattered. And that wasn't gonna happen unless and until Nate let him go back in. How to convince him, though, when he was so dead set against it?

You know how.

Oh, *God*. Mat shuddered, hands freezing in his sudsed-up hair. That hadn't been his voice; it was *Nikolai's*.

Nikolai, who'd taught him how to minimize pain. How to manipulate. How to use his body to make things easier.

Well, he wasn't going to feel sorry for considering that option now. Not when using the skills Nikolai'd taught him against the Cartel itself was such a perfect *fuck you*. And it would prove to Nate he wasn't too damaged and messed up to handle it, some delicate fucking flower who'd shatter under one more strike or rape. He could still make his body do his bidding. For Dougie, for revenge, for penance, to rescue everyone left to rescue, yeah, he could.

Besides, Nate was gorgeous, compassionate, kind, giving. Relentless in the best possible way. All the things Mat would've gone for, before. All the things that would've turned his head. So hey, if he *did* have to fuck someone ever again for any reason, Nate was a good choice.

And this was a good reason. The *best* reason.

That settled it. He rinsed the shampoo out, shut the water off. Rucked a towel over his hair—artfully messy, perfect—then swiped it over his chest, arms, and legs before wrapping it low around his hips. His eyes were drawn to the clean boxers and track suit sitting on the vanity, his fingers itching to pick them up, put them on. But no. Not this time.

He unlocked the door. Put his hand on the knob. Took a deep breath. Another one. He could *do* this. He *could*.

His skin itched like a dozen set of hands were teasing over it. The sensation of being naked, being naked where anyone could see, was like something out of a horror movie. The last time Coach Darryl had seen him like this, the man had fled on a four-hour run. The person before that? Well . . . that disgusting fuck was dead now anyway—Mat's only murder committed without a single regret—so no point in dwelling on him. Dougie had seen him naked too, but no way Mat was going *there*, especially if he had a single hope of getting it up for Nate.

He opened the door.

Strode into the living room like he owned the fucking place. Sat down on the couch right next to Nate.

Who looked up from his paperwork, eyes widening and the greeting on his lips freezing as he realized what Mat was—or wasn't—wearing.

Louise coughed in a way that kind of made Mat think she was covering a laugh, and left without saying a word.

"You, uh, you need someone to do some laundry for you?" Nate asked. He swallowed visibly. Mat watched his pupils dilate and thanked fucking fate that Coach Darryl wasn't here to see the shit he was pulling.

"Nope," Mat replied. Not bad. It sounded just like something he would have said before, when he was feeling horny and cocky. Almost his old self again, except his old self wouldn't be sitting here trying to dam a tidal wave of thoughts about being raped by his own fucking brother.

"Nice . . . shower, then?" Nate asked, practically squeaking, one hand clutching a file over his lap—presumably to hide some *evidence*. Obviously trying not to directly question Mat's decision to go naked.

Mat very gently reached out and pulled the file away. Yeah, *evidence* indeed, and quite a bit of it by the looks of the bulge in Nate's slacks. He'd expected to feel . . . what? Fear, maybe? Revulsion? Panic? Or possibly, on some wild outside chance, arousal, like he once would have? Instead he just kind of felt . . . nothing. It was a task, a chore, like any of the thousands of others he'd done for the men who held power over him this past year. Practically clinical, and in a way, that was its own kind of trauma. Couldn't he feel *something*? This numbness made him wonder if maybe Nikolai had shaped him into a mindless fuckdoll, after all.

"God, Mat, I'm sorry." Nate's expression was heartbroken, ashamed, horrified. He tried to cross his legs, but just ended up pinching his junk and dropping his foot back on the floor with a wince. "I am so, so sorry. This is— That is— I don't mean anything by it, okay? It's just—" He stood, snatching another file and holding it in front of his hips. Mat wished he'd stop being so fucking nice; this'd be easier if he weren't so *nice*. Mat was kind of starting to feel like the creeper here, forcing himself on another man, making him so uncomfortable. "I should go. This doesn't change anything about your case, or about our professional relationship. I'm just— I'm human, that's all, but I'm still an agent, and there are boundaries, and I understand that, and I just— I just need to get some fresh air or something. Fuck. I'm sorry. I'm so sorry. It won't happen again."

He started to back away, but Mat caught his arm. Caught his gaze. "What if I want it to?" he asked, and every single word was bitter in his mouth, but somehow it came out sounding sweet.

Nate's eyes darted to Mat's hand on his arm, back to Mat's face. To his lips. "What?" he breathed.

"You were a fan of mine before all this. Right?"

"Right."

"Came to all my fights, isn't that right?"

"Right."

Shit, no, he was going about this all wrong. Thinking about how dedicated Nate had been and still was, it was too sweet, too perfect, and Mat needed this to be dirty. "Wanted to *fuck* me, didn't you? Thought of bringing me home, maybe? Or maybe just getting me to blow you in a bathroom stall, quick and dirty?"

Nate's lips moved for a long moment before anything came out. He cleared his throat, swallowed hard. Said, voice thin, "*Be* fucked, actually."

Now he had him. Mat stepped forward again, closing the space between their bodies. Reached down and grabbed a big handful of what Nate was packing.

Nate moaned, just a little. Leaned away a little too, but didn't step back, didn't move Mat's hand. "Mat—"

"You never got up the guts to try though, huh? But I bet that didn't stop you jerking off to the thought." Mat rubbed him through the fabric of his pants, finding the outline of his shaft. "Did you? Did you jack off this big dick, thinking about me?"

"Mat," Nate tried again. He was panting. Lifted one shaking hand and touched it to Mat's wrist like he couldn't decide if he wanted to push him away or pull him closer. "W-what are you doing, Mat? You can't— *I* can't . . ."

"Can't *what*?" Mat narrowed his eyes, let a little anger, a little indignation bleed into his voice. "Fuck a rape victim? Is that it? Think you'll break me? Eleven months of whips and chains and drugs and cocks and plugs and fucking *fists* and my own—my own fucking *brother* didn't break me." He squeezed Nate's cock again, rock hard beneath his hand, even as Nate was wincing at his words. "You think *this* is gonna break me now?"

Nate reached up with both hands, but rather than drawing Mat in, he put his palms to Mat's shoulders and shoved. "It's fucking *wrong*, Mat! I know you're not going to shatter, I know you're still a man, I obviously—" he gestured to his erection "—don't just think of you as some victim, but that doesn't change the fact that it's wrong. I do want you, Mat, just as much as I ever did, and yeah, I did go to all those parties hoping to bring you home. But those days are over now. I'm not just some fanboy anymore. I'm a special agent on an important case, and you're my witness and the man I'm bound to protect. And when we crack this ring and I have to testify in court, I can't—the *case* can't—afford any conflicts of interest, you get me?" He scrubbed both hands through his hair, over his face. Looked like he was weighing the wisdom of his next words. "Not to mention you're a fucking head case right now. You and I both know it, and maybe you really want this and maybe you don't, but I can't know which it is, and I'm not convinced you can either."

Oh, *fuck* him. Mat felt the growl in his throat, found himself stepping forward before he could bring his body back under control. Nate stumbled back, hands out, placating, real fear in his eyes that drained the anger out of Mat in a heartbeat, left him sick and ashamed and fighting the urge to flee, to hide, to slam his fist into a fucking wall.

His posture and expression must've shown the change; Nate's placating hands dropped, his face gentling into sympathy. "And I'm not saying I blame you; fuck, I'd be huddled in a corner sobbing non-fucking-stop if I'd been through what you've been through. But . . . you need time to *heal*, and until you have . . ." He shook his head, tossed his hands. "It's unethical, and it's wrong." His expression hardened, all business, like he was intent on punishing them both. "And that's why I'm going to take the night off. Louise will stay here with you. She'll watch over you, so maybe you want to put some clothes on. I'm going to . . . I don't know. Take a long drive."

"Nate . . ." Mat mumbled. Bit his lip. This had gone all wrong. Completely wrong. He'd utterly fucked this up. Misread Nate. *Hurt* him, just like all those fuckers had hurt Mat this past year. Ruined everything good between them. Nate would be extra careful from here on out. No going back. "I'm sorry. Please, I didn't . . ."

Nate ignored his protests, his movements jerky. He packed a couple folders into his shoulder bag and hefted it over one arm, then gave Mat a raw, fierce look. "Don't be. I get it. Look, you're trying your best. I can't fault you for that. And to that end . . . Louise and I talked it over, and we agree. We can't afford to sit around much longer, or all the intel you have is going to go stale and we'll have nothing but some scary stories. We even got our AD on board. So we're giving our fake file another three days, and then we're sending you in. You'll have to sit in on the SWAT team briefings. Sign like three hundred waivers. And be willing to have your name smeared in the news." He looked directly at Mat, almost challenging. "And before you get the wrong idea, this was all set in motion before tonight. I was just waiting for the right moment to tell you. Guess this is as good a time as any. So, you know, you didn't end up needing to seduce me after all, huh?" He barked a laugh.

Mat winced again. God, fuck Nikolai. Fuck him for fucking up every good thing in his life, even after he'd gotten free.

"I'm sorry," he said again. He could say it a thousand times, and it would never be enough.

Nate pursed his lips, nodded, blinked a few too many times. "Yeah, me too."

And then he turned and walked away, taking with him all the unrealized potential they'd once shared.

CHAPTER NINE

Three days passed. Three days while Nate did every fucking thing he could to protect Mat from what was increasingly looking like the inevitable. The fake foster kid didn't get so much as a nibble, surprising no one. Which is how they all ended up in the Chesapeake field office, concocting a fake news story to feed the press.

Mathias Carmichael, 30, a former UFC fighter, was released from FBI custody yesterday and into the care of physicians at the Lakewood Psychiatric Facility after his tales of a multinational human trafficking ring yielded no evidence to support his claims. Carmichael has been diagnosed by Bureau psychiatrists as paranoid schizophrenic. According to Bureau sources, he spent the last eleven months in Mexico in an attempt to flee massive debts related to his participation in underground fighting rings. The FBI is unsure why he chose to return, but in light of his alleged crimes and his incompetence to stand trial, he has been committed to the mental health facility for four months of treatment and evaluation. His younger brother, Douglas Carmichael, 24, is still missing. The investigation into his disappearance remains open, with cooperation from the Mexican government. Both brothers disappeared last year, having fled their residence after Mathias's dealings with underworld bookies became violent.

Louise offered to do the press conference. Neither she nor Nate thought he'd be capable of holding his tongue and keeping his emotions in check in the face of questions insulting Mat's character.

Everyone watching and reading needed to be convinced, utterly convinced, that the FBI had given up on Mat, that his story had been completely discredited, that he had been abandoned to a system where, once again, it would be easy for him to slip through the cracks.

Except this time, the tracking chip beneath his skin belonged to the FBI. There was nowhere to hide a wire, not on a man who'd sooner rather than later wind up naked, all of his body cavities—

Couldn't even hide one in his damn nose without risking it breaking—and being discovered—beneath someone's fist.

Nate hated it. He knew it was the most sensible option, and that a trained fighter like Mat was pretty much ideal for a mission like this. If it had been Dougie, this wouldn't have been possible, but with Mat there was actually a reasonable chance of them pulling it off.

But Nate still hated it. Hated thinking of the pain and indignity Mat would be subjected to on the way to Nikolai. And they needed Nikolai, not some bounty hunter.

He hated the fact that somebody would be going on television, running Mat's name through the mud, calling him insane and incompetent and heavily suggesting he was responsible for his brother's disappearance and maybe even death. Hated that soon the 24-hour news cycle would be latching onto this story, maybe even the tabloids thanks to Mat's minor celebrity as an athlete. It would destroy his image. The things they'd say . . . just imagining the possibilities made Nate want to puke.

And sure, yeah, they'd fix it later—once it was safe to reveal the truth, Mat would be celebrated as a hero, brave beyond all comprehension. There'd be interviews and book deals and a movie of the fucking week, if he could tolerate the spotlight, and maybe even if he couldn't. But he had to survive this fucking *mess* first.

Nate briefed the SWAT team, Mat by his side, tall and unafraid at the front of a room full of heavily armed strangers. Mat signed the eight million forms. Went back to the safe house with Nate and Louise for the night; in the morning, they'd drop him at Lakewood Psychiatric, and then would come the press release and the news conference and the whole rest of the damn circus.

Of everything Mat was facing in his future, it was Lakewood itself that seemed to be drawing him up the shortest. He sat heavily on the couch, Lakewood brochure in hand—the one they gave to families of the committed—and threw Nate a look that could only be interpreted as tightly reined panic.

Good. Maybe he could still get Mat to back out.

"The staff won't know. They can't know. They're going to treat you exactly like any other paranoid schizophrenic. You might be restrained. You'll definitely be medicated. Locked in your room at night. Hopefully the Cartel will be quick to get you out of there—" *so you can suffer a different kind of hell.*

But that wasn't fair. They couldn't afford to have Mat back out now, and Nate should be talking him up, pumping him up like Darryl would before a fight, not scaring the shit out of him. He wished Darryl were still here—he'd know the right thing to say. But they'd sent him back home to his daughter and his gym to help maintain their cover story, so it was all on Nate now. "—and then you'll be one step closer to rescuing your brother, and taking these fuckers down."

Mat's fingers tightened around the brochure, wrinkling the heavy stock. "I can handle it," he said.

Nate reached out, took the risk, cupped a hand around Mat's neck and shoulder. Mat flinched but didn't shrug him off. "I know you can. You're a fighter. You're a goddamn warrior." Oh God, he was getting all choked up now. "You're a motherfucking hero, that's what you are."

Mat shook his head. "A fighter, maybe, but I'm no hero. Heroes are selfless, and I'm not. I want revenge. I want my brother back. I want to—" He pressed his lips together, swallowed hard, muscles flexing in his cheeks. "I want to try to . . . to *atone* for all those people I . . ." His gaze slid away from Nate's, to his hands still clenched around the brochure in his lap, and he finished, too soft, "Those people I hurt. Nothing selfless about that."

But Nate wasn't going to let Mat talk himself out of this. Wasn't going to let Mat take this away from himself. From them *both*, because shit, Nate needed this too. Needed it a lot more than maybe he rightfully should. He leaned forward, touching their foreheads together briefly as a substitute for the kiss they had never—and could never—share. "One day, when the things these people did to you aren't so raw, and the scars aren't so fresh, and you stop blaming yourself for what they made you do and stop feeling so damn worthless all the time? You're going to see what I see in you right now."

And my biggest fucking wish in the world—other than seeing you come back safe from this suicide mission—is to be there with you when it happens.

TO BE CONTINUED IN

THE FLESH
SEASON 5: RECLAMATION
CARTEL

www.riptidepublishing.com/titles/collections/flesh-cartel-season-5-reclamation

Dear Reader,

Thank you for reading Rachel Haimowitz and Heidi Belleau's *The Flesh Cartel, Season 4: Liberation*!

We know your time is precious and you have many, many entertainment options, so it means a lot that you've chosen to spend your time reading. We really hope you enjoyed it.

We'd be honored if you'd consider posting a review—good or bad—on sites like **Amazon, Barnes & Noble, Kobo, Goodreads, Twitter, Facebook, Tumblr,** and your blog or website. We'd also be honored if you told your friends and family about this book. Word of mouth is a book's lifeblood!

For more information on upcoming releases, author interviews, blog tours, contests, giveaways, and more, please sign up for our weekly, spam-free newsletter and visit us around the web:

Newsletter: tinyurl.com/RiptideSignup
Twitter: twitter.com/RiptideBooks
Facebook: facebook.com/RiptidePublishing
Goodreads: tinyurl.com/RiptideOnGoodreads
Tumblr: riptidepublishing.tumblr.com

Thank you so much for Reading the Rainbow!

AnglerFishPress.com

ANGLERFISH
PRESS
AN IMPRINT OF RIPTIDE PUBLISHING.

ALSO BY HEIDI BELLEAU

Dead Ringer, with Sam Schooler
The Professor's Rule series, with Amelia C. Gormley
First Impressions. Second Chances
Blasphemer, Sinner, Saint, with Sam Schooler

Rear Entrance Video series
Apple Polisher
Wallflower
Straight Shooter

With Rachel Haimowitz
The Burnt Toast B&B (a *Bluewater Bay* story)
The Flesh Cartel, Season 1: Damnation
The Flesh Cartel, Season 2: Fragmentation
The Flesh Cartel, Season 3: Transformation
The Flesh Cartel, Season 5: Reclamation

With Lisa Henry
Tin Man
Bliss
The Harder They Fall
King of Dublin

With Violetta Vane
Mark of the Gladiator
Cruce de Caminos

ALSO BY
RACHEL
HAIMOWITZ

Master Class
Master Class
SUBlime: Collected Shorts

Song of the Fallen
Counterpoint
Crescendo

With Cat Grant
Power Play: Resistance
Power Play: Awakening

With Heidi Belleau
The Burnt Toast B&B (a *Bluewater Bay* story)
The Flesh Cartel, Season 1: Damnation
The Flesh Cartel, Season 2 Fragmentation
The Flesh Cartel, Season 3: Transformation
The Flesh Cartel, Season 5: Reclamation

Anchored (Belonging, #1)
Break and Enter, with Aleksandr Voinov

ABOUT THE
AUTHORS

HEIDI BELLEAU was born and raised in small town New Brunswick, Canada. She now lives in the rugged oil-patch frontier of Northern BC with her husband, an Irish ex-pat whose long work hours in the trades leave her plenty of quiet time to write. She has a degree in history from Simon Fraser University with a concentration in British and Irish studies; much of her work centered on popular culture, oral folklore, and sexuality, but she was known to perplex her professors with unironic papers on the historical roots of modern romance novel tropes. (Ask her about Highlanders!) When not writing, you might catch her trying to explain British television to her newborn daughter or standing in line at the local coffee shop, waiting on her caramel macchiato.

You can visit her blog: www.heidibelleau.com, find her tweeting as @HeidiBelleau, email her at heidi.below.zero@gmail.com.

RACHEL HAIMOWITZ is an M/M erotic romance author and the Publisher of Riptide Publishing. She's also a sadist with a pesky conscience, shamelessly silly, and quite proudly pervish. Fortunately, all those things make writing a lot more fun for her . . . if not so much for her characters.

When she's not writing about hot guys getting it on (or just plain getting it; her characters rarely escape a story unscathed), she loves to read, hike, camp, sing, perform in community theater, and glue captions to cats. She also has a particular fondness for her very needy dog, her even needier cat, and shouting at kids to get off her lawn.

You can find Rachel at her website, rachelhaimowitz.com, on Tumblr at rachelhaimowitz.tumblr.com, and tweeting as @RachelHaimowitz. She loves to hear from folks, so feel free to drop her a line anytime at metarachel@gmail.com.

Enjoy more stories like
The Flesh Cartel, Season 4: Liberation
at RiptidePublishing.com!

Bump in the Night
ISBN: 978-1-62649-063-5

Strain
ISBN: 978-1-62649-070-3

Earn Bonus Bucks!

Earn 1 Bonus Buck for each dollar you spend. Find out how at RiptidePublishing.com/news/bonus-bucks.

Win Free Ebooks for a Year!

Pre-order coming soon titles directly through our site and you'll receive one entry into a drawing to win free books for a year! Get the details at RiptidePublishing.com/contests.

AN IMPRINT OF RIPTIDE PUBLISHING.